T0131562

"Years ago my daughters and wife were inhaling Robin Gunn's stories and loving them, so I had to take a peek myself to find out why. I did. Robin's characters are believable, and her stories have just the right blend of hope, broken hearts, disappointments, lighthearted fun, joy, and an eternal perspective. The Lord Jesus always plays a role, whether behind the scenes or in the thick of things. Robin lives the faith that's so evident in her books. She knows how to tell a story—and the stories she tells make an eternal difference."

RANDY ALCORN, AUTHOR OF *DEADLINE*

"When you read a Robin Gunn book, you know you're going to receive a tender lesson in what it means to belong to Christ—and you will be blessed for it."

FRANCINE RIVERS, AUTHOR OF *REDEEMING LOVE* AND
THE MARK OF THE LION SERIES

"Gratefully Robin's warmth, insight, and humor spill over from her heart onto the written page. She delights us with the well-woven fabric of a well-told tale and I'm certain Robin delights the Lord with her obvious passion for him."

PATSY CLAIRMONT, AUTHOR OF *GOD USES CRACKED POTS* AND
SPORTIN' A 'TUDE

"Robin Jones Gunn cares. She cares about her characters, she cares about her readers, and most of all, she cares about their mutual search for a life that pleases the Lord. Her novels are a delight to read—perfectly crafted, heartwarming, and fun. I'm always thrilled when one of Robin's books appears on the top of my to-be-read stack!"

LIZ CURTIS HIGGS, AUTHOR OF *MIXED SIGNALS, BOOKENDS,* AND *BAD GIRLS OF THE BIBLE*

"Robin Jones Gunn is one of those rare and wonderful writers who infuses her stories with bountiful doses of humor, wisdom, and warmth. Her books have touched and changed countless hearts and given a whole generation of readers a host of fictional characters who feel like dear friends!"

CAROLE GIFT PAGE, AUTHOR OF HEARTLAND MEMORIES SERIES

"Whenever I think of stories that touch the heart, I think of Robin Jones Gunn. They touch my heart and leave me wanting more. Reading a novel by Robin Jones Gunn is like spending time with a good friend…troubles are lighter and joys are deeper."

ALICE GRAY, AUTHOR OF STORIES FOR THE HEART BOOK COLLECTION

"Robin Jones Gunn writes from a heart of love. Her tender stories honor the Savior and speak truth to a world desperately eager to hear it."

ANGELA ELWELL HUNT, AUTHOR OF *THE TRUTH TELLER*

"Robin Gunn is a gifted and sincere storyteller who gets right to the heart of matters with her readers."

MELODY CARLSON, AUTHOR OF *HOMEWARD*

THE GLENBROOKE SERIES

#1 Secrets
#2 Whispers
#3 Echoes
#4 Sunsets
#5 Clouds
#6 Waterfalls
#7 Woodlands
#8 Wildflowers

ROBIN JONES GUNN

sunsets

a novel

THE GLENBROOKE SERIES

MULTNOMAH

SUNSETS

© 1997 by Robin's Ink, LLC
International Standard Book Number: 978-1-59052-238-7

Cover design and images by Steve Gardner/His Image PixelWorks

Scripture quotations are from:*Holy Bible,* The New King James Version
(NKJV) © 1984 by Thomas Nelson, Inc.
Also quoted: *New American Standard Bible* (NASB) © 1960, 1977 by
the Lockman Foundation

Published in the United States by Multnomah,
an imprint of the Crown Publishing Group, a division of
Penguin Random House LLC, New York

MULTNOMAH® and its mountain colophon are registered trademarks
of Penguin Random House LLC.

Library of Congress Cataloging-in-Publication Data
Gunn, Robin Jones, 1955-
Sunsets/by Robin Jones Gunn. p.cm. ISBN 1-57673-558-3
(alk. paper) I. Title.   1-59052-238-9
PS3557.U4866S86 1997   96-47448
813'.54—dc21   CIP

To Kevin and his indestructible cat, Chloe.

May your years together in Pasadena

be graced with exquisite sunsets.

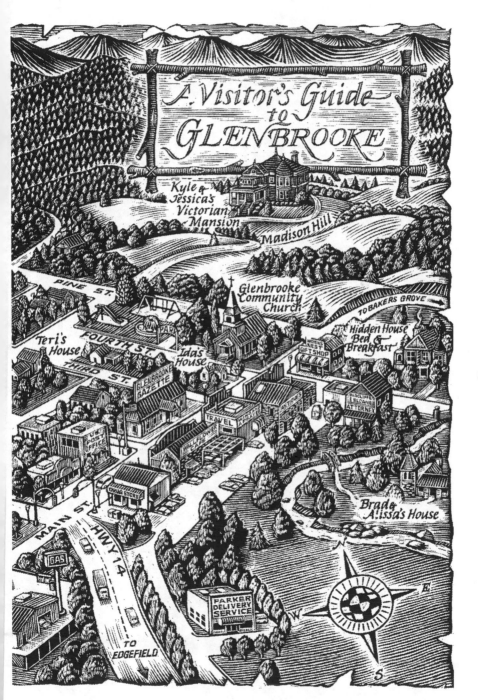

And they who dwell in the ends of the earth
stand in awe of Thy signs;
Thou dost make the dawn and the sunset shout for joy.

PSALM 65:8 (NASB)

Chapter One

"Coffee," Alissa muttered, pushing herself away from her cluttered desk, "a tall café mocha, and I need it now. You want anything, Cheri?"

"No, thanks," her co-worker said without looking up from her computer. "Are you getting this same strange reading on the Mazatlan cruise package?"

"Yes," Alissa said after checking the computer screen over Cheri's shoulder. "I got that reading when I tried to access the Alaska cruise package for the Andersens. But I'm not ready to try again until after I've had some coffee."

Cheri looked over the top of her glasses. "We open in five minutes."

"I know. I'll be back in four. Don't sell any cruise packages until then."

The line at Starbucks was shorter than usual. Alissa examined the pastries in the case. They had Cheri's favorite lemon bars this morning and lots of other incredible looking goodies.

She started her familiar mental workout. *Croissant. I want a croissant. But I shouldn't. Too much fat. I'll have a muffin. A low-fat blueberry. Or a bagel. I can have a bagel. A bagel with fat-free cream cheese.*

"What can I start for you?" the young woman behind the counter asked.

Alissa hesitated.

The customer behind her spoke up. "Cappuccino and a croissant."

"Excuse me." Alissa turned to the casually dressed man behind her. "I was next, and if you don't mind, I'm in a hurry."

He wore his long brown hair with a crooked part down the middle. A soft cocoa stubble curved across his broad jaw, and his gaze struck her with intense clarity. Green eyes. Green like the grass after it rains.

"So what took you so long?" he said with a teasing smile.

Alissa raised her eyebrows and decided this must be his idea of a joke. Since she had moved to Pasadena seven months ago, she had met plenty of men who acted as if the world were their footstool, and therefore they could put up their feet whenever they wanted. Southern California was full of that sort.

Turning to the woman behind the counter, Alissa said calmly, "I'll have a tall café mocha, a lemon bar, and a cinnamon roll. Thanks."

There was no point looking over her shoulder as she left Starbucks. The man with the intriguing green eyes wouldn't be watching her. Men used to watch her walk away. She could feel their gazes. Men used to offer to let her go first.

But that was thirty-two pounds ago. It had been far too long since a man had given her a second glance. Not that she blamed any of them. Much had changed in the life of Alissa Benson.

Wistfully, she remembered what it was like to be seventeen, sauntering through the sand at Newport Beach while everyone watched. That had been many summers ago, back when the ends of her long, blond hair had danced in the wind like the mane of a wild horse.

Today, a long, linen blazer covered her rounded hips, and her shoulder length, wavy blond hair was caught up in a twist, clipped flat against the back of her head. She rarely wore her blue tinted contact lenses anymore. Makeup was something she bothered with only on special occasions, of which there hadn't been many lately.

Alissa's live-in companion was a cat named Chloe, and her favorite weekend pastime was reading. At twenty-six she was living the life of a sixty-year-old. And she was safe.

"She's right here," Cheri said, motioning to Alissa as she opened the door. "I'll put you on hold, Mr. Brannigan."

"Line two," Cheri said to Alissa. "And your landlord is on line one."

"Oh, terrific," Alissa muttered. She handed the pastry bag to Cheri. "I picked up a little something for you."

A smile spread across Cheri's face. "Did you bring me a lemon bar? You are a honey!"

"Don't touch my cinnamon roll!" Alissa playfully responded as she slid behind her desk and reached for the phone. "Good morning, Mr. Brannigan. Did your wife tell you I was able to reserve two nights for you at the Heathman?"

With a few clicks on the computer keyboard, she tried to pull up the active file of the Brannigans as he said, "We've decided to stay three nights. Can you add one more night for us?"

The computer screen froze. Alissa tapped on the keys. "Certainly, Mr. Brannigan. May I call you back to confirm that?"

"I'll wait for your call," Mr. Brannigan said.

Alissa knew he would. The Brannigans had to be the most active retired couple she knew. In good health and possessing excessive spending money, they traveled constantly. And with Alissa's efficiency and excessive good manners, she was their only travel agent.

"Okay. Thank you, Mr. Brannigan. Good-bye."

"Cheri?" Alissa said. "Did we go off-line?"

"I've called the repairman. I don't know what the problem is. I guess all we can do is take messages. Don't forget your landlord. Line one."

With a push of a button and a deep breath, Alissa picked up line one. "Clawson Travel Agency. This is Alissa."

"Ms. Benson," the landlord said with forced friendliness. "You have not responded to the notice we sent you last month. I have left messages on your machine at home, but you have not returned the calls. I found it necessary to call you at work to ask for a reply."

Alissa turned away from Cheri and the client who had just entered the shop and was seated in front of Cheri's desk. "I'm going to need more time to decide."

"I'm afraid there isn't any more time. I must know today by five o'clock."

Alissa heard the click as he hung up, but she kept the phone to her ear as if the answer she needed would come sometime after the dial tone. Her condo complex had been sold a month ago. The new owner required all renters to sign a new lease that included an increase of $150 a month and a minimum commitment of two years. Alissa had never lived anywhere for more than two years. It was a nice condo but not her dream home. During the past month she had found nothing else in her price range. Yet the two-year commitment scared her. She had already been in Pasadena and at the same travel agency for seven months. That in itself was almost a record.

She heard a slight rustling sound and realized a customer was now seated in front of her desk. "Okay. We'll work on that and get back to you then," she said into the dumb receiver that she still held to her ear. "Good-bye."

Turning to hang up and greet her customer, Alissa forced a smile back on her face and said, "Yes, how can I—" She stopped. It was the guy from Starbucks. "How can I help you?"

He took a slow sip from his Starbucks cappuccino and looked at her with his grass green eyes. "You're having trouble with your computers this morning?"

It crossed Alissa's mind that perhaps this guy had followed her here and somehow overheard Alissa and Cheri say they had computer problems. For a brief flash, Alissa felt flattered that this man had apparently sought her out.

"Alissa?" Cheri called over. "Excuse me for interrupting, but Mr. Brannigan is on the phone again. Do you want to take it?"

"Sure." Alissa put on her headset. "Excuse me a moment, please," she said to the green-eyed stranger. "Yes, Mr. Brannigan?"

"My wife wanted me to ask about the special you advertised for the Alaskan cruise, but I forgot when I called earlier. Is there still room on the June trip?"

"I'm having difficulty accessing the information on those cruises this morning. Would it be all right if I called you back this afternoon? That way I'll know about the extra night at the Heathman as well."

Alissa hung up and turned her attention to the man at her desk. "What can I do for you?"

"Do you have local access, or do you have to go through a central clearing agency?" Brad asked.

"Excuse me?"

"For the cruises," he said, getting up and coming over to her side of the desk. "Do you have a local server for your info? Pull up the file. That might tell me." He reached over Alissa's shoulder and clicked on a few keys.

His forward approach startled Alissa. First at Starbucks and now this. Who did this guy think he was? "I'm sorry, but I can't allow you to do this."

Alissa was glad to see Cheri come over to offer her support.

"Alissa? This is Brad Phillips. I thought you two had already met. Brad works down the street at The Computer Wiz." Cheri kept her voice professional. "I called him this morning."

"Oh," Alissa said, feeling foolish for allowing herself to think this man had come looking for her. She rose from her work station and offered Brad her seat. "All yours," she said.

Then, reaching for her coffee and cinnamon roll, which Cheri had put on a paper plate for her, Alissa took the customer seat on the other side of the desk. She might just as well make some phone calls.

"All righty then," Brad said, punching the keys at top speed. The screen miraculously unfroze. "We have lift off."

Alissa punched in a phone number and spoke into her headset. "Yes, I'm checking on reservations for the Brannigans for the nights of June 10 and 11. Would it be possible to add the night of the twelfth as well?…Wonderful. Three nights confirmed then. Thank you very much."

"Here's your problem," Brad said. "No, wait. Oh, I see. This is a strange way to do this." He sipped his coffee and stared at the screen, obviously content to carry on his one-sided conversation. "Why did they take this out of binary? It doesn't have to go that route."

Alissa reached into her in-basket for a list of apartments

she had been calling the last few days. She started at the top and phoned each one that wasn't already checked. Her questions were simple, "Do you have any immediate openings? What is the price range?" She circled four potential apartments on her list and planned to visit them on her lunch hour.

Brad's running mono-conversation came to a halt. "I think we've got it here. What date was Mr. Brannigan interested in? And that was the Alaska cruise, wasn't it?"

"Thank you. I can take it from here." Alissa said.

"Oh, right," Brad said. "Strict customer confidentiality around here." He got up and offered her the chair with the same gesture she had used on him.

"You're back in business," Brad said, tossing his empty coffee cup into the trash. His friendly smile lingered in Alissa's direction only a moment before he stepped over to Cheri's desk and began to work on her computer.

Alissa checked on Mr. Brannigan's cruise. The program functioned perfectly. Even Mazatlan was coming up.

After gathering the information for her customer, she took her half-eaten cinnamon roll into the back room and shoved it into the small refrigerator. Glancing at her reflection in the microwave oven, she pushed up her glasses. She didn't like the feeling that had followed her back here. It was a cloud of hopelessness. A low buzzing in the deepest corner of her heart reminded her that she had lived hard and fast during her high school years, and now she was used up. The locusts had stripped her emotions bare. She didn't consider herself worthy of the attention of a man, any man.

Come on. Snap out of this slump! Don't take yourself down this path. Put a smile on your face.

She did, but it hardly seemed to matter. When Alissa returned to her desk, Brad was gone. She noticed a slip of paper next to the computer. The note read, "Duplex for rent" followed by a phone number. It wasn't her handwriting. She guessed Cheri or their boss, Renée, had left it since both knew she had been apartment hunting. Renée only worked afternoons. Perhaps she had left it yesterday, and Alissa hadn't noticed it with all the commotion this morning.

It didn't matter. It was another lead for an apartment, something she desperately needed. She called and made an appointment to have a look that afternoon.

It ended up being her last stop after four discouraging apartment complexes. The duplex was situated in an older part of town, down a quiet, tree-lined street. That was reason enough for Alissa to feel hopeful.

But when she pulled up in front, she felt certain this dream duplex would be out of her price range. The building resembled twin cottages complete with shuttered windows and flower boxes. It looked like something she had seen in a small town in Europe. Lots of greenery, lace curtains on one side, and stepping stones around to the back made the scene very inviting.

Next door, to the right, stood a grand, villa-style house. It was white with a blue tile roof and two verandas off the top story. A colorful variety of flowers lined the walkway.

"Hello. Are you Alissa?" A middle-aged brunette with a toddler girl on her hip stepped out of the large house.

"Yes. You must be Genevieve."

"Yes, and this is Mallory. I'm sorry I was in such a hurry on the phone. I didn't give you much information."

Alissa noticed Genevieve's accent. People had told Alissa that she, too, had a "potpourri" accent from all the places she had lived. She wanted to ask Genevieve where she was from but hesitated. She was cautious, not wanting to be impolite. That was how her proper Bostonian grandmother had taught her to behave.

"It's this side over here."

Alissa was pleased to see Genevieve was gesturing toward the unit with the lace curtains. "Is it available right away?"

"That's what I didn't have time to explain to you. My husband, Steven, and I are the landlords, but we actually have a tenant already. Shelly Graham. I don't suppose you know her?"

Alissa shook her head.

"Shelly's a flight attendant. Since she's gone so much of the time, I'm helping her find a roommate."

"Oh. I didn't realize a roommate was involved."

"I apologize for not making that clear to you over the phone."

Alissa didn't want to walk away. From the outside, at least, this was far more desirable than anything she had looked at all month. "What about the other side of the duplex? I suppose that's taken?"

"Yes, it is."

Mallory laced her pudgy fingers in her mother's thick, shoulder-length hair. It was the color of dark brown sugar. Alissa noticed how pretty Genevieve was. Here it was the middle of the day and she was at home with a toddler, yet she wore gold hoop earrings and makeup to highlight her clear, gray eyes.

"How did you hear about the duplex?" Genevieve asked.

"Someone left me a note at work. I'm not sure who it was."

"We haven't advertised," Genevieve said. "It's all been through referrals. I wonder who it was?"

"I really don't know."

"Have you found another place?" Genevieve asked.

"Not yet, but I have a few options." Alissa thought of the one small apartment she had just looked at that was immediately available if she wanted to sign a six-month lease. It was a dark downstairs unit with badly stained rose-colored carpet.

But it was the only one on her list that allowed pets. And she would never give up Chloe.

"Do you allow pets?" Alissa ventured.

"Small ones, yes. Shelly had a kitten when she first moved in but gave it to our girls since she was traveling so much."

"Whiskers." Mallory said, then hid her face in her mom's neck.

"My cat's name is Chloe," Alissa said, trying to draw out the little girl.

"Would you like to have a peek inside the duplex?" Genevieve asked.

Alissa agreed, and as they walked up to the front entrance, Genevieve said, "It would actually be like having a part-time roommate since Shelly is gone so much."

"Like Daddy," Mallory chimed in and hid again.

"My husband is a commercial pilot. He flies a route to the Orient." She turned the key in the front door, which Alissa could now see was a two-part, dutch door. It added even more charm to the unit. As they stepped inside, she caught her breath.

"The furniture is like mine! Did Shelly buy the wicker pieces at Pier 1 Imports?"

"I don't know."

"And this poster of Portugal. I have one of the same place."

"I would say there's a good chance you and Shelly would get along. The unit has two bedrooms and a dishwasher but only one bathroom. My favorite feature is out here." She led Alissa through the spacious living room and out the back door. "This is our garden."

Alissa stopped and tried to drink it all in from the small landing that opened to lush green grass. Tall trees provided a canopy from the June afternoon heat. A brick trail lined a neatly kept rose garden and led to a wooden archway that housed two small benches facing each other. To the right side, toward Genevieve's home, lay an intricate maze of colorful flowers lining the brick walkway. A swing hung by long ropes from a thick-trunked tree, and a small wading pool glimmered in the sunny spot of the common yard.

"This is beautiful," Alissa said.

"Thank you. I love to garden."

"This is more than a garden," Alissa said. "This is…"

"This is home," Genevieve stated.

With a catch in her throat, Alissa swallowed and nodded. It had been a long, long time since she had felt like anywhere was home. Yet she had to agree. If any place on earth felt like home, this was it.

"I'll take it," she heard herself say.

Chapter Two

T wish it were that simple," Genevieve said. "You see, the other part I didn't explain yet is that it needs to be Shelly's choice. I'm only helping her out by showing the place. She would, of course, like to meet and interview you."

"Of course. When will she be back?"

"I'll have to check her calendar. She's usually gone four days at a time."

Alissa's heart sank.

"I can try leaving a message for her, if that would help. She could call you in a day or two, and perhaps you could chat on the phone."

"I'm in a difficult situation," Alissa said. She briefly explained about the landlord and needing to sign the lease agreement tonight or let the condo go.

"I see your problem," Genevieve said. Mallory had hopped down and was stalking a butterfly in a bunch of Shasta daisies. "I wish I could make the decision for Shelly. But I can't."

"No, of course not. I wouldn't expect you to. I have to get back to work. I'll give you a call this afternoon, and maybe we can figure something out."

Back at the office, three customers were waiting, and both Cheri and Renée were on the phone and had customers at their desks. Alissa was nearly five minutes late. A stack of six messages waited for her.

"Who was next?" she asked.

An older couple rose together. He pulled out the chair at Alissa's desk for the woman and made sure she was situated before he sat down. Alissa thought it was sweet to see a couple in their sunset years being polite to each other and holding hands.

"What can I do for you?"

They looked at each other tenderly, and the woman said, "We'd like to go to Italy."

"Sounds wonderful," Alissa said, smiling at the white-haired woman who wore slightly smeared red lipstick and had a bright gleam in her eye.

"Spare no expense," the balding man said. "All the best hotels. Rome, Florence, Venice. Nothing's too good for my Rosie."

"Oh, Chet," the woman purred.

Alissa reached in the side drawer for some brochures on Italy and smiled at the charm of this couple. "We have several tour packages available, or if you'd like, we can arrange the accommodations, and you can take the sightseeing at your own pace. How long would you like to stay?"

"A month," he said. "Minimum. We'd like to keep our own schedule. And don't rent a car for us. We'll take the trains. First class, of course. Do they still offer those rail passes?"

"Yes. We can arrange Eurail Passes for you. When did you want to begin your trip?"

"Anytime after the fifteenth. That's our wedding day."

Alissa smiled again. She tried to guess if this was their golden anniversary. They looked old enough to have been married for fifty years.

Fifty years. What would it be like to spend fifty years with the same person?

"Would you like to start out in Rome or Venice?"

"Which is more romantic?" Rosie asked. Alissa thought she caught a hint of mischief in Rosie's eyes.

"Rome is beautiful, especially this time of year before the late summer heat. I've never been to Venice, but of course it's a fabulously romantic city." Alissa opened the brochure and pointed to a photo of a gondola. "Hundreds of canals to explore. Lots of history."

Chet leaned forward and said with a wink, "Don't know if we'll have time to explore all the canals. We'll be busy making our own history."

"Oh, Chet," Rosie said pressing her cheek against his shoulder.

"Which one do you want to start with, honey? Venice or Rome?"

"Venice."

"Venice it is." Chet winked again at Alissa and said, "Reserve us the best suite in the whole city for our first night. It's our honeymoon."

"Your honeymoon?"

They nodded.

"That's wonderful. Congratulations." Alissa felt slightly off balance. They had a strong attraction and so much affection at their age. "Did you meet around here?"

"Oh, no," Rosie said. "We met in Des Moines back in '43. We were high school sweethearts."

Alissa leaned back. She had to hear this story.

"Chet went off to war, you know."

"But we were promised to each other," he added. "Secretly."

"My parents didn't approve of his family," Rosie confided, lowering her voice and shaking her head. "I kept his ring hidden, and he sent his letters to my girlfriend's house. We planned to elope the moment he returned home, before my parents had anything to say about it. Then the letters stopped coming. I waited and waited."

"They listed me as deceased," Chet said. "Can you imagine? I took a tiny bit of shrapnel in the noggin. Right here." He leaned forward so Alissa could get a good look at the top of his bald head. Sure enough, there was a two-inch long scar in the shape of a lightning bolt.

"They carted me off to some second-class army hospital where my ID got mixed up with someone else's. I didn't find out until I was ready to come home six months later, and she was gone."

"Gone?" Alissa asked.

Rosie shrugged her shoulders. "I married Joe. I didn't have a choice. Everyone in town believed Chet was dead."

"She really didn't have a choice," Chet added. "You've never met her parents. They wanted her to marry an Elderidge boy since the day she was born. Elderidges had all the money, you know."

Alissa nodded. "So what happened?"

Cheri stepped over and placed a note in front of Alissa. It read, "Please call Mr. Brannigan right away."

"Would you two please excuse me a moment?"

Chet glanced at his watch. "Oh, dear, look at the time. We have to go, honey. The florist is expecting us in ten minutes, and you know how slow I drive." He chuckled and grinned, exposing lots of gold in his back teeth. "We'll have to come back and see you tomorrow morning."

"Okay," Alissa said reluctantly. She felt as if someone had yanked her away from a suspense novel right at the good part. "Tomorrow morning would be fine. I'll put together a tentative itinerary for you, and we can discuss it then. Shall we say nine o'clock?"

Rosie and Chet looked at each other. "Don't we meet with the caterer tomorrow at nine?" Rosie asked.

"I believe it's the preacher at nine and the caterer at eleven." Chet stood and helped Rosie from her chair. Alissa noticed for the first time that Rosie's left arm hung limp.

"I'll be here all day tomorrow," Alissa said. "Come in whenever you can. I'll look forward to seeing you then. I'm eager to hear what happened."

Rosie gave Alissa a little-girl grin. "It's like any good love story, dear. It has a happy ending."

Alissa could see that. The two held hands on their way out the door.

Cheri motioned for Alissa to take the next call as it rang through to her desk. Slipping on the headset, she answered the call from Mr. Brannigan. "How are you, Mr. Brannigan?"

"We've decided to cancel at the Heathman altogether and go on the Alaska cruise instead. We'll take the ten-day package."

"All right," Alissa said, swiftly entering the change into his electronic folder on the computer. "And which cruise did you want? The June cruise begins on the fifteenth, and the deposit is due ten days ahead which makes it…" She flipped through her desk calendar. "Tomorrow. Are you comfortable with that?"

"No problem. Put it on our account, and we'll set sail on the fifteenth."

Alissa hung up and with extra care planned a twenty-eight-day Italian tour. This was the part of her job she loved the most. Because she enjoyed traveling, whenever she planned an itinerary, it was as if a little piece of her stowed away and went on tour with the clients. Alissa wondered as she printed out Chet and Rosie's schedule if she would be seventy before she ended up with the right man.

Then, as her own secret signature and blessing on the travel plans, Alissa kissed her fingertip and blew the kiss toward the still warm copies. Her action made her think of her dream to have her own travel agency someday. She would call it A Wing and a Prayer and would specialize in helping people realize travel opportunities they didn't know were available to them. Alissa had a lot of dreams. But she had put them on hold far too long.

After work, she drove by the duplex. Again, the street, the front of the house, and the memory of the garden out back filled her with a peace that had been missing for a long time.

"Lord," she whispered, "I haven't asked you for anything in a long time. This duplex seems like the perfect home for me. Is this where you want me to live? I don't know what you want from me anymore. If you want to know what I want, this is it. As long as Shelly is a normal person, that is. At this point, only you can answer that. Okay, Lord? Do we have an understanding here? It's down to the final hour. I need an answer. Please."

No answer rolled in through her open car window. No fingers wrote yes or no in the sky.

"I wish you wouldn't make me trust like this. I wish you'd make decisions like this a little easier."

After letting out a heavy sigh, Alissa popped her car into gear. She drove past the duplex and down the street, no further along in her decision-making than she had been an hour ago.

As soon as she unlocked the front door of her condo, Alissa called for Chloe. The big, midnight black cat with a white patch on her nose came out of the bedroom with an affectionate "meow." Alissa lifted her and went into the living room. They settled in the middle of the wicker love seat, where Alissa began to stroke Chloe and to line up her options one more time. "I don't know what to do, Chloe. Should I go on faith and assume I can get the duplex?"

Chloe meowed.

"Oh, excuse me. Should I assume *we* can get the duplex? You'd love the backyard, Tiger. It would be your jungle, and you'd even have Whiskers to keep you company."

Chloe meowed again.

"I know. It sounds too good to be true. That's what I thought."

A silent moment stretched between them.

"You know what? I'm going to do it."

Alissa jumped up, taking Chloe under her arm into the kitchen. "We're going to sign off on this place and hope and pray and pray and hope we get the duplex. I told Genevieve I'd call her and we'd try to work something out. Let's call her."

Chloe jumped onto the counter as Alissa fished in her purse for the apartment list. She called Genevieve and asked if she had heard from Shelly yet.

"Not yet. I left a message. Hopefully she'll call this evening. I gave her your number. I didn't think you'd mind."

"No, of course not. I hope she calls, too. Thank you."

Just as Alissa hung up, the doorbell rang twice. "Go see who it is, will you, Chloe?"

Chloe meowed, and Alissa roughed up her fur, saying, "I was only teasing. I'll get it. As always. Come with me." She picked up her pet and went to the door. The new landlord stood there with the papers in his hand.

Alissa hesitated a bit before saying, "I'm not going to sign. I'm going to move."

The short man looked furious as he snapped the papers

back and said in a controlled voice, "Then you must be out within two weeks. It is the law."

"Yes, sir, I understand. I'll be out in two weeks."

The phone rang, which offered Alissa an excuse to close the door on the man. She grabbed the receiver and balanced it on her shoulder. "Hello?"

It was Shelly. Alissa felt a little tremor of goose bumps dance up her arm. Whenever coincidences like this happened, Alissa felt as if God was alive and right there with her rather than watching from a distance.

"Thanks for calling back. I suppose Genevieve told you I'd like to talk to you about the duplex."

"She did. And she told me you liked the place. Apparently we have matching furniture or something."

"The wicker," Alissa said, feeling comfortable with Shelly's lively voice. "I have the love seat and one chair to the set."

"Sounds like a match! Will you fill out a credit check and all that preliminary stuff, and do me a favor and drop it by Genevieve's so she can run it through? Then when I come home next Monday night, we can get together and decide if our personalities match as well as our furniture."

"Okay. I can do that."

"Great! And you have a cat?"

"Yes, Chloe. She's been with me through thick and thin for almost seven years now."

"She sounds like a sweetie. I have to run. I'll give you a call on Monday. Nice meeting you over the phone."

"Nice meeting you, too."

Alissa hung up and headed for the refrigerator. "A little cream to celebrate, Chloe? Looks like we won't be out on the streets." She poured the half and half into a saucer and placed it on the floor. Chloe immediately entered into the celebration.

Alissa recognized the familiar feeling coming over her.

For the past few years, her relationship with God had been a tug-of-war.

Not that she thought God was always wrong and she was right, nor that she always expected to have her own way. But after all she had been through, she needed proof, evidence of his supreme power. Facts, not feelings. She had had enough feelings for one lifetime.

Whenever she tugged on God's rope, she felt the tug back. Back and forth, back and forth, struggling with no peace.

She wasn't about to let her side of the rope go slack. Because if she let go now, she was afraid she would lose God forever, the same way she had lost every other significant person in her life.

Chapter Three

*A*lissa took a little extra time getting ready for work the next morning. She washed and curled her hair and put on some makeup. Today she needed to drop off the papers at Genevieve's, and being around her the day before had made Alissa feel frumpy.

She also thought of Rosie's sweet face and her red lipstick. Here Alissa had chided herself for living the life of a sixty-year-old, but Rosie's life and her appearance showed that she was taking much better care of herself than Alissa was.

More than a year ago Alissa had diagnosed her lack of attention to her appearance. She had figured if she looked good, men were attracted to her. When men were in her life, she got hurt. Solution? Go plain. Gain weight. Avoid men.

Even though Alissa had perfected her male-repellent technique, it hadn't brought the contentment she had longed for. So many hurts. So little healing.

As she applied her lipstick, she thought of Rosie's slightly smeared red lips. Had they gotten that way after a big smooch from Chet? Or was it hard for her, at her age, to put on her lipstick evenly?

Alissa knew how difficult it could be for an older woman to manage her makeup. Her grandmother had asked Alissa to do her personal care tasks for her during the last eight months of her life when she had become too shaky to handle the tasks herself. Alissa had combed her grandma's long, ivory hair each night and had smoothed lotion across her wrinkled cheeks. Every morning she had washed her grandmother's face with a warm washcloth, rolled her hair on top of her head in a round twist, and told her to pucker up as Alissa applied the lipstick. Her grandmother always wanted the red lipstick. "Firecracker Red" the bottom of the tube had said.

Alissa wondered if Rosie wore firecracker red. It was obvious Rosie's lips could still start a fire in Chet.

Perhaps those subliminal thoughts were what prompted Alissa to be nice to her own lips this morning. It wasn't their fault she didn't plan to use them on men anymore. They deserved a little pampering.

Alissa felt so good as she drove across town to work she didn't even think about stopping at Starbucks. "Good morning, Cheri," she said brightly as she walked in a few minutes early.

Cheri looked up and said, "I like your hair. It looks great that way."

"Thanks." Alissa considered complimenting Cheri, but she looked the same as always, which was perfect. She had a tidy, trim figure, and she wore coordinated, jewel-toned career apparel, which she mixed and matched. Cheri's black hair was in a super short cut that allowed her to get out of the shower, shake once, and take off. There didn't seem to be anything new to compliment her on.

"Did I tell you about that older couple yesterday?" Alissa asked, adjusting herself in her chair and putting on the phone headset. "Chet and Rosie. They're getting married a week from Saturday, and they must be in their seventies. They are so cute. I'm doing an Italian tour package for their honeymoon."

Cheri smiled. "Warms your heart, doesn't it. Did you find a new apartment?"

Before Alissa could answer, the phone rang, and she took it. "Yes, we can book group tours to the Holy Land. How many would be in your party?"

The morning sped by with nonstop calls and customers. It seemed everyone had suddenly realized it was June and time to plan a vacation. Not until Renée arrived at noon and told Alissa to take her lunch break did she realize she hadn't seen Chet and Rosie.

"If an older couple comes in asking about their itinerary for Italy, it's on top of my in-basket. But I'd like to be the one to go over it with them, if they don't mind waiting."

Renée, a large woman with red hair in a bouffant style, took her position as manager seriously. She worked part-time because she also ran a home business selling cosmetics. After managing this travel agency for seventeen years, she was looking for something more flexible. That's what the home business seemed to provide, but not enough money was coming in yet for her to quit the agency.

"I'll keep an eye out for them," Renée said. "And please try to be back in an hour today. I understand about the apartment hunting yesterday, but we've been so busy we need all hands in the office."

"I'll be back at 1:00," Alissa promised. She drove right to

Genevieve's and dropped off the papers, which she had picked up that morning on her way to work and had filled out. She also had purchased a potted yellow mum as a gift for Genevieve.

Mallory answered the door with a shy, "Hello."

Genevieve appeared at the top of the stairs, holding a pair of tennis shoes. In the entryway hung a brass chandelier with three tiers of lights covered by frosted glass domes. It made for a beautiful setting as Genevieve moved down the stairs to the polished hardwood floor where Alissa stood.

"Hi," Alissa said, wondering if she had overdone it by bringing the flowers. "I wanted to bring a little contribution for your garden."

"Thanks. It's lovely. Please, come in," Genevieve said. "Would you like something to drink?"

Alissa followed her to the spacious kitchen and pulled up a stool at the center island. Genevieve had decorated every-thing in flowers, not in bright or overwhelming colors, but in quiet pastels. The wallpaper was a subtle, neutral grass with a border of wildflowers midway up the wall. Cursive writing appeared on the flowered border, making it look like labeled packets of flower seeds or pages from a gardener's journal. The string of flowers from this mock diary made for a soothing bor-der. Dried flowers hung from the ceiling over the sink, and a swag of dried flowers arched over the french doors that led to the common garden.

"This is a beautiful kitchen," Alissa said.

"Thank you. I like it here very much. Is iced tea okay?"

"Yes, thank you."

Genevieve handed her the tall, blue-tinted glass of tea along with a long spoon and a china sugar bowl. "I'm glad Shelly caught you last night. I'll get the credit check started right away. Is there anything unusual we should be aware of?"

"I don't expect anything unusual on the credit report itself, but I had to leave one of the questions blank and that may slow the process."

"Which one?" Genevieve asked, scanning the paper.

"Under references. They asked for a relative, but I don't have any."

"None?" Genevieve asked. Mallory had removed a boxed drink from the refrigerator and was holding it up for her mother to poke in the straw.

"None." Then, because she knew it was so unusual, Alissa hesitatingly explained. "My dad died when I was sixteen. My mother died six years ago, and my grandmother passed away four years ago. As far as I know, I have no other living relatives."

Something pinched the corner of Alissa's heart as she said the words. In a way it was a lie. She did know of one other living blood relative. But that one didn't count. Shawna wasn't hers to claim.

"Mommy?" Came a voice from the couch in the adjacent family room. "May I have something to drink?"

"Sure, honey." Genevieve reached for another boxed drink and walked over to the couch. "Poor little angel," she said. "Her last week of school, and she came down with chicken pox. Have you had them? I should have asked before inviting you in."

"Yes, I had them when I was six."

As Alissa watched, a little face framed with mussed up blond hair appeared over the edge of the blue couch. She turned shyly to spy on Alissa. Red dots speckled her forehead and cheeks.

Without warning, tears from a deep fountain surfaced in Alissa's eyes. The girl couldn't be more than eight or nine, the same age as Shawna, the baby Alissa had given up for adoption.

Alissa had kissed her baby good-bye when she was less than a week old and had placed her in the eager, grateful hands of a couple who had longed and prayed for a child. She always knew she had done the right thing, especially since Shawna's father had been killed in a surfing accident before he even knew Alissa was pregnant. It was all a long time ago. The fruit of her reckless, misguided, and painful teen years.

"This is Anna," Genevieve said. "Honey, this is Alissa."

The little patient took a lingering moment to meet Alissa's blue eyes. Even Alissa's glasses couldn't hide her glistening tears from this observant patient.

"I'm hot, Mommy," was all Anna said.

"I know, love. Try drinking this. I'll get you a washcloth." Genevieve's words were so steady and calming, they even comforted Alissa. Her tears stopped right at the brim of her eyelids.

"You have your hands full. I should go," Alissa said, taking a quick sip of the iced tea. "Oh, this is delicious tea."

"I use fresh mint from the garden. Nice isn't it?"

"When we lived in Germany, we had a neighbor who grew mint in a window box."

"Really? You lived in Germany?"

"My father was in the air force. We lived lots of places."

Genevieve retrieved a washcloth from a drawer in the kitchen and wet it with tap water. "I grew up in Zurich," she said. "Have you ever been there?"

"Yes, several times. It's a beautiful city. How long have you lived here?"

"Seventeen years. Ever since I married Steve."

"And you have two daughters?"

"Three. Fina is at school. She's fourteen."

"I had a friend in school named Fina. From Josephina, right?"

Genevieve looked up from the couch where she had

placed the cool cloth on Anna's forehead. "You're the first American I've ever met who knew that. I certainly hope everything works out. It would be delightful having a neighbor who actually knows what I mean when I say 'francs' and doesn't think I'm referring to some sort of hot dog!"

Alissa smiled. She had to agree. Genevieve and her girls would make wonderful neighbors. "Maybe I'll see you Monday, when Shelly returns."

"Good. I'll look forward to it, Alissa."

"I hope you feel better, Anna."

A soft "thank you" drifted up from the couch.

Alissa hurried to her car, thinking of how peaceful Genevieve's home felt. It wasn't just the wallpaper or the magnificence of the house. It was Genevieve. She exuded a steadiness and charm that Alissa admired. And Genevieve's girls seemed to have inherited it from her.

Driving through the nearest fast food place on her way back to work, Alissa ordered a hamburger, fries, and large Coke. But then she changed her mind. "Can you please make that a chicken salad, no dressing, and an iced tea?"

You think you're starting some kind of pointless diet? a voice inside her chided.

No, I'm tired of hamburgers, that's all.

But the truth was Alissa wanted to make a fresh start. She didn't know exactly what had caused the shift in her attitude, but she did know she was on the road toward some changes. And her eating habits were just one of them.

She arrived at the office a few minutes before one o'clock and had time to consume half her salad in the back room before returning to her desk. The duplex was much closer to work than her condo. Her hopes were getting set on moving in, and she had no idea what she would do if it didn't work out. The cave apartment with the dirty, rose-colored carpet barely seemed feasible after picturing herself as Genevieve's neighbor.

She and Cheri went out for a bite to eat after work on Thursday. After Alissa told Cheri all about the duplex and how much she hoped it would work out, Cheri cautioned her with a phrase that stuck with Alissa. "You know," Cheri said, "you can't depend on people or houses to make you content. You have to find contentment within yourself."

Alissa knew she was right. Still, she wanted to argue by saying, "Yeah, but it makes it a lot easier to be content when the people and houses are there, too."

The next afternoon Alissa thought about leaving work a little early to pick up some packing boxes. But Mr. Brannigan called requesting that Alissa fax him a detailed list of the types of services and entertainment options available on their Alaskan cruise ship. She was just about to run the list through the fax machine when the front door opened, and Chet and Rosie shuffled in.

"Hello!" Alissa greeted them. "How are you two? Please have a seat at my desk, and I'll be right there."

They looked a little weary but none the worse for all their busy wedding plans. Alissa ran the list through the fax machine and eagerly joined her clients.

"The first thing I need is your last name. I forgot to get it the other day."

"Michaels," Chet said. "That's my name, of course. As of a week from tomorrow I'll share it with my Rosie."

Alissa felt the same warm feeling coming over her she had felt the last time they were in. She leaned forward and said, "You must tell me the rest of your story! You left with Rosie marrying Joe. Then what happened?"

"I came home," Chet said. "Shocked my mother so, an ambulance came and carted her off to the hospital."

"Your poor mother!" Alissa said. "After everyone thought you were dead."

"Everyone but Rosie. She knew I was still alive."

"But you still married Joe? How did you know Chet was alive?"

"Here," Rosie said, patting her heart. Her lips bore their red flame well today. "I knew his soul hadn't left this earth. I knew he was still alive. But there was nothing I could do. The wedding was set, and I had agreed to marry Joe." She shook her head. "Oh, the things we do when we're young and foolish."

Don't I know.

"I managed to postpone the wedding for a month," Rosie continued. "I convinced Joe we needed to have everything in order. Every day I prayed and watched out the window, waiting for Chet to walk up that pathway to my front door. Finally, I couldn't stall any longer. The night before our wedding I went into my parents' room and sat on their bed and told them everything. How Chet and I were promised to each other, how I knew he wasn't dead. I told them I couldn't marry Joe. I had to wait for Chet to come home."

"What did your parents do?"

Chet shook his head. "She doesn't like to talk about it. But I'll tell you. Her father struck her. Right across the mouth. Told her never to speak such foolishness again. She would marry Joe Elderidge, and that was that."

"How awful," Alissa said. She couldn't imagine anyone hitting this delicate-boned woman with the flame red lips. Her face was made to be kissed, not slapped.

"Joe was nearly the only man in town available for marriage," Rosie explained. "He was partially deaf in his left ear, so the army issued him a 4-F classification, and he stayed home while all the other boys were shipped off. I knew I should be grateful for the chance to marry. Many of my girlfriends were destined to become spinsters."

The phone rang, but Alissa ignored it, hoping Cheri or Renée would see how involved she was. "So you married Joe," Alissa said, prodding. "And then Chet came home. What happened when you saw him?"

"I didn't see him. My mother made sure of that. The week after Joe and I were married, she and Joe's mother arranged for us to move to Houston."

"Why? Did they think Chet was alive, too?"

"I don't think so. I think they wanted to teach Joe and me how to get close to each other. As long as we were in Des Moines we both had lots of family and friends. In Houston we only had each other."

"Each other and the bottle," Chet muttered, shaking his head.

"Joe drank," Rosie explained.

She didn't need to say any more. Alissa's mother had died of alcohol poisoning after many years of struggling to kick the addiction. Because of that Alissa had never gotten drunk, even during her wildest, most rebellious years. She had sipped wine coolers and shared bottles of beer with boyfriends, but she never had let herself get drunk. She knew what it was like to live with an alcoholic, and her admiration for Rosie swelled to the point she wanted to reach across the desk and take this sweet woman in her arms and hug her close.

"I'm sorry," Alissa whispered.

Rosie looked down, then lifted her cheerful, hope-filled face back up. "You can imagine what happened the day Chet actually showed up! He shocked his mother and then went to my house and nearly sent my mother to the hospital with a fainting spell as well. But my mother was strong."

"Strong!" Chet said, making a face. "The woman was a tyrant! She wouldn't let me in the house and cast me out as if

I were a demon returned to haunt her. All she would tell me was that Rosie didn't love me. Rosie loved Joe, and they had left town as soon as they married. The woman threatened my life if I ever tried to contact her daughter."

"But you did, didn't you?"

"Not right away. It was all pretty overwhelming to me, as you can imagine. I'd lie awake at night doubting that Rosie had ever loved me. I almost convinced myself that as soon as I'd left, she had taken an interest in Joe." Chet looked at his halo-haired fiancée, and a tender smile warmed his face. "Then I got the letter."

"Excuse me," Renée said, stepping up behind Alissa. "I'm sorry to interrupt, but it's a little after five, and I wondered if you needed some more time." Renée always wanted to be the last one to leave and lock up. It was obvious she was ready to go now.

"I didn't realize it was that late. We haven't even gone over the itinerary yet," Alissa said, hunting for their file.

"We need to be on our way, too," Chet said.

"Why don't I take two minutes to go over this with you," Alissa said. "And then we can finalize everything after you've had a chance to study the plans more carefully." Gathering her thoughts, she opened the folder and tried to find her voice. Her mind was filled with questions. *Who sent the letter? What did it say? Did Chet go to Houston in search of Rosie?*

She went over the departure times with them, smiling at Chet's relief that their flight didn't leave until late morning. "I'm not much of a morning person anymore," he commented.

"Now," Alissa continued, "I have you flying out of LAX on the morning of the sixteenth. I thought since the wedding was on the fifteenth you might like to stay at one of the hotels near the airport your first night and then get a fresh start in the morning."

She opened the hotel brochure for them, pointing out the pictures of the bridal suite. "It's a lovely room. You'll be treated to complimentary champagne, chocolates, breakfast in bed the next morning, and the room has a hot tub."

Rosie appeared to blush. "Sounds lovely," she said. "What kind of a room did you find for us in Venice?"

A smile spread across Alissa's face. "Just wait until you see this." She opened the next brochure in their file and with great pleasure described the luxury hotel she had found for them near the romantic Piazza San Marco.

This is why I love being a travel agent, she thought as she watched the couple's eyes shine in anticipation of their honeymoon travels.

Chapter Four

*A*lissa attacked the chore of packing up her condo with vigor. She still had to meet with Shelly on Monday before the final decision was made, but it all felt so right. Certainly everything would fall into place.

By Saturday afternoon she was in the thick of it, going through her bedroom like a twister, leaving nothing in her path that could be wrapped and boxed. She used to joke about how she never had to spring clean because she always moved before the task became necessary.

Digging through the back of her closet, Alissa pulled out four boxes that were still wrapped with packing tape from her last move. Or maybe it was from the move before that. Hard to tell.

Why am I hauling this stuff around if I don't even know what's in it? I probably won't miss it.

She plopped down on her bedroom floor and tore open the boxes. They were full of clothes—two sizes smaller than what she wore now. Alissa remembered packing them and telling herself she would fit in them again. Now, even if she lost that much weight, the outfits were so different from her current style, she probably wouldn't wear them.

As she pulled out a few of the pieces, each item seemed to release a picture in Alissa's mind. Each snapshot was of events that had happened when she had worn that outfit. The navy blue mix and match pieces she had taken on her trip to Japan. The white shirt she had worn for seventy-two hours straight when her grandmother went into the hospital.

Then came a neatly folded dress, short and black. She had chosen that dress for the first time she had met Thomas at Chang's. Alissa sniffed at the bodice. Did she imagine it, or did it smell like Chinese food? What a wicked night that was. She let the dress crumble into a mound in her lap. Then she allowed her memory access to the places in her mind and heart she had kept locked for two years. Every thought and memory of Thomas Avery tumbled over her with frightening clarity.

They had met at church. It was a mutual attraction. He was on the worship team, and she spotted him her first week there. She was living in Phoenix at the time. A large travel company had opened a corporate office and had transferred her from the agency where she worked in Atlanta. The first thing she did after moving into her apartment was find a "rockin" church. That was her style at the time—contemporary services, seeker friendly, lots of people, and a platform for her to stand on and sing out her heart.

She found the perfect church, and tall, gorgeous Thomas Avery was the perfect man. There was only one problem. He was married.

Alissa was a different person then. She was so on fire for Jesus. And she was slim and energetic with a healthy salary to support her clothes habit. Never did she wear the same outfit twice on Sunday mornings. Lots of single men were interested in her. But she was used to that. None of them intrigued her the way Thomas did.

The first time she shook Thomas's hand and looked into his strong face was right after she had given her testimony at a Sunday evening service. She had been attending for almost two months and had shared about her past with one of the women in the singles group. The next day the pastor had called her at work and asked if she would be willing to share on Sunday night. He also said he had heard she liked to sing and would she grace them with a song after her testimony. Of course she saw it as a high honor and went out that afternoon to buy an appropriate outfit.

She practiced in front of the mirror all week. By Sunday night her words were honed.

"I led a rebellious life as a teenager. My father died when I was sixteen, and my mother was an alcoholic."

Alissa went into detail about the party scene she became immersed in and the different guys she was involved with. "I remember one time we were staying at Newport Beach for summer vacation, and my mother was so drunk she threw a vodka bottle at me. I was used to that from her. What I remember the most wasn't being upset with her but being mad at myself because I'd forgotten to take my birth control pills, and my date was waiting for me. He drove off without me, and I broke down and cried all over this girl I hardly knew. She was so innocent and sweet, and I felt so used up. I wished I could be like her."

After more details of the wretchedness of her life, she told how she had been with one guy who died in a bodysurfing accident while he was stoned. She hadn't really cared.

"Everything inside me was dead. Then I found out I was pregnant with his child. It seemed impossible that something could be alive inside me when I was so sure I was dead."

She told of her difficult decision not to have an abortion, and then how she had given up the baby girl for adoption. There wasn't a dry eye in the congregation.

"Then Christy, the girl I cried all over that one night, shared with me how to become a Christian, and I got saved."

A roar of applause had filled the church, the pastor had given her a warm handshake, and Thomas had gazed at her from the front row with piercing eyes. Alissa had felt higher than a bird.

Then, like a bird, she sang her heart out in a praise song she had learned at her church in Atlanta. She tried not to stare at Thomas as she sang. He cried through the whole song. The tears only made his strong face more desirable.

When he stepped forward after the service to shake her hand, his rumbling voice said, "I wrote that song."

They stood in front of the church talking until only four other people were left in the building. Then he walked her to her car and stood there another hour, opening up his heart to her.

Thomas had graduated from a Christian college as a music major and wanted to become a worship leader at a church. But he was hindered by his wife refusing to attend church. They had married his second year at college and both had worked hard to make it through. After college he was hired as a music pastor in Idaho. They were married only two years when his wife turned against him. He didn't know why. He couldn't understand.

As they stood in the parking lot, he told her how hard the last eight years of his marriage had been. He had lost his position at the church in Idaho and had moved to Phoenix when his brother offered him a job. After ten years in his miserable marriage, he was about to give up everything until hearing her testimony and song. Maybe he should try writing more songs.

Even though it felt a little awkward for this married man to be so open with her, Alissa's heart went out to him. All those years in a loveless marriage. All his musical talent going to waste.

He called her at work two days later saying he had written a song and would she be willing to meet him that night at Chang's Chinese Restaurant to help him with one part he just couldn't get right.

Alissa lifted the black dress and sniffed for the scent of Chinese food again. Was it her imagination? No, the essence of sweet and sour sauce was definitely still there. In her flood of memories there was only the sour. All the sweetness she had felt when she drove to meet him that night was long gone.

Perhaps she had been too trusting. Or perhaps she knew exactly what was happening and didn't have the maturity to resist this older man. Whatever the problem, the trap set for Alissa had been a wide one, and she had fallen in without hesitancy.

They met regularly and talked on the phone daily. Alissa's thoughts were filled with Thomas. What made it so intense was that they only talked. They didn't touch. After all, he was a married man. They were both Christians. This was a spiritual friendship. She was helping him with his music, and he was helping her recover from her past.

Thomas taught Alissa about "forgiving God." She had never heard that concept before in any of the churches she had attended. He explained that with all the painful experiences from her past, the only way she would be able to move forward was by telling God she forgave him for all the awful things he had allowed to happen to her.

At the time she had only slightly questioned his theology. Now she knew it was all backwards. It was the most damaging way of thinking she had encountered in her Christian life. It put her in charge, not God. But she didn't realize how flawed that thinking was at the time.

Then came their debut.

Five weeks after they had met, Thomas had perfected two of his new songs and arranged for him and Alissa to sing together in church. When their harmonized voices filled that auditorium, Alissa had never felt so fulfilled. They were a hit. The thunderous applause showed they were blessing people, serving God together. Two weeks later they sang again.

Thomas was different from any other Christian man she had known. He put a "twist" on all the basics of Christianity she had been taught. She couldn't understand why his wife had turned against him. What moved Alissa the most was when Thomas talked about how he longed for children of his own. He shared with her the intimate details of why that was never going to happen with his wife and how sad he felt that, at thirty-two years old, he knew he would never be a father.

The night after their fourth duet at church, Thomas walked Alissa to her car and asked if they could go somewhere to talk. They went to Alissa's apartment. She fixed coffee, and Thomas cried. He confessed to her his deep longings for her. He wanted to leave his wife and marry Alissa. Together they would have the music ministry he had always dreamed of, and together they could have children. He made it sound so logical. Why would God want him to stay in bondage to an evil woman? God wanted him to be happy. He needed to be free of his wife to serve God.

Even now, sitting on her bedroom floor, Alissa remembered her response to Thomas. She had sat there, listening in horrified silence. As his words washed over her, she saw clearly, for the first time, how intertwined she and Thomas had become. All of her illusions, all of her justifications and excuses melted away. She was left with the cold reality of what she had allowed to happen.

"I couldn't live with myself if I knew I was responsible for the breakup of your marriage," Alissa told Thomas.

He had cried and pleaded, saying, "Don't you see? You didn't break up anything. My wife did. Years ago. You are the one who has brought life back to me. I can't live without you." He took her in his arms and wept on her shoulder.

Alissa knew what would happen next. After all these weeks of having a "spiritual" friendship, they were about to cross the line into a physical union. She, who had been physically pure ever since she had turned her life over to the Lord, was about to change that. Although she struggled fiercely with her impulses, the voice inside her heart spoke loud and clear, "No!"

With a strength that came from some place beyond her own frail flesh, Alissa pushed him away. She rose to her feet and firmly said, "I can't do this, Thomas. I won't."

He crumbled, broken and lost. "What will I do? What will I do without you? You can't do this to me!" He cried for what seemed like a very long time.

Alissa stood firm. "You need to leave. Now."

Gathering himself together he headed for the door saying, "You were the best thing that ever happened to me, Alissa. I don't know if I can keep on living without you."

With bars of steel protecting her bruised heart, Alissa had said, "I refuse to be manipulated, Thomas. You need to get your life together. I need to get mine straightened out, too. But not like this. Not the way we've been going. It's not right."

She opened the door for him to leave, and Thomas slumped against the doorway. "This is it then, isn't it? You really mean it, don't you? You won't take me back."

Alissa shook her head. All the strength and tenderness that had drawn her to Thomas had now turned to mush, and she wanted him and everything about him to vanish from her life. Without looking back, Alissa turned from Thomas, who was still crying. She disappeared inside her apartment. Then she bolted the door.

The next step had seemed simple to her. Phoenix was a big city. She was a big girl. She would find another church and avoid all married men. She had learned her lesson, as painful as it had been, and she was ready to move on. At least she hadn't done something really stupid and fallen for his pleadings.

However, the next Sunday she slept in, and the Sunday after that and the Sunday after that. Then she went on a weekend cruise for work, and before she knew it, three months had passed, and she hadn't visited any new churches. That was more than two years ago.

Now, with the box of clothes open before her, Alissa felt as if the Thomas experience had happened to someone else. That wasn't she. The woman she was now would never have fallen for a man like that. It seemed so long ago.

Wiping the few tears that had come along with the memory and drawing in a deep breath, Alissa carried all four boxes of her Phoenix clothes down to her car and stacked them in the backseat. Tomorrow morning they would be in the Goodwill donation bin. That season of her life needed to be gone—from her closet and from her memories.

In every way, she was ready to move on.

Chapter Five

Sunday morning dawned clear and warm, but Alissa stayed in bed. She was emotionally exhausted from reliving the Phoenix nightmare.

In a strange way, she knew she had begun to purge herself of the strong effect the events had had on her. By recalling everything from start to finish, she felt good about herself. She had done the right thing to move on with her life. If she knew a church to attend in Pasadena—a safe church—she probably would have ended her two-year hiatus and attended this morning.

Instead, she returned to her packing. But she continued her self-evaluation while she wrapped items and wedged them into boxes. Her inability to emotionally connect with anyone other than Chloe was probably the worst consequence of her Thomas experience. She trusted no one. And rarely opened up. What would it be like to have a roommate? Would Shelly want to talk late into the night, or would she be on the go so much that they would only communicate through notes left on the refrigerator?

By Monday night, her questions were all answered. Shelly called Alissa at work and invited her to come to the duplex. Alissa arrived at 5:15 and knocked on the lower half of the dutch door. The top portion was open, and harp music floated from the heart of the duplex.

"Hi, Alissa?" Shelly scurried to the door with a dish towel in her hand. "Come in, come in." The scent of cinnamon followed her.

Alissa liked her at once. Only a few other women had brought out that response in Alissa, including a girl named Christy, the innocent one who had shown Alissa the path to Christ.

Shelly resembled Christy in some ways. She had long, silky hair the color of a fawn's. Her eyes were clear and a soft brown tone, arched by curved brows. Her smile was bright, and so was her outfit—a short green top and white cut-off jean shorts. And she was barefoot.

Alissa had worn a suit to work that day, hoping to appear professional and successful when she met Shelly. She had curled her hair, which now hung in a soft curl a bit past her shoulders. She had put in her contacts that morning, too. They tinted her eyes a cool shade of aqua.

Alissa felt this was a high school summer day all over again, and she was making a new friend.

"I'm so glad to meet you," Shelly said, shaking Alissa's hand and welcoming her in. "That's a beautiful necklace. Did I tell you the credit check came through? No problem. Everything is clear. Did you see the bedroom last time you were here?"

Alissa had rarely heard anyone talk so fast yet still make sense. Shelly's voice was smooth and clear. Alissa guessed she was younger by about two years. Maybe three.

"No, I only saw the living room."

"Well, then, let me take you on the grand tour. This is the kitchen. I was just cleaning up so don't mind the mess. I was in a baking mood when I got home. Would you like a cookie? Snickerdoodles."

"No thanks," Alissa said. She noticed how much larger this kitchen was than the one in her condo. Shelly had a unique kitchen table that Alissa paused to examine.

"I made that," Shelly said. "It's not a tree stump. It just looks like one."

A thick, ridged "stump" seemed to protrude from the linoleum floor and held up a round glass tabletop. A bowl of avocados sat in the middle of the table with a small mixed bouquet to one side. The chairs were black wrought iron with woven straw seats. It had to be the most unusual table Alissa had ever seen, and she loved it.

"This is wonderful! What is it?" she asked.

"I don't know. I found that stump thing at a junkyard and bought the glass top. The chairs came from an old patio set. I painted them, and a friend of mine strung the seats. If that's what you call it. I don't know what that kind of weaving is. She was taking a class, and this was her final project. Cool, huh?"

"Yes. Very fun. I like all your cupboard space."

"Oh, this place is full of storage space. Let me show you the closets in the hall. And wait until you see the walk-in closets in the bedroom!"

They ventured down the hallway, and Shelly opened each door as they went. The first room was an extra large bathroom with a long window. The wooden frame around the window was painted a mossy green to match an old dresser in the corner that Shelly used for towels. On top of the dresser was a big bouquet of flowers, and in the inset window frame was an arrangement of clear glass bottles with colored water in them, shooting rainbows across the white tile floor.

Everything about the duplex was lovely, and Alissa was amazed how the decorating matched her taste and her ideas of what was artistic.

Shelly opened the bedroom door at the end of the hall and said, "I hope you have a lot of furniture. This is the bigger bedroom. I was going to turn it into a sort of office-guest room but I never got around to it."

They stepped into a gigantic, empty room. The walls were covered with travel posters.

"Sorry," Shelly said. "I didn't take those down yet. Genevieve said she would send a painter over to freshen this room up before you move in. I think he's coming tomorrow. Or maybe it's Wednesday. Anyway, if you have a specific color you'd like him to paint it, we could let Genevieve know. She wouldn't mind at all. She's terrific, isn't she?"

Alissa nodded but found no words to voice her agreement. She felt choked up. It was as if some long lost relative had found her and was welcoming her into the family. It felt so different from any other living situation she had been in.

"Check it out," Shelly said, pulling up the pleated shades to the two back windows. The room instantly was flooded with evening sunlight, and all the dust fairies came to life, dancing merrily on the hardwood floor.

"It gets pretty hot in here in the afternoons if you keep the shades up. But that's only in the summer. The sun seems to be in just the right position between those two trees to pour itself into this room."

Alissa stepped forward to examine the view out the back. It was beautiful: the grass, the rows of colorful flowers in Genevieve's garden to the right, and straight ahead, the wooden archway at the end of the brick path. She couldn't ask for a more picture-perfect view and decided her desk would go right there, in front of the window.

With a smile and a heart full of contentment, Alissa turned to Shelly and said, "Well? I don't know what else to ask."

"Do you think we should maybe talk a little bit and see if we feel we're compatible?" Shelly asked.

"That's probably wise," Alissa said. She couldn't imagine them not getting along.

"Let's go into the living room." Shelly settled herself on the cushioned seat of her wicker sofa, among several embroidered pillows. Alissa took the chair by the window and felt the filtered sun warming the top of her head. The harp music lilted its way around them, and the bowl of bright red roses on the wicker coffee table gave off a sharp, spicy fragrance.

"You first," Shelly said. "Tell me all about you."

Something at the top of Alissa's throat suddenly froze shut. She didn't do this. People didn't just freely step into her life. "There's not much to say," Alissa began. "I'm a travel agent, as you know. I've been at this agency for seven months. Before that I was at the corporate office of an agency in Phoenix. I was there about two years and in Atlanta before that."

Shelly nodded and kept listening.

"I don't know what else you'd like to know. I have one cat, Chloe, who goes with me wherever I go. My father was in the air force, so we moved a lot while I was growing up. I think that's why I still like to travel today. I usually go on two trips a year. Sometimes three, if the agency pays."

"Besides traveling, what else do you like?" Shelly asked.

"Reading. I read a lot. That's about it."

"No interesting men in your life?"

"None."

"Wait until you meet Jake, next door," Shelly said, a playful smile blooming on her face. "He's an actor. Well, a wannabe actor. He has an agent and everything, but he hasn't gotten his big break yet. He was in a commercial, though. It aired a lot last winter. You probably saw it. It was for that new pain reliever. He was a mechanic. He held up a wrench and his line was, 'When the job is this big, there's no substitute for the right tool.'" Shelly's brow furrowed, and her voice deepened as she imitated Jake's TV debut.

"Then he holds up a bottle of the aspirin and says, 'And there's no substitute for the right pain reliever when it comes to headaches as big as mine.'"

"I think I missed that one," Alissa said, smiling.

"He thinks he's famous now. Only that was his last part, so he's been working as a waiter at Chez Monique's over in Santa Monica."

"I've heard of that place. It's supposed to be really nice."

"Oh, it is! He makes great tips." Shelly let out a low giggle. "If you really want to bug him when you meet him, call him Mr. Wartman. That's his name, Jacob Wartman. But, of course, his agent changed his last name to Wilde. He goes by Jake Wilde in the Hollyweird circuit."

"Hollyweird?" Alissa questioned.

Shelly laughed. "That's what I call it. Jake is always good for a story, and every one of them is weird."

"Weird Jake, huh?"

"Jake's not weird. Just his experiences. He's working on getting his pilot's license right now. I met him through Steven and Genevieve. I work for the same airline as Steven, and he tried to fix me up with Jake." Shelly rolled her eyes and shook her head. "Was that ever a disaster! But I found out about this side of the duplex and moved in the next week-end. They had a married couple who were moving out. Jake and I are great buddies now. So don't worry; there's nothing going on between us. Besides, I'm never home. That's part of the reason I decided to get a roommate. It seemed pointless for this place to be empty and go unused for half the month. Especially for what I pay."

"That probably should be my next question," Alissa said. "What do you pay?"

She was pleased to find out that with splitting the rent she would pay two hundred dollars less per month than her condo had cost her. It seemed a perfect arrangement all the way around.

"So, what do you think?" Shelly said. "I don't smoke, and I keep the TV in my room nice and low. Oh, and I eat more than anyone I know, so when I'm home, I'll cover the majority of the grocery bill."

"Have you lived here long?" Alissa asked.

"Only a year or so. I came from Seattle. That's where all my family lives. My dad's a minister. His father was a minister, as was his father. And my great, great, great—did I get too many greats in there? Anyway, how about you?"

"There definitely are no ministers in my family tree," Alissa said.

"I guess I should have asked about you and God earlier. You're not a Buddhist or anything are you? I mean, not that you couldn't still rent the duplex if you were. It's just that religion can often be a dividing point in friendships, and if that's going to be a real difference between us, we should talk about it now."

"I don't think it will be a problem. I'm…" Alissa hesitated. It had been a long time since she had labeled herself for anyone. "I'm a Christian," she said.

Shelly sat still, eyebrows slightly rounded up. She seemed to be waiting for Alissa to define that starting point.

"I haven't gone to church in a while, but I'm on good terms

with God, if that's what you're wondering."

"No, I didn't mean to judge you or anything. It's just that so many people say they're Christians, you know. Well, maybe not everybody. But both the guys next door are, and so is Genevieve. I think it just makes it easier when we get together and stuff. We're all coming from the same place, you know?"

Alissa noticed Steven wasn't included in the list. But she was too relieved Shelly hadn't asked for more explanation to ask where Steven stood. She also felt more comforted than threatened to know that she would be around Christians.

Several years ago Alissa would have been the one grilling Shelly, asking her if she had a personal relationship with Christ and if in all her years of church going she had ever repented of her sins and asked Jesus to come into her life. That zeal had drained itself from Alissa's life after the Phoenix experience. Now she would have felt like a hypocrite trying to evangelize anyone when she wasn't even attending church.

In a larger sense, Alissa was interested only in that which would bring about fresh new starts and positive changes in her life. There was no point in dredging up Phoenix again or her checkered church experiences. She knew she had given her heart to the Lord that summer day on the beach with Christy, and she knew Jesus was her best friend. For now that was the only place she knew to go back to. Because Shelly reminded her of Christy, Alissa felt a beginning sense of hope that she might get closer to God again.

"What do you think?" Shelly asked. "You want to move in?"

Alissa nodded. "If it's okay with you."

"Of course!" Shelly said, hopping up and giving Alissa an enthusiastic hug. "This will be terrific. Now do you want a snickerdoodle? How about something to drink? I went to the store on my way home from the airport, and I have all kinds of good stuff."

Alissa followed her into the kitchen. As Alissa trailed a bit behind, she tried to remember the last time she had felt a friendly touch like Shelly's hug. It had been far too long. She had exchanged handshakes at work and pats on the back from Renée. But it had been months since anyone had offered a friendly hug, and even longer since she had offered one.

"Actually," Alissa said as Shelly held up a pitcher of orange juice, silently inviting refills, "I think I better go. What's the next step?"

Shelly shrugged her shoulders and said, "Move in, I guess. Genevieve will have some lease papers for you to sign. Did she tell you they ask for a minimum of a year?"

Alissa flinched slightly. Then she realized a year was fine. She preferred six month commitments, but a year, in this case, would be fine.

"Okay. I'll start to move in this weekend, if that's all right with you."

"Terrific. I'm here until Thursday, and then I fly until next Monday. So why don't you stop by and pick up a key. I'll have one made tomorrow. You can sign the papers at Genevieve's then. And be sure to tell her about the paint, if you have a favorite color or something. Otherwise, when the guy comes this week, I think he'll just do it in some off-white shade. That's what my room is. Oh, I didn't show you my room, did I? Do you want to see it?"

"No, that's okay. I really should get going."

"If you can stop by tomorrow, for the papers and paint and everything, maybe we could decide about extra furniture. There's room for more in the living room, like your wicker love seat. It just looks full now because I crammed every empty corner with plants. They're good for the atmosphere, you know, especially because this place is closed up so much of the time. You're welcome to rearrange any way you want." Shelly poured herself a glass of juice. "Sure you don't want some?"

"No thanks."

"You'll find I'm not very picky about most things. Except shoes." Shelly wiggled her bare toes. "I should have lived in the Orient because I don't think shoes should be worn in the house. The guys next door have to take off their muddy clod-hoppers before they come in here."

"That's fine with me," Alissa said, glancing at her heels and checking the rugs covering the hardwood floor to see if she had tracked in any dirt. "From now on, I'll take off my shoes at the door."

"Great," Shelly said, her wide smile lighting up her face. "This is going to be so fun! By the way, how did you find out about it? From Genevieve?"

Alissa thought about the slip of paper she had discovered on her desk. Neither Renée nor Cheri knew anything about it. "I honestly don't know."

Alissa drove back to her condo, trying to solve the mystery of the note. No conclusions came to her. It reminded her of the mysterious letter that had brought Chet and Rosie together. She had been wondering about it since last Friday. They hadn't come in to confirm their travel plans, so first thing tomorrow she would call them to make sure everything was set. She puzzled over how she could ask about the letter without intruding.

As she entered the freeway traffic, she glanced up at the evening sky. The only nice thing about smog was it produced soft amber and peach hues as the sun set. At this moment the sky looked soothing. She loved sunsets. They reminded her of heaven. And tonight, heaven seemed closer than it had in a long time.

Alissa wondered if perhaps she really did have a guardian angel. Maybe God was trying to do something to draw her back to himself after all the years she had felt so abandoned.

Instead of turning south toward her condo, she pulled into a strip mall and parked in front of a paint store. Fresh beginnings called for freshly painted walls—and not off-white. A soft yellow, perhaps, like the sunset.

Chapter Six

$\mathcal{I}$ like it," Shelly said the next day as she held up the paint sample card in Genevieve's kitchen. "It looks like moonlight."

"It's called Golden Sunset. You don't think it'll be too yellow?" Alissa asked, offering another swatch of a lighter tone.

"I don't," Genevieve said, smearing some peanut butter on a slice of bread and handing it to Mallory, who sat on a stool next to Alissa. "That's a wonderful, neutral shade. I think it will give the room a nice, soft, sunny tone. But it's completely up to you. Let me know which one you decide on, and I'll call it in to the painter today."

"Mommy, can I have some juice?" Mallory asked.

Genevieve reached in the fridge for the juice and pulled out the iced tea pitcher as well. "More tea for either of you?"

"I'd like some, please," Alissa said. "I love the mint in this."

Genevieve poured the tea and gave Mallory a boxed drink. "You see if you can get the straw in this time," she said with a loving look at her littlest one.

Mallory tried, but the straw bent. She tried again and got it in. "I did it, Mommy!"

"I knew you could. That's my girl!"

"I'll go with this one," Alissa said, laying the "Golden Sunset" sample down on the counter like a playing card. "Did I need to sign some papers?"

"I have them here," Genevieve said, stepping over to the table and reaching for a file that bore Alissa's name on the tab. "This is the lease form, and this is the cleaning deposit addendum."

Alissa looked over the papers and signed them, feeling no regret for making a year's commitment.

"Are you wearing contacts?" Genevieve asked.

Alissa looked up surprised. "Yes, I am."

"I just noticed because when you were here before you had on glasses, and you look quite a bit different without them. When I have my glasses on, people barely recognize me."

Alissa was aware that people were noticing she was taking a little more care of herself lately. This morning she had climbed on the scale and was shocked to see she had lost two pounds. She had no idea how that had happened, except during the last week she had been on the go with her packing and everything. She had had no time for snacking.

At work Cheri had complimented her on her hair again and suggested she let it grow out more. She had pulled it back in a low ponytail for so many weeks, it had grown more than she had realized. Now that she was wearing it down with a slight curl on the ends it seemed even longer.

The lipstick touch up and squirt of perfume she had applied in the car before coming to Genevieve's front door had more to do with her next appointment than with meeting with Genevieve and Shelly. At 1:30 Alissa was meeting Chet and

Rosie at their home to give them the tickets and to finalize the itinerary. It seemed only logical to Alissa that one could not call on Chet and Rosie without looking one's best.

"Are you going to need help moving in on Saturday?" Shelly asked. "The guys might be around. Do you know if they'll be here, Gen?"

Genevieve shook her head. "I don't know."

"They're really nice," Shelly said. "After you get used to them."

Genevieve smiled. "Ideal neighbors as long as you don't mind their occasional bongo-fest. Isn't that what they call it?"

Mallory jumped into the conversation. "Jakey has a big bongo, and he lets me play it."

"Drums," Shelly explained. "It's their tribute to the beatniks of the '50s or something. It all started one night when we watched this hilarious beach party movie. What was it called? Anyway, through the whole movie this one guy played bongo drums and would say stuff like, 'Butterfly on a sourdough radio.' Crazy stuff like that. None of it made sense, but it kind of rhymed. Sort of."

Genevieve reached over to wipe off Mallory's sticky fingers before she hopped down.

"We watched the movie twice that night just because of that beatnik bongo guy. That was on a Friday night, and the next morning the three of us decided to go to the Saturday market. A guy was there with bongo drums." Shelly's light-hearted laugh filled the kitchen. "So these guys bought, I don't know, six drums. All different sizes. And that night they sat outside in the backyard with these silly little berets on their heads, beating their drums and making up ridiculous rhymes like a bunch of kooks until after midnight."

Genevieve smiled. "It was really quite funny. For about the

first hour. Then we all wanted them to go to bed."

"Thanks for the warning! I noticed you both waited until after I signed the papers before you told me this minor detail regarding the beatniks next door."

Genevieve and Shelly burst out laughing. It felt good to Alissa. She couldn't remember the last time she had said something spontaneous that made people laugh. She muttered jokes to Chloe all the time, but she never laughed. It almost felt as if a part of Alissa was coming out of deep freeze and some of the feeling was returning to her extremities.

Glancing at the oak-framed clock on the wall, Alissa said, "I need to go. I have an appointment with one of my clients. You would love this couple. Sometime I'll have to tell you their love story. That is, after I hear the whole thing."

She slid off the kitchen stool and headed for the door. "Oh, I almost forgot." Alissa reached into her leather briefcase and pulled out two coloring books. "For Anna and Mallory," she said, handing them both to Mallory. "How is your sister feeling?"

"She's fine. Can I have this one?" Mallory held up one of the cartoon coloring books.

"Sure. Give the other one to Anna for me, okay? I'll see you both sometime Saturday." Alissa looked up at Genevieve and Shelly. "And I will call if I need help. Thanks."

"Did you get the key?" Shelly asked.

"Right here," Alissa said, holding up her key chain. "I guess I'm official now."

Mallory moved closer, and with an impish grin on her face she said, "Thank you for the present."

Alissa smiled at the button-nosed toddler. "You're welcome, little Lady Bug. I'll see you later."

Mallory held up her arms, inviting Alissa to lift her in a hug.

Gladly, Alissa scooped up the child and pressed her cheek against Mallory's in a warm hug. She set the little girl down and waved to Genevieve and Shelly.

All the way to Chet and Rosie's the scent of peanut butter lingered on her cheek. Alissa didn't want to wipe it off.

She liked being hugged by Mallory. She loved sitting around selecting paint colors with her new friends. This was the life she'd never had as an only child. She hadn't gone the college route that included dorm rooms and sororities. Her schooling had come through night classes, and the only club she ever had belonged to was a mail order book club.

She found Chet and Rosie's bungalow in the hills of Altadena and parked in the cracked cement driveway. The house was yellow with white trim and looked as if it had been built in the forties but kept in good condition. A lovely pink climbing rose bush covered a trellis by the front door, and the welcome mat looked brand new.

Alissa rang the doorbell and adjusted her skirt's waistband, making sure the seams were straight.

Rosie answered, her lips red, her cheeks flushed. "It was so good of you to come all the way up here. We've been in such a scurry getting everything in order. Do come in."

"It was no problem at all," Alissa said, glancing around the small living room. Boxes were everywhere. "Did you just move in?"

"These are all Chet's things. I've lived here a number of years." Rosie clasped her hands and shook her head. "There is so much to do. The movers brought it all in over the weekend, but how does one combine two lifetimes in one small home?"

"Is Chet here?"

"No, he's out running errands for me. Why don't we slip out to the patio and have some lemonade?"

Alissa felt privileged to be invited into this dear woman's

life and out on to her patio. Following Rosie through the cluttered kitchen, she stopped at the refrigerator where Rosie handed her the pitcher of lemonade. Rosie found two glasses in the cupboard by the sink, and they wove their way out to the back patio.

"What a lovely patio and backyard," Alissa exclaimed as they pulled out the chairs from a new patio set. The open umbrella over their heads still smelled like plastic. Beyond the cement slab where they sat was a small patch of grass bordered by a flower garden and a huge blooming cactus tree. The majority of the shade came from the tall trees lining the fence on their neighbor's side. Alissa noticed how quiet it was. Along the side fence grew a winding honeysuckle bush providing an intoxicating fragrance. She could picture the love birds enjoying many meals here in their secluded nest.

Rosie lifted the pitcher and poured with her wobbly right hand. "How do you like the patio furniture? Quite an extravagant set, if you ask me. Chet picked it out yesterday."

"I like it very much," Alissa said. "Thanks for the lemonade."

"Do you need sugar? I made this from the lemons off our tree. Did you see it in the front? We have so many lemons. I'm sure we'll drink ourselves silly with all the lemonade I'll be making this summer."

Alissa sipped the drink. "Mine's fine," she said. "Very good."

They were silent a moment as they sipped their lemonade. The phone lines along the back fence issued a low humming sound. Rosie smiled. She looked refreshed. Alissa wanted to hear the rest of Rosie's love story and why the letter Chet had received had changed everything.

"Were you able to make all those reservations for us?" Rosie asked. "My, that's a lot of work for you."

"Yes, everything fell right into place. I don't mind a bit. It's not a lot of work, really. Not like it used to be when letters were all written by hand or on a manual typewriter." Alissa hoped the clues would prompt Rosie to pick up the story where she had left off at the letter.

"Do I need to sign anything?" Rosie asked.

Alissa reached for the file in her leather briefcase. "I don't need any signatures," she said. "But I would like to go over everything with you. Should I go ahead now, or should we wait until Chet returns?"

"I suppose you could tell me, and then if Chet has any questions, he could give you a quick call this week."

"That would be fine. Let's start with the tickets." She opened the vouchers and went over the departures and arrivals step by step. "I've listed all of the information on this sheet here, in case some of these vouchers seem a little confusing. You're confirmed for each of the hotels for the nights listed. You'll find those right here." Alissa pulled another printed sheet from the folder.

"My, you went to a lot of work," Rosie said.

Alissa reached over and gave Rosie's right hand a little squeeze. "And I enjoyed every second of it."

Rosie responded warmly by giving Alissa a squeeze back. It was then that Alissa realized what she had done. She had made the first move to reach out and show affection. It was so natural with Rosie. She was so different from Alissa's Bostonian grandmother, who had spent her every waking hour instructing Alissa on everything from how to enter a room, to how to begin a sentence. Rosie, just by being Rosie, welcomed affection and acceptance.

Leaning closer, still grasping Alissa's hand, Rosie said, "If you find a line of work you love, stay with it, dear. I loved children and would have gladly made raising children my life's work."

"Did you and Joe have a lot of children?" Alissa asked cautiously.

Rosie pulled away her hand. "Goodness, no!" she said with a gentle chuckle. "Ours was a rocky marriage in so many ways. I tried everything to please Joe—his favorite meals, I even dyed my hair." She shook her head. "He knew how badly I wanted to start a family. He insisted we couldn't afford to have children, and he didn't want to take any chances. Only he had children anyway. One that I know of in Houston and one from a business trip to Toledo."

Alissa's eyes grew big. How awful. How terribly awful. And with Chet still alive and in love with her. Alissa covered her mouth with her hand and let her eyes pour their sympathy out on Rosie.

"There was all the drinking, you know. Sometimes he would be gone for weeks. I wouldn't know where he was, and then he would come home drunk and sleep for days. He lost his job, so I took in laundry and cleaned the floors at the elementary school to keep food on the table. What I longed for more than anything was a child of my own. But as much as I begged him, Joe wouldn't give me that."

Alissa couldn't contain herself any longer. "Is that when you finally wrote to Chet?"

Rosie looked confused. "I never wrote to Chet."

"But the letter. Last week he said when he received the letter, it changed everything."

"Oh," Rosie said, her expression brightening, "that letter. I didn't write it. My best friend, Meg, did. You see, Meg moved to California not long after I married. She was my maid of honor. She had a cousin out here who owned an orange grove. Meg said she planned to be the first woman on the docks in Long Beach when all those lonely sailors came home after the war. She thought she had a better chance of finding a husband out here than back in Des Moines."

"So Meg wrote to Chet?"

Rosie nodded. "She did. Meg was the only one I confided in. She knew what my marriage was like. I never expected her to tell a soul. Then she heard about Chet coming back to Des Moines alive. It took her nearly five months to work up the courage, but she wrote to him and told him where he could find me. That's all she told him. Meg knew it wasn't her place to share any of the personal confidences I'd entrusted to her."

"Good for her. I like Meg," Alissa said.

Suddenly Rosie's expression changed. "Then you must meet her. She'll be at the wedding Saturday. You will come to our wedding, won't you? Chet and I would be honored to have you as one of our special guests."

Alissa quickly put aside her plans to move into the duplex, and with a smile she said, "Rosie, I wouldn't miss your wedding for anything!"

"Good," Rosie said, patting Alissa's leg. "Two o'clock on Saturday at Descanso Gardens, the Rose Garden."

Just then they both heard the back door open and Chet's warm voice call out, "Rosie-o, Rosie-o. Wherefore art thou, Rosie-o?"

Rosie gave Alissa a little-girl look, scrunching up her nose. "He always says that. Isn't he adorable?" With her head held high, she called out in a twittering voice, "Out here, my love! And Alissa is here, Chet."

"Well, hello there," he greeted Alissa with a friendly smile as he pulled up a seat. "I suppose you're going to want some money from us pretty soon."

"It's all detailed here in the folder. I've included the tickets along with the itinerary."

Chet gave Rosie a loving, adventuresome look and said, "Only four more days, my true love."

Alissa watched the tenderness transmitted between them. In a slight way, she felt as if she were intruding. But in a grander, deeply wonderful way, she felt as if she were being allowed to witness a miracle, to share a secret.

She knew exactly what she wanted to buy them for a wedding gift. A garden shop in the Old Town section of Pasadena made customized plaques and signs. Alissa could envision one hanging next to the honeysuckle on the garden wall. She would order a big wooden heart with the grand declaration, "Love Spoken Here."

Chapter Seven

When Alissa returned to the office, she felt exhausted. It was as if she had driven to Houston, Long Beach, and Des Moines as Rosie moved from place to place in her story. What mesmerized her was how Rosie could be so beautiful and poised after such a painful life. Did Chet do that for her? Was it possible for one completely true, sincere love to cancel so much hurt and pain? How did Rosie keep from being bitter?

All the way back to the office Alissa had tried to figure out what had happened after Chet received Meg's letter. Each scenario she pictured took her down a long, winding road in her imagination. Every angle Alissa worked factored Chet and Rosie getting together, as they were now. True love conquers all, right? But why were they reunited at seventy instead of at thirty? She knew some pretty detailed chunks of the story remained to be told.

The only thing that helped Alissa get her mind off Chet and Rosie was the stack of phone messages waiting for her. The afternoon flew by, as did the rest of the week.

On Friday after work Alissa drove by the duplex. She knew Shelly would be gone, and now, with Rosie and Chet's wedding on Saturday, she wouldn't be moving in until Sunday. At least she could move some of the plants around and check on how the paint turned out in her room.

Turning the key in the door, Alissa was glad to find it opened with just a touch. She entered the cool, quiet duplex and noticed a pair of Birkenstock sandals by the door. She remembered to slip off her flats and padded silently into the house.

On the table was a fresh bouquet of garden flowers and a sign that read, "Welcome home, Alissa!" First she smiled. Then she felt a tightening in her chest. She was home. Finally. Everything felt as if it had fallen into place.

Then she heard a noise. Alissa held her breath, listening intently for another sound.

There it was. Faint, but definitely inside, not outside. A slight tapping sound. She glanced around quickly, finding only one of the wrought iron dining room chairs to use as she stalked the intruder at the end of the hallway. The noise came again from behind her closed bedroom door. Alissa carefully pushed open the door and stepped in, her heart pounding, with the chair raised above her head.

A man with long brown hair, wearing a tattered work shirt was bent down under her window, fiddling with something on the wall.

"What are you doing here?" Alissa demanded, ready to heave the chair at him and run.

"Hey!" he cried, seeing her armed and dangerous. "Don't shoot! I'm doing you a favor."

He turned and she looked carefully at his face, something

she knew you were supposed to do before filing a police report. Then it hit her that she had seen that scruffy face before. She lowered the chair and put her hand on her hip.

"What in the world are you doing here?" she said, confronting the green-eyed computer guy.

Brad Phillips stood up and shook the hair out of his eyes. He said, "I live here."

"You do not. I live here!"

"Okay, you like specifics? Fine. I live there." He used both hands to point toward the common wall between the two sides of the duplex.

"You live next door?" The coincidence sent her brain spinning. "What are you doing in my bedroom?"

"Wiring your wall," he said as if it were the most natural thing in the world. "Genevieve told me you wanted to put your desk under the window. That outlet would never let you run a light and phone or fax machine off the same juice. So I rewired it."

He calmly brushed past her and headed for the front door. "You know," he said without looking at her, "you might consider thanking me instead of threatening to throw furniture at me."

"Thanks for fixing my electricity," Alissa muttered, her heart still in a flutter.

"I don't mean thank me for the electricity," Brad said, slipping his feet into the Birkenstocks. "Thank me for getting you this duplex."

"Excuse me? You didn't get me this duplex."

"Oh yeah?" Brad said, sticking out his chest as if she had just challenged him and he was up for the duel. "Who did?"

Alissa had no answer.

"I'm the one who left the note." He tipped an invisible hat

to her and said. "Welcome, neighbor." He opened the door, about to go, then turned and said, "You know, if there's ever anything I can do to help, just holler. Or better yet," he said, nodding at the dining room table, "why don't you just, you know, throw a chair at me or something?"

"I thought you were a burglar!" she said defensively.

"Do I look like a burglar?"

Alissa looked him up and down and let her expression answer for her.

He looked her up and down.

Alissa cleared her throat, took her hand off her hip and for a silent moment they stood there, forcing themselves to breathe the same air.

Brad spoke first. "Genevieve tells me you're moving in tomorrow. You need any help?"

"It'll have to be Sunday," Alissa said. "I have something going on tomorrow."

"So do I," Brad said. "Why don't you move in tonight? Jake's working, but I'll help."

"That's okay," Alissa said.

"What? You already have help?"

"No, but…"

"You're not packed?"

"I'm packed," Alissa said, irritated at his pelting questions.

"Then move in tonight. It's better at night. Cooler."

"Oh, all right," she said, deciding she didn't have the energy to fight this guy. "We can at least start."

"Now, don't let me put you out any," Brad mocked. "I'm only trying to help out here. You don't have to say thanks or anything."

"You have a thing about people saying thank you, don't you? What? You need a lot of praise? A lot of affirmation from your peers?"

"I just think people should have a few manners and say thank you every now and then."

"Oh, manners," Alissa said with a deep laugh. "And you are going to teach the world about manners? You, the man who cuts in front of people at Starbucks?"

"I didn't cut. You were stalling."

"I was thinking."

"Thinking?" Brad said, flipping his hair behind his ear. "At Starbucks? What is there to think about? It's coffee."

"I have the right to think about what I want to order without being harassed by some impatient customer." Alissa stated. She couldn't believe she was talking this way. Ever since she had stepped into this duplex, it was as if she were a different person. No, it wasn't when she walked into the house. It was when she saw Brad. He pulled all the raw edges of her emotions to the surface and yanked on the loose strings one at a time.

"Do you want to get your stuff? Or should we stand around here all night and fight?"

"Fine," Alissa said throwing up her hands. "Let's go. We'll have to rent a trailer."

"No we won't," Brad said. "I have a truck."

"I'll drive my car, and you can follow me over," Alissa said. "If you can keep up, that is."

She climbed into her sedan and glanced at Brad in the rearview mirror. She couldn't understand how she had so quickly moved from being sweet, polite, slightly hesitant Alissa to an all-feelings-out, in-your-face, who-do-you-think-you-are-anyway Alissa.

Avoiding the bumper-to-bumper freeway traffic at 5:45 on a Friday evening, Alissa led Brad to her condo via a dozen side streets. She decided the personality transformation was due to the emotional exhaustion she felt after an intense, full week at work and then coming home every night and staying up until midnight or later packing.

In all her rushing around, she had barely eaten anything all day either. Hopefully something was left in her refrigerator.

When they arrived at the condo, Alissa didn't have to check the refrigerator. The minute she unlocked the door, Brad got to it before she did. "You have any special plans for these plums?" he asked.

"No. Is there anything else in there?"

"No other recognizable real food. Just yogurt, cottage cheese, celery, carrots and—just a sec." He opened the milk carton and took a sniff before drinking right from the carton. "No more milk," he said. "Anything in here?" He opened the freezer and found it empty except for two Weight Watchers frozen dinners she had bought earlier in the week and hadn't had time to eat.

"Are you on a diet or something?"

Alissa felt her face blushing, and she tried to avoid his question.

"So let's just get it out in the open. I'll bet you were one of those beauty queens. In high school."

"Excuse me?" Alissa leaned against her kitchen counter. She really couldn't believe this guy.

Brad chomped off the end of a carrot. "In high school, you were so beautiful you didn't know what to do with it so you used it to your advantage until it got you in trouble." He snapped off another chunk of carrot. "Then you decided to kill off the beauty queen part by adding pounds. But she's still there, you know. So here you are at what, twenty-five?"

"Twenty-six," Alissa grudgingly offered.

"Twenty-six, and you're still trying to find a balance between who you are on the inside and the curse you were handed at birth."

"The curse, huh?" Alissa folded her arms across her chest.

"The beauty. You're beautiful, you know. It can be more of a handicap than being born with a physical defect. The beautiful women never know if people, men in particular, are nice to them because of their looks or because of who they are on the inside. So the women with the beauty handicap spend their pre- to mid-life years distrusting men. That's you."

Alissa unfolded her arms and put her hands together, applauding Brad in jest. "Oh, thank you, great Freud. How has the world gotten along all these years without your wisdom?"

Brad shrugged and tossed the top of the carrot into the sink. "It's a mystery, isn't it? So, what do you want to move first? The furniture or the boxes?"

She was steaming mad. This guy had to go. "You know what? I'm going to change my clothes, and when I come out of that room, I want you to be gone."

"See? Right there," Brad said, opening the freezer and pulling out two of the microwave dinners. "You don't know what to do with someone who is honest and trustworthy. You run, you push them away. Now what would be the point of my leaving? You'd have to see me again. We're neighbors. What do you want? Chicken piccata or vegetable lasagna? Forget I asked. You can have the lasagna."

As Brad was ripping open the boxes and tossing them into the microwave, Alissa stomped into her bedroom and slammed the door. There was nothing she could do with her anger. Everything was packed so she couldn't find anything to throw. Plus, she had nearly thrown one chair today. How many chairs did she have to threaten this clown with to get rid of him?

Okay, calm down, Alissa. You can do this. You're a professional. You've dealt with worse than his kind at work. Take a deep breath. You'll be fine. Change your clothes, eat some vegetable lasagna, and haul some boxes over to your new home. You'll be fine. You can do this.

She pulled on a pair of jeans and a T-shirt and wrapped her hair on top of her head, holding it in place with a silver barrette. Washing her face helped, even though all her towels were packed and she had to dry off with toilet paper. She sat on the edge of her tub, letting all her fired-up emotions burn themselves out.

Feeling calmer and more in control, she walked out the bedroom door and found her microwave dinner waiting for her on the counter. Brad was gone. And so were half the boxes she had stacked up in the living room. She had no idea how he could have hoofed it to his truck with so many boxes so fast.

Silently eating her lukewarm vegetable lasagna, Alissa decided what to do next. As long as she was going to move everything tonight, she might as well clean out the rest of the kitchen cupboards and empty the refrigerator. She still had to clean the condo to get her deposit back. But she could do that Sunday.

Going at it with all the energy she had left, Alissa filled the last four packing boxes with goods from the cupboards and then emptied the refrigerator.

When Brad walked back in her open front door, she looked up, wondering what this encounter would bring. Brad plunked a Big Gulp on the counter. "Peace offering," he said. "Diet Coke. Okay?"

"Thanks."

"See how nice that is?" Brad said and then drew a long slurp up the straw of his drink. "I do something nice, and you say thank you. That's nice."

Alissa should have kept her mouth shut, but the statement tumbled out. "I hate diet drinks. But thanks anyway."

Brad flipped his hair behind his ear and said, "You're kidding."

"No. It's the artificial sweetener. I don't like it."

"Well, that's your problem. Do you know how much sugar is in a regular Coke?"

"You're saying I have a weight problem?"

Brad's eyes widened in disbelief. He slapped his forehead and said, "I come here, I look in the fridge. All you have are carrots and diet frozen dinners. I try to be nice so I buy you a beverage that corresponds with the contents of your refrigerator. This does not take a brain surgeon. But no, you eat diet food but don't drink diet drinks. Okay."

"I appreciate the thought," Alissa said. He didn't perk up so she added the magical, "Thank you."

"You're welcome," Brad said. "What goes next? The rest of the boxes or the furniture?"

Alissa felt he had closed her off. Maybe that was a good thing. At least they wouldn't be at each other for the rest of the night.

And they weren't. They worked in tandem, quickly, quietly like two old jogging buddies running the track silently in sync with each other.

Just to be nice, Alissa drank about a fourth of the diet Coke. It wasn't bad.

They delivered the last load of stuff to the duplex at twenty after midnight. She thanked him out in front of the duplex. He said, "You're welcome" and went inside his half of their domain. Alissa entered her jumble-tumble duplex and was glad Shelly wasn't there to see the mess.

So that's that. I have the ideal home and roommate, but my neighbor is impossible. I'm going to plan right now to see as little of him as possible.

Alissa barely got her bed made in her new room before she fell into it and slept a dreamless sleep. She hadn't set an alarm, so she was shocked to find it was after ten when she woke up the next morning. She had needed that rest. But now she had less than four hours to clear the house a bit, find some nice clothes, and shower and dress for the wedding.

Like a worker bee on a mission for the queen, Alissa dashed around the place, unpacking clothes, filling her drawers in the bathroom with her cosmetics, and reshuffling the boxes in the kitchen. She and Shelly hadn't talked through which dishes to keep. Since they both had complete kitchens, Alissa was going to propose they keep their favorite things, even if they had duplicates, and store the rest or have a garage sale.

She didn't think much about Brad as she scrambled around the house. He was going to be one of those unavoidable nuisances. Everything else about her new friends and new home was perfect. Almost too perfect. But Brad took care of that. He was the negative that balanced out the positives.

Showered and dressed in a slimming navy sundress, her hair down and curled, Alissa slid her contacts into her eyes and finished applying her makeup. She felt excited about watching Rosie come down that aisle to at last be united with her dear Chet.

Alissa grabbed her car keys and wallet and swished out the front door. The door to the other duplex shut the same time as hers. There stood Brad, dressed in black slacks, a white shirt, and striped tie, with his hair slicked straight back and his face shaved. He obviously had a hot date.

Brad lifted his sunglasses and looked at Alissa. "Hi."

"Hi," she said.

They stood there awkwardly glancing at each other, and then down at their shoes and over at their cars parked on the street.

"Well, I have to go," she said.

"Me, too," Brad said, flipping his sunglasses back in place.

They walked down their tandem walkways and split to go to their cars. Alissa unlocked her door and said over her shoulder, "Have a nice time."

"You, too," he called back. "I don't know how much fun I'm going to have." He slipped into his truck, rolled down the window, and called out, "I'm going to a wedding."

Chapter Eight

$\mathcal{A}$lissa froze in mid-entrance to her car. She couldn't get in until she settled the question that had arisen in her mind. Brad started his engine and was pulling away from the curb when she ran back and flagged him down. He stopped, and she went over to his rolled down window.

"This is really a ridiculous question." She caught a whiff of his aftershave and knew that he must be going to a wedding with a date. She couldn't imagine a guy like Brad cleaning up so nicely unless it was for a woman. Plus it was June. Lots of afternoon weddings were going on today.

"What?" Brad asked.

"By any chance is the wedding at Descanso Gardens?"

"Yeah. You want a ride somewhere?"

Alissa closed her eyes and breathed in slowly. "It's not Chet and Rosie's wedding, is it?"

"Yeah!" Brad lifted his sunglasses and looked her in the eye. "How did you know?"

"Because that's where I'm going."

"How do you know them?" Brad asked.

"I'm their travel agent. They're going to Italy for their honeymoon."

"That's right," Brad said. "You can thank me for that little bonus in your paycheck. I sent them to you."

Alissa put her hand on her hip. "You did not."

"Yes, I did. I met Chet at the dentist a couple of weeks ago. See? I had this filling replaced back here." He opened his mouth and pointed to a lower molar.

"I'm not interested in your dental history!"

"That's where I met him. He asked me where I thought he should go on his honeymoon. I told him Italy. Then I told him about Clawson Travel."

"Wait a minute. You told Chet to go to Italy at the dentist's office, and he made his honeymoon decision based on your opinion?"

"You find that so hard to believe? That someone actually valued my opinion?"

"Well…"

"Boy, you never let up, do you? Come on, get in. We're going to be late. No use both driving to the same place."

"All right, but I'll drive. My car's cleaner."

"Your car's cleaner? Who's going to see your car? Your car is not going to the wedding. It has to wait for you in the parking lot."

"My gift for them is in the car."

"So? Go get it. I've already started my engine. Not to mention I've wasted a gallon of gas sitting here talking to you."

"Well, excuse me!" Alissa said. "Drive yourself over. I don't need a ride from you."

"Fine," Brad called as she walked away. "I was going to tell you the story, but never mind."

Alissa stopped in her tracks. She decided it would be worth enduring a ride to the wedding with Brad to hear the rest of Rosie and Chet's love story.

"Okay! Okay! Just a minute," she yelled. She grabbed her sunglasses from the visor and the wrapped gift from the front seat, then hurried over to the passenger side of Brad's truck. He was revving the engine as she approached the door.

"Very funny. You're wasting gas, you know," she said, trying to slide gracefully across the seat. The floor was one big mound of used fast food bags. The distinct scent of French fry grease rose from the abyss. "Gross! Can't we take my car? Where am I supposed to put my feet?"

"Buckle up, baby. Brad's at the wheel." He squealed the tires as he rammed down the street, burning rubber at the stop sign.

"Now do you feel important and in control?" Alissa chided. She carefully planted her heels on top of a crumpled Burger King bag. "You know what it is with your kind? You never grow up. You think power is synonymous with maturity. If you can show you're in control of something or someone, that must make you an adult." She crossed her arms across her middle as Brad peeled through the intersection. "You need constant affirmation. You're an eternal adolescent, trying to prove something."

"That's pretty good," Brad said. "Did you get that from psychotherapeutic systems? I took that class last semester."

Alissa could not believe this guy. "That's all you're going to say?"

"I think you're right," Brad added. "You're very insightful. Anything else you want to add to your conclusions?"

"Yes, would you mind rolling up the window and turning on the air conditioning?"

"Sure."

She was surprised he was so agreeable. But her goal was to return to the topic that had motivated her to come with him in the first place. "So, tell me their story. I just heard up to the part where Meg sent Chet the letter telling him Rosie was in Houston."

Brad looked over at her. "What are you talking about?"

"Chet and Rosie's love story."

"Their love story? I meant the story of how I convinced him to go to Italy. As in the immortal words of Indiana Jones, 'Ah, Venice.'"

Alissa stared at him in disbelief.

"Did you ever see that old movie about the couple who went to Venice on their honeymoon? I was telling Chet about it at lunch."

"Wait a minute. I thought you met in the dentist's office."

"We did. Then I took him to lunch. McDonald's for chocolate shakes. That's all we could eat after our dental work. I told him he needed to take Rosie on a gondola ride. That's about as romantic as it gets. Either that, or I told him to take her to St. Mark's Square with all the pigeons. That was at the end of the movie. They ran into each other's arms, and all the pigeons fluttered up around them. It was awesome."

Alissa slowly turned her head, peering at Brad over the rim of her sunglasses.

"What?" he said returning her gaze, then looking back at the road.

"That's your idea of romantic? These people are seventy years old, okay? They are not going to run into each other's arms through a plaza of pigeon goo."

"Pigeon goo?"

Alissa ignored him and plunged forward. "And just how romantic is it to sit in a gondola with some fat guy in a striped shirt wearing a bow on his hat looking over your shoulder?"

"Obviously you've never been on a gondola," Brad said.

"And you have?"

"Not yet."

"Not yet, huh?"

"It's one of my goals."

Alissa shook her head and stared out the side window again. Her idea of the romance of Venice would be whispers in a private corner of a candlelit café. Or a walk across one of the bridges, stopping in the middle for a long, lingering kiss.

Pigeons! I can just see Rosie trying to shoo a flock of pigeons out of her hair.

"So you don't know how Chet and Rosie got together?"

"Sure I do. They met in high school."

"I mean recently. How did they end up together recently?"

"I don't know." Brad drove into the Descanso Gardens parking lot. He pulled an embossed invitation from his pocket to check the wording. "Rose Garden," he said. "Which way? Does it say on your invitation?"

"No."

"Did you bring your invitation?"

"I didn't get one."

"Oh, really? Are you sure you're invited?"

"Yes, I'm sure. Let's go find this place. We're probably late."

"And whose fault would that be?" Brad asked, leading the way.

"I didn't say it was your fault. It's nobody's fault. Look, I think the wedding's over there."

They followed a winding path down to an archway covered in ivy, red roses, and baby's breath. A minister in a black suit stood behind the arch, and several dozen chairs were set up on either side of the white runner. Beyond the arch stretched a lovely garden of roses.

Chet stood to the side, looking handsome in his black tux and deep red rose boutonniere. The photographer was snapping shots of Chet as the guests shifted in their seats.

"See?" Brad said. "They wouldn't start without us."

Brad and Alissa slipped into two open seats in the second row behind an older woman in a big hat covered with silk flowers. Alissa had to adjust to the side to see around her. Right after they sat down, a string quartet began to play. Chet approached the pastor solemnly, his hands folded in front and a grin the size of Miami on his face.

The music switched tempo slightly, and the thirty or so guests stood to observe the eighth wonder of the world—a woman clothed in white, coming down the wedding aisle.

Rosie looked stunning. Her hair was brushed out full in a halo of white. Crowning the top of her head was a wreath of gardenias, red rose buds, lavender statice, and delicate baby's breath.

Her dress had lace and pearls across the bodice and down the long sheer sleeves. It gathered at her waist and flowed in delicate, airy layers to the ground. She seemed to float past them.

In her hands she held a cascading bouquet of red roses woven with white ribbons; large, white gardenias; and baby's breath.

The instant Alissa looked at Rosie's face, tears welled up in her eyes. She turned so Brad wouldn't see and tease her. Never had she seen a woman look so beautiful. Rosie's firecracker red lips were pursed together, trembling as an endless stream of tears flowed down her cheeks. She had eyes only for Chet. Nothing could stop this woman, who was so powerfully, deeply, painfully in love, from reaching that altar.

Alissa felt a gentle tap on her shoulder and glanced down to see Brad's fingers offering her his handkerchief. She took it without looking at him. The guests were seated, and Alissa noticed the handkerchief was already wet. With a glance over at Brad, she knew why. Tears still clung to his lower lids.

They watched the couple join hands before God and the witnesses. Alissa still felt choked up, knowing how this woman had endured and how she had promised herself to Chet so many years ago. Now they were finally being married. Their true love had weathered it all.

The words the minister spoke only convinced her further of that truth. He read Scripture of how real love comes from God alone. The couple prayed aloud, holding hands and thanking God for his mercy, his grace, and his goodness to them.

The minister asked the couple to repeat after him, Chet first. "I, Chester Andrew Michaels, take thee, Roseanna Marie, to be my lawfully wedded wife, to have and to hold, to cherish from this day forward. For better, for worse, for richer, for poorer, in sickness and in health, as long as we both shall live."

Rosie repeated the vows, her voice quavering but strong.

The minister then explained how a ring is an endless circle and as such is a perfect symbol of their love.

Chet slipped a ring on Rosie's left hand that appeared to be limp and useless. He worked with her gently, coaxing the fingers to uncramp enough for him to place the ring on her finger. Mission accomplished, he held the bouquet for her so she could place a ring on his finger.

"As a pledge," Rosie said, repeating the words Chet had said while putting the ring on her finger, "and in token of the vows between us made, with this ring, I thee wed."

They both wept now. Unashamedly, with unveiled faces. Their joy seemed to know no bounds.

The minister then served the couple communion, something Alissa had never seen before at a wedding. It seemed like a fitting, sacred seal on their union before God. Turning the couple to face their guests, the minister said, "By the power vested in me by God and the State of California, I now pronounce you husband and wife." He paused slightly with a grin on his face before saying, "You may kiss the bride."

Chet looked deep into the eyes of his wife. He reached his wrinkled hands up to her tear-streaked cheeks and took her face in his hands. Then tenderly drawing her to himself, he laid a full, one-minute smacker on her that made even the minister blush. The guests were beginning to look at each other and chuckle under their breath.

Chet and Rosie victoriously marched down the aisle, as the guests rose and filed in line to follow them to the reception area. They gathered nearby in a lovely garden alcove with chairs forming small groups to encourage conversation. In a gazebo, a table full of silver trays and crystal serving bowls was laden with a sumptuous feast fit for a king and queen. The string quartet had relocated in the south corner of the garden area and was playing lilting, celebratory music.

"Looks good," Brad mumbled in Alissa's ear. She knew he meant the food, although she was drinking in the beauty of the plethora of yellow, red, white, and peach roses that encircled the gazebo.

On impulse, Alissa grabbed his arm and pulled him away from the food area back to where she stood in line. In a low voice she instructed him, "You're supposed to greet the couple first. Didn't your mother teach you anything?"

Brad shrugged and gave her a little boy smile. "She taught me to beware of single women who try to grab me at weddings."

Alissa rolled her eyes and turned away. Over her shoulder she said, "Don't worry. You're not my type."

"Then how about that guy?" Brad nodded toward a suave,

black-haired man in an expensive dark suit who was at the front of the receiving line kissing Rosie. A petite brunette in front of him took his arm. She was holding the hand of a little girl in a fairy princess dress. The girl turned to the man, held up her arms, and asked her daddy to pick her up.

"He's married," she muttered between clenched teeth.

"Good to see you at least have some scruples. Leave those married men alone," Brad said.

His words stung. Of course he didn't know about Thomas. But the truth was, she hadn't left a married man alone. Not that she had ever intended for it to go the way it did. But she should have stayed far away from him.

Don't do this to yourself. Alissa drew in a deep breath. It was as if all the forces of destruction were raining down on her, trying to destroy this wonderful experience. She wouldn't give in to remorse, not even one pinch.

"There's one," Brad said, tapping her shoulder and pointing to an older Hispanic man with streaks of gray hair starting at his widow's peak and blending into his thick, dark coiffure.

Alissa turned to Brad and said, "Do you mind finding some other fanciful little game to keep you amused while you wait to congratulate the happy couple? You're really bugging me."

"Have you figured out why?" Brad asked.

"Why what?"

"Why you and I seem to bug each other."

"You mean you don't have this affect on all the women you meet?"

"Not that I ever noticed. Except maybe Wren."

"Your first wife?" Alissa teased. "The one who divorced you after one week?"

"Never been married," Brad said. "Wren's my sister. Her real name is Lauren. You remind me of her in some ways."

"Wonderful."

Alissa was relieved to be the next person in line. She planted a sweet kiss on Rosie's cheek. "You're beautiful," Alissa said, grasping Rosie's hand. "I'm so happy for you!"

"Thank you so much. I'm delighted you came."

"And so am I," Chet said, leaning over and kissing Alissa's cheek. She quickly responded in kind. Then, as Chet noticed Brad, he looked over the top of Alissa's head and said, "Brad, you came! Rosie, this is the young man who brought me home that day after the dentist."

"So nice to meet you," Rosie said, receiving Brad's kiss on her cheek. "You were a lifesaver that afternoon. Thank you so much." Turning to Alissa she explained, "Seems my Chet can't hold his Novocain. It had the strangest effect on his sense of balance. This young man wouldn't let Chet drive home. Why, it's quite possible he saved my husband's life!"

A warm glow of appreciation spread over the newlyweds and their hero, Brad. *Terrific!* Alissa thought. *All this guy needs is a bigger head.*

"Do you two know each other?" Chet asked.

Neither of them answered at first.

"We found out last night that we're neighbors," Alissa said.

"How wonderful!" Rosie said with a pleased smile. "When we get back from our honeymoon, we'll have to have the two of you over."

"If you're going to serve more of that peach cobbler," Brad said, "I'll be there."

"We'll give you a call when we get back," Chet promised.

"Have a great time," Alissa said.

"Oh, we will!" they said in unison.

Alissa moved forward in the line, her emotions tangled up in a strange mixture. She was overjoyed for Chet and Rosie. At the same time, it bothered her that Brad seemed to have such close access to "her" Rosie and Chet. They were her treasured new friends, and she didn't want to share them with anyone, especially not Super Hero.

Chapter Nine

*A*lissa held her plate of gourmet delicacies in one hand and the sacred bouquet, which she was holding on to for Rosie, in the other. With a discerning eye, she scanned the guests seated in semi-circles on the lawn. Brad was still in the food line.

Which one is Rosie's best friend, Meg? she wondered. A large woman with very short, white hair caught Alissa's attention. The woman's soft lavender dress was adorned with a diamond-like necklace and matching diamond stud earrings. As she ate, she observed with a smile all that was going on around her. To Alissa, the woman seemed the sort of adventuresome spirit who would have stood on a dock in Long Beach fifty years ago, checking out all the sailors.

"Pardon me," Alissa said. "Is anyone sitting here?"

"No." The woman smiled, showing her wide front teeth. "Please join me. I'm Meg. You must be the travel agent Rosie told me about."

Alissa was surprised at first, but then, with only thirty or so guests, she was probably the only one Meg didn't know. "Yes, I'm Alissa." She extended her hand, and Meg took it firmly in hers for a friendly handshake.

"I'm Brad," the sudden shadow said. Alissa had hoped he would find someone else to torture. He nodded at Meg and sat next to Alissa.

Alissa decided to try the technique that had worked so well on boys like Brad in junior high. She ignored him.

"I've heard Rosie speak of you, too," Alissa said, crossing her legs and focusing on Meg. "She told me you wrote a letter to Chet letting him know where he could find Rosie after he came home from the war."

"Oh, yes," Meg chuckled. "And a lot of good that did. You do know what happened when he showed up on her doorstep in Houston, don't you?"

"No," Alissa said, leaning forward. She couldn't wait to hear this.

"They hadn't paid the electric bill." Meg popped a grape in her mouth.

Alissa waited.

Meg made small circular motions with her free hand. "That's why Rosie had all the candles lit in the living room. It was a hot summer night, and the front window and curtains were open. Joe had been asleep on the couch when Rosie came in the front room to check on him, to see if he was sober enough to eat some dinner." She dropped another grape in her mouth and made Alissa wait for the rest of the story.

"Joe got up from the couch and was furious at her for waking him. He lunged at her but was too stupefied to do anything other than fall on her. She held him up and helped him back to the couch where he tumbled down, taking Rosie with him."

Alissa had a difficult time understanding where all this was leading. "What about Chet?"

"Chet saw the whole thing from the taxi parked out front. In the dim light, it looked to him as if they were dancing by candlelight and joined in a romantic embrace on their way to the couch. He told the cab driver to take him back to the train station. That night he took the first train out of there, which happened to be going to Mexico City."

"You can't be serious!" Alissa said. "Didn't he ever call her?"

"No. He thought she was in a loving, thriving marriage. Chet was a gentleman. He wasn't about to break that up."

"So did he settle in Mexico City?" Brad asked. "His Spanish is good."

Alissa glanced over her shoulder and gave him a "go away" look.

Brad pulled away at her glare and said, "He ordered his milk shake in Spanish, okay?"

"He didn't stay in Mexico City," Meg explained. "He ended up in Brazil on an American civil service project. He built bridges or something. The money was good, and it seemed the only cure for his broken heart. Of course, Rosie was the one who needed a cure by this time. I begged her to come to California and live with Fred and me. I was afraid Joe was going to permanently hurt Rosie. And he finally did, you know."

Alissa shook her head. "What happened?"

"Her left arm," Meg said, raising her corresponding arm. "He broke it at the elbow, permanently damaging the nerves. Six months after the cast was off, she wrote to tell me her fingers on her left hand were going numb. I told her it was because of Joe. She wouldn't believe it. And she wouldn't leave him."

Brad jumped in and asked, "Why not?"

"Things were different then. A promise was a promise. For better, for worse, you know. She stayed with him till the day he died."

Alissa shook her head. "How long ago was that?"

"Oh, nearly thirty-five years ago by my guess." Meg picked up a dainty triangle sandwich and put the whole thing in her mouth. "That's when she finally came to California. She cleaned house for my cousin, Walter. He owned a huge orange grove in Redlands and had a big hacienda to go with it. Walter's wife, Angelina, died when their fifth child was born, so Rosie took over. She loved those babies as if they were her own. Amelio was her favorite."

Meg pointed with her manicured finger at the man with the graying widow's peak hair. "That's Amelio over there. He composes music for movies now. In Hollywood. Rosie was the one who taught him how to play the piano."

"Excuse me," Brad said. "I'm going back for more. Can I get you two ladies anything?"

"Something to drink would be nice," Meg said. "Thank you."

Alissa glanced at the plate in her lap. She hadn't eaten a bite. She couldn't think of eating or drinking while Chet was in Brazil and Rosie was raising someone else's five children.

"No, thanks," she said. She focused back on Meg, eager for the next morsel of the unfolding story. "Please go on. Did Rosie contact Chet in Brazil? She was free of Joe. Why didn't she try to find Chet?"

"She did when she first came to California. I helped her. We wrote letters and made phone calls. But Chet had quit the engineering group, and no one seemed to know where he was. His parents were deceased. His brother never recovered from the war and was in a sanitarium. It was all dead ends."

"Rosie must have been shattered."

"Not completely. She had a spiritual experience in California at some kind of tent revival meeting. I'll say this for her: when she made her commitment to Christ, she kept it the way she kept all her commitments—completely. She was in church every Sunday with those five kids in tow. She told me she prayed every night for Chet."

Brad returned with a glass of punch for Meg and one for Alissa. Alissa accepted the unrequested glass from him without a thank you and asked Meg, "Where was he all this time?"

"Chet?" Meg took a slow sip and gave Brad a smile along with a thank you. "He was still in Brazil, of course."

"What happened with Walter?" Brad asked, sitting back down.

"Walter?" Alissa said, glancing at Brad. "Who cares about Walter?"

"Oh, well," Meg said, "I can answer that! Rosie cared about Walter. Or rather, Walter cared about her. He was sixteen years her senior, but a fine man in every way. Mind you, he was my cousin. Came from good stock." Meg winked and took another sip of the punch. "My, this is lovely. Is there a hint of almond in this?"

Alissa took an obligatory sip. "Yes, perhaps. So, did Walter marry Rosie?"

Meg leaned back, her shoulders shaking as she chuckled. "He certainly tried to! I've never known a man to propose as many times as my cousin. She loved him dearly, but like she would love a favorite uncle or older brother. She turned him down, of course, always hoping one of her many letters to Chet would reach him and he would come riding up to the hacienda on a white stallion to save her. Oh, how that girl could dream.

"Of course," Meg continued. "I couldn't blame Walter for

falling in love with her. She was beautiful. So graceful, you hardly noticed the way her fingers were beginning to curl in on her left hand. It was as if all the pain from her years with Joe had evaporated. She ran that ranch, and she raised those kids and continued to do so after Walt was killed in that accident."

Meg shook her head and took another sip of punch. "One of the ranch trucks overturned with a full load of oranges. He was gone before they got him to the hospital. The court awarded Rosie custody of the kids. Their deceased mother had no relatives living in the U.S., and none of Walter's brothers wanted them. Amelio was in his first year of college, and Anita, the baby, was starting junior high. That's Anita over there. She married the son of a ranch hand. He's much younger, but look at her. She doesn't look her age, does she? And look at that angel baby." The little girl in the fairy princess dress stood patiently by her mother, nibbling on a strawberry. "Cristiana may be the only child they're able to have, though. The birth nearly killed Anita."

"Nice meeting you, Meg," Brad said, suddenly standing, his empty plate in his hand. "Let me know when you're ready to go, Alissa."

Alissa found herself swallowing a smile. Why was it all men made quick exits whenever women began to talk about childbirth?

"You have to tell me," Alissa said, turning her attention back to Meg, "what happened to Chet? What was he doing this whole time in Brazil? Why didn't he receive Rosie's letters or try to come looking for her again? Did he just give up?"

"I don't think so," Meg said thoughtfully. "People change, you know. By the time Walter died, Rosie had her hands full with those children. And then Martin entered the picture. Oh how he made her life a living nightmare!"

"Wait," Alissa said, not ready to hear about Martin. "What

about Chet? What kept him in Brazil so long?"

"Oh, well, that's easy. It was Hannah."

Alissa sat back, not sure she wanted to know about some Brazilian floozy who had the audacity to make Chet forget about his Rosie. And hadn't Rosie already gone through enough trials? Why did God send this Martin guy into her life?

"Auntie Meg," a tall, tanned, middle-aged man said, stepping up and offering his hand to her. "You promised me a dance."

Meg took his hand, and he helped hoist her from the chair. "Carlos, this is Alissa. Carlos is Rosie's middle boy. He coaches at the high school in Redlands."

"Nice to meet you," Carlos said with a polite nod. "We better get on that dance floor before everyone else gets the same idea."

Alissa had been so absorbed in the story she hadn't paid attention to the portable dance floor behind her, nor had she noticed Rosie and Chet taking their first dance together. She looked down at her full plate. A strawberry was about all she could muster to lift to her mouth. For the first time since Chet and Rosie had invited her on this journey into their fifty-year love affair, Alissa was glad to take a break. She had so much to digest.

Glancing across the room, she noticed Brad standing by the table, engaged in conversation with Amelio, the composer. Alissa couldn't imagine what they had in common, unless it was Brad's famed bongo drum collection. Content to sit in her chair and watch the celebration go on around her, Alissa thought about Meg's comment that Rosie had made a commitment to Christ and how Rosie had kept her commitment so completely. Alissa didn't feel she could say the same thing about the promises she had made to God many years ago. So much had happened in her life. For some reason she felt she had the right to straight-arm God and hold him at a distance.

It didn't appear that Rosie had done that, in spite of all her heartaches. Her face had such a deep beauty to it, not just because of her love for Chet. It was obvious it went much deeper than that.

That night, as Alissa lay awake in her new room, listening to the night sounds of determined crickets and a twittering bird who refused to go to sleep, she thought of nothing but Chet and Rosie.

I hope they like the hotel suite I arranged for them. It's all so romantic. True love never dies. Passion is alive within a human heart until death, and even then it can live on just as strong in memory.

Alissa gave up trying to sleep and wrapped herself in her favorite plush, peach-colored robe. She padded out to the kitchen and poured herself a glass of juice. Tomorrow she would attack all these boxes.

When Brad had driven her back from the wedding that evening, it was nearly seven. They both had been unusually quiet on the ride home except for his ribbing her for forgetting the present and leaving it on the front seat of his truck.

She'd simply replied she would take it over when the couple returned from Italy. They weren't going to have time to open gifts before then, anyhow.

Placing her glass in the sink, Alissa checked the green numbers on the microwave clock: 11:52. She unlocked the door that led to the backyard, and opened it to a midsummer's eve fairyland. The full moon smiled on the silent garden, turning everything golden.

The night air was cool but not cold. Alissa stepped outside barefoot, and Chloe, who had stirred from her spot on the couch, came alongside, rubbing her fluffy fur against Alissa's leg.

"How you doing, baby?" Alissa whispered, picking up her long-time companion. "You like our new home?"

Chloe purred and settled herself in Alissa's arms, eager for her head to be stroked. This appeared to be as soothing for Chloe as it was for Alissa.

Alissa walked in the cool, damp grass as she stroked Chloe. They settled on one of the bench seats under the vine-trimmed arch. Alissa imagined a hundred sets of eyes watching them from behind the fox-gloves, pansies, and daisies. It was an image she'd adopted from her favorite childhood book about a special garden where every summer the fairies gathered to sing and dance. They drank evening dew from the bluebells and played petunia trumpets. At the slightest sound of human feet, the fairies would hide, watching with unblinking eyes, waiting for the human intruder to leave.

"It's okay," Alissa whispered to her imaginary friends. "I won't hurt you. You can come back out to play."

Then she realized how silly she had just been, talking to the fairies. She hadn't done that since she was ten years old. She hadn't even thought of fairies since then. What brought back this image from her days of childhood innocence?

Alissa looked up at the moon. She couldn't remember the last time she had felt his approval as he gazed down on her. Probably since she was a child. Alissa used to think of the moon as God's face. She was most comforted when it was a full moon and he was smiling on her. But he was always so, so far away, so removed from her life. He only appeared every now and then, when the celestial conditions were cooperative. But the moon did follow her everywhere she moved around the world—Germany, Argentina, California, Massachusetts, and Hawaii. But he was never involved in her life, watching from a distance. Was that how God really was?

Before she had turned eleven, Alissa had begun to read beyond her age level. The books had transported her from childhood to adulthood in a few short pages. No longer did she think of fairies dancing in the night. Instead, her dreams turned to boys, and her thoughts turned to how she could get boys to notice her.

It wasn't hard. She was beautiful and acted older than her age. She received her first "promise" ring from a boy on her twelfth birthday. Every few months, and sometimes every few weeks, she had a new boyfriend. By the time she was fifteen, she had pretty much experienced everything she had read about on the pages of those novels. None of the rings had held any true or lasting promises. Nothing lasted in her life. Nothing gave her hope.

When she opened her heart to the Lord at age eighteen, it was as if her innocence had been restored. She zealously read her Bible from cover to cover within the first six months of her conversion. She told Jesus she loved him all the time, and she told everyone she knew that they needed Christ.

That was eight years ago. Now, rather than feeling as if she were in love with Jesus, she thought of their relationship as a cordial agreement. She would live a sin-free life to the best of her ability, and he would keep an eye on her and make sure she didn't become an alcoholic like her mother. What this arrangement didn't have room for was celebration, a grand rejoicing such as she had witnessed with Chet and Rosie today. Or even a fanciful dance in the moonlight like her imaginary fairy friends, who simply danced because it was summer.

Alissa felt as if her emotions were on cruise control. She was moving down the road of life without much variation. Nothing really bad had happened since Phoenix. But nothing really good had happened either—except for maybe Chet and

Rosie and moving into this charming new home.

Chloe nestled closer to Alissa's warm robe and wrapped her tail around her backside. "Come on, baby," Alissa said. "Let's go back inside." She checked on the moon one more time and padded across the bricks to her back door.

To her shock, the door had closed on its own, and it was locked. She stole through the cool grass in her bare feet and checked the front door, even though she already knew it would be locked. Chloe stopped purring as Alissa checked her bedroom window. She had left it open about two inches for the fresh air, but the security locks were in place behind the tightened screens. She was locked out.

A car pulled up out front. She heard the engine turn off and the door close. Alissa hoped beyond hope that it would be Shelly, coming home a few days early. She skittered around to the front, still holding Chloe close. A tall, broad-shouldered man, wearing a white shirt, black slacks, and black bow tie, strode up the path headed for Brad's side of the duplex. Alissa tried to duck behind one of the tall cypresses along the side of the house, but Chloe meowed loudly. The man turned toward her, startled.

He stopped and stared at her in the moonlight. Alissa curled and uncurled her cold toes, realizing how ridiculous it would be to run. The man came closer, and she could see his clean cut auburn hair, his perfectly chiseled features, and his engaging smile.

"Alissa, I presume?" His voice carried the timbre of a Shakespearean actor, his face the tenderness of a big brother.

She nodded.

"I'm Jake. I heard you had a cat."

Alissa grinned at her new neighbor. He certainly looked like a movie star. "This is Chloe," she said.

Jake studied the moon. "Nice night for a walk."

"Yes, it is," Alissa said.

"Well, nice meeting you."

"Nice meeting you," Alissa said, feeling foolish for having locked herself out. How could she tell this guy? Worse yet, what could she do about it?

Jake turned to go, and Alissa impulsively followed him. He turned to look at her over his shoulder.

"Can I ask you something?" Alissa said, stopping when her cold feet touched the hard bricks. "By any chance do you know if Shelly keeps a key hidden anywhere?"

Jake covered his mouth with his hand to hide his grin. He appeared to be thinking about Alissa's question. "Brad might know."

Alissa's eyelids fluttered in frustration as she pursed her lips together. She did not want to wake up Brad with the admission that she had locked herself out. "That's okay," she said. "Never mind. Thanks anyway." She turned to go into the backyard where she could hide. Maybe a light would still be on at Genevieve's, and Alissa could work up the nerve to bother her new landlady for a spare key.

"I could help you crawl through a window," Jake suggested, coming after her.

Alissa thought that was the nicest thing any man had ever said to her. Obviously Jake had sized up the situation, but he wasn't going to embarrass her by making her admit her dilemma, nor was he going to force an encounter with Brad on her. She liked this guy.

Chapter Ten

$\mathscr{W}$ ell," Alissa said, trying to hide her embarrassment over locking herself out, "I checked my bedroom window, and the security lock is in place. I'm sure Shelly locked her window. The only other one, I guess, is the bathroom."

"Let's have a look," Jake said.

He followed Alissa and Chloe around to the side of the house and rattled the pull up bathroom window. "Aha!" he said, jiggling the window until it easily slid up. "You really should check these windows before you go to bed, you know. Anyone could break in." With that, he hoisted himself up on the wide wooden windowsill and slid into the bathroom. "Go around to the front," he said. "I'll let you in."

Alissa trotted around and found Jake standing at the open front door with the porch light on. Between the bathroom and front door he had managed to slip Shelly's blue-and-white-checkered apron on over his formal waiter outfit. "Welcome home, honey," he said in a playful, high-pitched voice. "I've made all your favorite foods for dinner."

Lowering her head, Alissa hid her smile and walked in past him.

"Now you just put up your feet, honeybunch," Jake continued in his Harriet Nelson voice. "I'll fetch your pipe and slippers for you."

"Thanks," Alissa said, putting Chloe down and wiggling her cold toes into the warm rug.

Jake took off the apron and hung it back up on the hook in the kitchen. "Any time. Welcome to the neighborhood. I think you'll like it here."

"I think I will, too."

"Don't let my roommate scare you. He looks like an escapee from a forced labor camp, but deep down he's really a terrible person. I mean a nice person."

Alissa smiled. "If you say so."

"Sleep tight. Don't let the bed bugs bite," Jake said.

"There are bed bugs here?"

Jake put the back of his hand to his mouth as if he were telling her a secret. "I hear they enter through open bathroom windows after midnight."

"I'll be sure to close mine."

"I already did. You'll find the itemization on my bill."

"Thanks again," Alissa said.

Jake gave her one of his winning smiles. If she had seen that smile on a pain reliever commercial, she would have believed his headache was all gone. "I'll see you later," he said, slipping out and closing the door behind him.

Alissa was sorry he was gone. She thought he was an engaging person as well as entertaining. If he had stuck around, they could have made coffee and sat around talking all night. That would certainly be more fun than trying to sleep.

But to her surprise, she fell right to sleep as soon as she

double-checked the bathroom window and her feet began to warm up under the covers. As a matter of fact, Alissa slept well every night for the first week and a half in her new room.

Shelly was proving to be the perfect roommate, open and talkative, but not pushy. She was extremely considerate of Alissa's privacy.

They worked out the blending of their furniture and belongings and decided to hold a garage sale at the end of the month.

Work continued to be busy, and Jake and Brad only gave an occasional wave in passing as the week turned into the weekend and then eased into the next week. While her other three duplex-mates all seemed to have on-the-go lives, Alissa was content to come home from work, sit down with a good book, and listen to everyone else come and go.

On Alissa's twelfth night at the duplex, the phone rang in Shelly's room at 2:30 in the morning. She knocked on Alissa's door, waking her with the words, "Can you take the phone? It's someone named Rosie, and she says it's important."

Alissa sprang from her bed with her heart pounding. She reached for the cordless phone in Shelly's hand. "Rosie, is everything okay?"

"Alissa?" came the voice from the other end. "Why, you sound as if you're in the next room, dear. We had such a hard time trying to figure out how to call you. I hope it's okay that we called you at home. You left this number on our itinerary."

"Yes, of course, it's fine. Are you two all right?"

"Oh, yes, we're fine. But we want to come home. Do we have to stay for the rest of the trip?" She sounded like a child after her first week of summer camp.

Alissa motioned for Shelly to go back to bed. "It's not an emergency," she whispered.

Her sudden fear that one of them had suffered a heart attack or slipped on the pigeon goo was for naught. Alissa actually felt like laughing at Rosie's timid voice asking to come home.

"You can come home any time you want," Alissa said. "Have you had enough of Italy?"

"I'm afraid we have. We ended up changing our hotel reservations, and we stayed in Venice the whole time instead of taking the train down to Florence. We were supposed to leave yesterday, but we were so tired. You don't know what being on your honeymoon does to a person, especially at our age!"

Again Alissa resisted the impulse to giggle. "I'll make all the arrangements for you in the morning and fax the information to your hotel. Can you hang in there one more day until I can get you on a flight?"

"We can last another day," Rosie said. "I wouldn't mind one more gondola ride."

"Well then, you take one more gondola ride, and I'll get you back home as soon as I can."

"Thank you! What's that?" Rosie said, apparently listening to Chet in the background. "Oh, Chet says, '*Ciao*, baby.' He likes to practice his Italian words."

This time Alissa did laugh. "Tell him '*Ciao*' from me. Good night."

"Oh, goodness! Is it night there? I suppose I didn't think about that. I called the travel agency, and no one was there."

"It's okay," Alissa said. "Bye, bye." She hung up and thought how Brad was going to love it that Chet and Rosie liked riding in the gondola. She would never live that one down. She didn't even want to ask if they had made the pigeons flutter at St. Mark's Square.

It took nearly three hours the next morning to work

through all the arrangements for their flight home and to cancel their hotels in Florence and Rome. That Friday afternoon they arrived in LA. Alissa arranged for a limo to pick them up and to take them home to their love nest.

Even though she was dying to check on them, she waited until Sunday morning to give them a call. No one answered, and she began to be concerned. She tried again that afternoon. Chet answered the phone.

"I'm so glad you're home," Alissa said. "I tried this morning but didn't catch you."

"We were at church. How is everything with you?"

"Fine. I wanted to make sure you arrived okay and to see if you had a good time."

"Wonderful! Simply wonderful. Here, say hi to Rosie."

"Hi, Rosie. It's Alissa. How are you doing? Are you getting settled in?"

"Oh, yes. Thank you for calling. We're so tired, though."

"That's normal. The jet lag will take a few days to wear off. I'm glad you had a good time. Call me if you need anything, okay?"

"I don't think we'll be taking another trip for a while," Rosie said.

"I didn't mean just travel arrangements. Let me know if there's anything I can do for you." Alissa wondered if she was being condescending. She meant it as a friendly gesture. But then, she realized, even though they were elderly, this couple had just been halfway around the world and back. They probably wouldn't call her if they were running low on milk.

"We'd love to have you over in a few weeks," Rosie said. "I'll give you a call."

"Wonderful," Alissa said. "I'll look forward to it."

Right after Alissa hung up, Shelly stepped into the living room. She had changed from her Sunday dress into shorts and a T-shirt. "Genevieve and I are going for a walk. You want to go with us?"

"Sure."

Alissa and Shelly met Genevieve at her front door, where she was watering her potted plants. "Hello," she said when she saw Alissa. "I was hoping you would join us. How are you doing? Getting settled in okay?"

"Yes. I really like it here. Your garden is so beautiful; I love looking out my window at it."

"Did you put your desk there like you thought you would? Under the window, I mean," Genevieve asked as the three began to walk down the sidewalk with Alissa in the middle. It startled her how fast a pace they set. This wasn't a leisurely afternoon stroll; these women were serious about walking.

"Yes, it's perfect."

"And did Brad come over to fix the electrical wiring?"

"Yes." Alissa decided the less said about that incident, the better.

They turned east at the corner and headed uphill. Alissa was already breathing hard and felt frustrated that she was so out of shape. Genevieve and Shelly seemed to be able to keep talking, with their breathing only slightly elevated as they hoofed it uphill. Alissa listened and answered in monosyllables when necessary. She kept up with them, feeling the perspiration beading up on her forehead.

The neighborhood was beautiful. Their walk along the tree-lined streets was lovely, and the conversation delightful. At the end of their forty-five-minute trek, Alissa made a decision. She needed to do that every day. Her mind felt clearer, not to mention her pores. Genevieve had said along the way that she took this route four times a week, and anytime Alissa wanted to join her, she was welcome to.

Before the inspiration of the moment could give way to

sore leg muscles, Alissa said she would like to walk with Genevieve the next morning.

"I'll see you at 6:30 then," Genevieve said on her front lawn. "And did Shelly tell you about our picnic on the Fourth?"

"I don't think I told you yet," Shelly said. "We're going to barbecue in the backyard. What did we have last year? About thirty people?"

"At least that," Genevieve said. "Steve will be home on Thursday this week and off for the whole weekend. Isn't that a nice change!"

"I'll be working that weekend," Shelly said. "Sorry I'm going to miss all the fun."

"We'll save you some cake," Genevieve said. "Last year the girls and I made a big flag cake. I had red, white, and blue sprinkles everywhere in the kitchen for weeks."

They went their separate ways, and after she washed up, Alissa meandered back into the living room. Instead of curling back up with her book on the couch, she walked into the kitchen where Shelly was unloading the dishwasher.

"Would you like to do something tonight?" Alissa asked.

"I'd love to, but I already have plans with some of my friends from church. I usually work Sundays, you know, so this is sort of a vacation day for me." Shelly put the last plate in the cupboard and said, "You're welcome to come with us, if you'd like. We're just going out for dinner."

"No, thanks anyway. I have some things to do." Alissa opened the refrigerator and took out a bottle of peach-flavored iced tea. "Was this mine or yours?"

"Doesn't matter," Shelly said. "I'm not that picky about stuff like that. Whatever you find in there, any time, help yourself to it. The guys sure do." She leaned against the counter and pulled the clip out of her ponytail, shaking out her long, silky hair and letting it fall freely down her back. "You know what I just realized? The guys have hardly been over since you moved in. I wonder if they feel they don't have to keep checking on me all the time now that I have a roommate."

"Or it could be they're afraid of me," Alissa said, opening the bottle of tea and taking a drink.

Shelly laughed. "Right. You're such a threatening person." She laughed some more. "I'm glad you moved in, Alissa. This is working out better than I had hoped. I don't think you scare anyone, especially Brad and Jake. Don't they feel like brothers to you?"

Alissa shrugged. "I don't know. I didn't have any brothers."

"Sisters?" Shelly asked.

Alissa shook her head.

"Lucky you! I have three sisters, and we were all two years apart. Makes for constant cat fighting around the house. No offense, Chloe," she said to the cat, who had come wandering into the kitchen to see what was happening.

Alissa picked up her cat and massaged the back of her skull.

"Where do your parents live now?"

"They're both dead."

"I'm sorry," Shelly said.

Then a familiar awkwardness set in. Alissa knew it well. It was that moment of shock when people realized Alissa was a bona fide orphan. They always felt compelled to somehow fix it. She expected Shelly to now extend an invitation that, for every holiday from here on, Alissa was welcome to join her family.

Instead Shelly perched herself on the counter, took a cookie from an open bag beside her, and said, "Tell me about you."

"Me?"

"Yes, I want to know you."

No one had ever wanted to know her before. She felt all

her defenses rise up around her.

"There's not much to tell. My dad was in the air force. We lived a lot of places. My mother…," she hesitated. Knowing that Shelly came from a long line of ministers, she didn't want to bring up the alcoholism. "My mother used to like to sing."

"Do you?" Shelly asked.

"I used to. I don't any more."

"I can't carry a tune unless it's in a Walkman," Shelly said, smiling at her own humor.

"You have a really soothing voice," Alissa said, glad for a chance to take the attention off herself. "That's one of the first things I noticed about you. Are you sure you don't sing?"

"Positive! Every Christmas they made me the narrator in the church play. My three sisters were always the angels, and they got to sing and wear the halos."

Shelly popped another Chips Ahoy in her mouth and said, "I believe I can blame all my adult trauma on never getting to wear the white robe and gold halo. Instead, I had to say, 'There went out a decree from Caesar Augustus,' and 'There were shepherds abiding in the fields keeping watch over their flocks by night.'"

There was a knock on the door, and Shelly hopped down to greet her friend, who stood at the half-opened dutch door. "Come on in, Lori. I want you to meet Alissa. Alissa, this is Lori."

The two exchanged polite nods and hellos.

"I was trying to talk Alissa into coming with us. Why don't you finish convincing her while I get ready." Shelly disappeared into her bedroom, leaving Alissa alone with Lori.

"You're welcome to come," the tall, fair-skinned woman said. "It's not a real big deal. We're going to Mi Piace. I've been craving some of their pasta all week. We always have a good time."

Alissa smiled courteously and said, "Thanks, but I really have some things I need to do." The last thing she wanted to do was break into an established group that always had a good time when they got together. Party crashing may have been her style in her younger days but not anymore.

They talked about how nice the duplex looked with Alissa's furniture in it and some of the plants outside. Lori asked Alissa what she did, and when Alissa said she was a travel agent, Lori asked for the name of the agency, saying she would be in to arrange a flight for her family's big Thanksgiving reunion in Oklahoma.

Shelly entered the room, looking bright and ready for some fun. "So, did she convince you?" Shelly asked Alissa. "Are you coming?"

"Not this time. But thanks for the invite."

"Next time then," Shelly said, grabbing her keys from the basket on the counter.

As soon as they were gone, Alissa felt sad. Part of her wished she had gone with them. That part of her coaxed her to believe it wasn't too late to revive her social skills. She needed to change. She couldn't live the life of a hermit forever.

In an illogical compromise, Alissa took herself out to the movies. She ate popcorn until her stomach hurt. She regretted it the next morning when Genevieve showed up at 6:30, ready to walk.

Alissa did her best to keep up with Genevieve, and at the end of their loop, she felt as if she had definitely had a workout. They agreed to meet again on Wednesday morning, and Alissa spent the rest of Monday and all of Tuesday complaining to herself about her sore leg muscles.

As Genevieve and Alissa rounded the corner on their way back home Wednesday morning, Brad came out his front door and stood watching them. He had on slacks and a short-sleeved, casual shirt. Alissa hadn't seen him since the wedding and was surprised that he was kind of dressed up—for Brad, anyway. He didn't look grungy, but he wasn't formal either; he looked like a normal person.

"Brad!" Genevieve greeted him. "Haven't seen you around. How are you?"

"Doing fine. I'm off to a sales breakfast." He walked past them with only a glance at Alissa. "Hope you ladies have a wonderful day."

"You and Jake know about our Fourth of July barbecue, don't you?" Genevieve asked.

"Yeah, Jake told me we're going to do a rerun of last year. Sounds great. We'll bring the ice cream."

"Good. See you around four then." Genevieve waved good-bye to Brad and Alissa at the same time and kept up her long stride on the way to her house.

As Alissa stepped into the shower, she enjoyed the soothing water pouring over her. It felt good. And so did she. Business had been exceptionally good in June, and she expected a bonus this week. She was down another pound on the scale, despite all that stale popcorn. And Brad had treated her like an average person. True, he hadn't said much to her, but she decided that was better than the verbal fencing that had marked their first few encounters. Life was good, and she was looking forward to this barbecue more than a person who had a normal social life would.

Chapter Eleven

*T*he travel agency was closed on the Fourth, so Alissa slept in—or at least she tried to. But her body was used to waking up early and wouldn't let her fall back asleep. She finally gave in at 8:10 and climbed out of bed. Instead of showering, she decided she wanted to go for a walk. Genevieve wasn't planning on walking this morning, but Alissa felt fine about going by herself. She liked the way she felt after exercising.

As she took off on the familiar uphill route, she discovered it was warmer than when they usually walked. She wished she had brought along some water. To distract her thirsty thoughts, she played her favorite mental game, thinking about Rosie and Chet. She tried to decide who Hannah was and how she had managed to capture Chet's heart. It could have happened like Meg had said: people change, and it had been a long time since Chet had had any contact with Rosie. Maybe he had given up hope of ever being with her.

Hope was a terrible thing to lose, Alissa decided. She had

teetered on the brink of that abyss herself. Even now, with circumstances going so well for her, she didn't have much to look forward to. What she needed was something to hope for, some kind of dream to propel her forward.

She had her dream of running her own agency. But she hadn't spent much time thinking about that lately. Maybe she needed to put some of those thoughts back into motion.

As much as she hated to admit it, the only frayed bit of a dream she had had lately was to get married. She desired stability, a home, children, and someone she could feel safe with, even after he knew all her intimate secrets, someone who would love her for who she was.

Alissa picked up speed the last two blocks and ended up at her front door sweaty and ready for a shower. As she entered the kitchen, she thought of Shelly's words from the previous Sunday, "I want to know you."

It seemed too good to be true. But perhaps Shelly was someone Alissa could trust. And while a roommate certainly wasn't a husband, Shelly might turn out to be a close companion for Alissa. Of course, Shelly wasn't there at the moment. Instead, Alissa was alone—and had to face the assignment of making potato salad for thirty people by four that afternoon. After her shower, she set about her task with concentrated effort, deciding to try to forget the loneliness she felt.

Halfway through peeling the potatoes, there was a knock at her front door. Alissa poked her head around the corner of the kitchen to see the sweet little face of Genevieve's daughter Anna peeking over the top of the open dutch door.

"Hi," Alissa said. "How are you, Anna?"

"Fine."

"Would you like to come in?"

She nodded, and Alissa wiped her hands before reaching

for the knob. "Have you finished the cake over at your house?"

Anna nodded again. "It's a flag."

"Yes, I heard about this cake. I'm making potato salad. Would you like to help me?"

Anna shyly nodded again. Her wispy blond hair was held back on the sides by two barrettes with sunflowers on them. She wore overalls with a sunflower embroidered on the front-centered pocket. Apparently she had been informed of Shelly's rules about shoes because she took off her white sandals when she entered the house.

"Do you have an apron?" Anna asked.

"As a matter of fact, we do." Alissa lifted Shelly's blue-and-white-checked apron from the peg on the wall and tied it around Anna's pencil-thin waist. The apron slid right off.

"My mom ties it under my arms," Anna said, lifting both arms so Alissa could wiggle the apron up and try tying it again. The little girl looked so cute with the apron covering her whole front.

A deep longing welled up inside Alissa so powerfully that she had to brace herself against the counter. Her memory of Shawna would never go away. The counselor had told her that. But she hadn't told Alissa how to deal with these overwhelming moments along the way, when the "what if" questions loomed so large. *What if I'd kept her? What if she were standing in front of me today, just like Anna? What if I hadn't agreed to sign the adoption papers so quickly? What if I could relive my teen years?*

The answer to the last question was always simple. *I never would have been so sexually active.* But because Alissa couldn't go back and change that reality, she sucked up her courage and moved forward.

With a smile to her innocent guest, Alissa said, "Are you ready to make potato salad?"

Anna nodded.

Alissa lifted Anna up to the counter, holding her close for just a second and breathing in the scent of her sun-warmed hair. Alissa's only comfort was knowing that somewhere the Christian couple who had been so overjoyed to adopt her Shawna were probably lifting her the same way, holding her close, and showering her with kisses.

"Anna," Alissa said, swallowing her tears and looking into the face of the young one who gazed back at her from the countertop. "I want you to know you are a very special little girl, and I like you very much."

Anna gave Alissa a shy smile, indicating Anna had soaked up every word.

A few hours later Anna seemed to have decided Alissa was her favorite grown-up. Twenty or so adults gathered in the backyard, but everywhere Alissa went, Anna followed. Genevieve had set up a long table in the shade where Alissa added her contribution of the potato salad.

"I hope you didn't put pickles in it," Jake said, leaning over, examining Alissa's creation. His dark hair was cut shorter than when she had seen him last, and he had been working on his tan. Alissa wondered if a man like Jake would ever be interested in her. His fresh-scented cologne met her nostrils, and she felt a little overpowered by his good looks and strong presence.

"We didn't put in any pickles," Anna answered for both of them.

"Good," Jake said, dishing up a heaping scoop. "I'm not a pickle fan, especially sweet pickles." He gave a slight shiver. "They should be outlawed."

"Where's Brad?" Anna asked.

"He's around here somewhere," Jake said, glancing over his shoulder. "Probably looking for some pretty woman to flirt with."

"Alissa is the prettiest one here," Anna said, giving her new friend an admiring smile.

Alissa felt herself blushing as an amused grin spread across Jake's clean-shaven face. "You know why, don't you?" Jake said to Anna. "It's because we only allow beautiful women to live on our street. It's a rule. Every woman on this block must be at least as adorable as you, Miss Anna." He gave Anna a tender wink and moved on down the food line.

A swell of emotions caught in Alissa's throat. She could never have her own daughter back, but perhaps she could always have a special friendship with this little girl who now stood beside her. Anna held out a paper plate with wobbly hands, silently asking Alissa to dish up some potato salad for her.

The evening floated by in interesting conversations and loads of food. Alissa enjoyed being a part of it all, but what she enjoyed most was Anna's companionship. Genevieve's husband, Steven, had gifted the garden with a new bench swing on a stand, which was positioned under the shade of the large trees lining the back side of the yard. Alissa and Anna spent the twilight hours there, away from the laughter of the crowd, swinging and talking.

"Did you know God made all these trees?" Anna asked. "How did he do it?"

"I'm not sure," Alissa said, looking up and seeing the greenness of the leaves anew, through this child's eyes. "God is pretty amazing, isn't he?"

"Yes, he is," Anna answered softly. "I asked Jesus into my heart. Do you have Jesus in your heart?"

"Yes," Alissa said with a tender smile. "Yes, I do. I gave him my heart when I was eighteen years old. At the beach. That was a very happy day."

Anna nestled her head against Alissa's shoulder, and

together they watched the rest of the party carrying on around them. Jake and Brad were clearing a spot on the brick walkway to set off the fireworks. Like two little boys, they began lighting their toys before the sun had completely set. Anna hopped down and joined them when they enticed her in their direction with a lit sparkler. But Alissa was content to watch from a distance, her attention focused on Jake.

Both Jake and Brad were terrific with the six or so children who were at the gathering. The men sometimes let the kids light the fireworks, but most of the fountains, Piccolo Petes, snakes, and shooting candles were brought to life by Brad's matches. He was more into this than any of the kids. Alissa felt a tenderness for him that hadn't been there before.

What am I doing? I'm watching these guys as if I were a teen, staking out my next target. They are my neighbors. And if I'm going to stay on good terms with all my neighbors, I certainly can't date either one of these men. That would ruin everything. I like it here. I want to stay. I can't be dreaming up some false hope just because I'd like some attention.

After the last fountain was lit and the sulfur haze had begun to dissipate, Genevieve lit the last sparkler and placed it in the middle of her gorgeous flag cake. With a shout of "Happy birthday, America!" she held up the cake and added, "And may God bless America."

Alissa joined the rest of the party, lining up for cake and ice cream.

"You going to stick around for our bongo-fest?" Brad asked, sliding up to Alissa. It was the first time he had talked to her in a week or so, and she wondered what direction their conversation would go. Would he psychoanalyze her for being an observer rather than a participant during the party? Would the bantering they had going at Chet and Rosie's wedding start up again?

"If you talk me into it," she heard herself say. *Where did that come from? Am I trying to flirt with him? What happened to my vow to be only neighbors? Friends?*

Suddenly Alissa felt young. The heaviness of her complicated past, the loss of Shawna, and all her other hurts seemed to break up and scatter like a gray rain cloud that sits threateningly on its haunches until the wind blows it away. Alissa felt as if the skies over her were clearing.

"If I talk you into it?" Brad repeated, raising an eyebrow. "How much convincing do you need? It's the coolest thing we do around here, and it's by invitation only. Consider yourself one of the few. The inner circle. How could you turn that down?"

Chloe, who had been hiding out in the daisy patch during the party, now strolled up to Alissa and rubbed her warm fur against Alissa's leg. In a burst of lightheartedness, Alissa scooped up her cat and said, "Only if Chloe can come, too. Invite me, invite my cat."

Brad shook his head. "You really know how to torture a guy, don't you? What is it with women and cats? My sister has a cat, too. Do they really keep you company?"

"This one has. Seven years now. I've never had a relationship last seven years with anyone before." As soon as the words were out of her mouth, Alissa felt her heart pounding. She couldn't believe she had just given away such a big chunk of her personal life, especially to a man who told her she was afraid of her beauty and that's why she had put on all her weight. What would he have to say now about her lack of relational skills?

"Well, then, Chloe," Brad said, giving her a civil pat on the head, "may you live long and prosper."

Alissa edged away from commenting, glad he hadn't launched into a critique of her relationships. She was beginning to sort of like this guy, as a person, and she didn't want his good points to be canceled out by a wrong turn in the conversation. "When do the festivities begin?" Alissa asked.

"When you hear the beat, man," Brad answered, "when you hear that crazy beat."

Alissa heard the beat, all right. She had gone inside Genevieve's to help carry in the last of the party goods when a distinctive beat started up.

"Bongo-fest?" Genevieve asked. She smoothed her long hair back from her face and gave Alissa a questioning look before picking up a dish towel.

"So I've been told," Alissa said, sliding the last bowl into the dishwasher. "Anything else need to go in here?"

"That should be the last of it," Genevieve said. "You are going to join them, aren't you?"

"I guess so. At least I received an official invitation."

"Then you must go. It's so much fun. If only I were young again…" Genevieve's voice trailed off, leaving Alissa to wonder. Did Genevieve regret being married or simply being on the edge of mid-life?

Genevieve quickly changed the subject. "My Anna is quite taken with you, Alissa. I hope you don't mind. She may pop over to see you more than you would like. Just send her home whenever you're not in the mood for her company."

"I don't mind a bit. She's a very special little girl."

"Yes, she is. God has gifted us with three special daughters." Genevieve put down her towel and stepped closer to Alissa. "If this is none of my business, please tell me. But Anna said you have given your life to Christ."

Alissa nodded. "When I was eighteen. I have to admit, though, I haven't been real faithful in my church attendance since I moved to Pasadena. But I am a Christian, if that's what you're wondering."

"I know a person's faith is a personal thing, but I'm so glad you're a believer. I came to know Christ only two years ago through a friend who took me to Bible Study Fellowship. I began to study the Bible, and it all came alive. Do you know what I'm saying?"

Alissa nodded. She had felt that alive once, that zealous about her faith in God. Somehow the fervor had dissipated and was now little more than a polite acknowledgment of Christ as her Savior. Was he the Lord of her life? Probably not.

Outside the open kitchen window, the bongo beat picked up a companion, and two bongos thumped in rhythm. It was the kind of musical reverberation that could be felt up through the feet, under the skin, and close to the heart.

Genevieve reached over and touched Alissa's arm. "We're sisters in Christ," she said. "That means more to me than I can tell you. We can help each other grow."

Genevieve's soft gray eyes sparked with warmth. "I'm here for you," she said softly.

"And I'm here for you," Alissa repeated. She had never said those words to anyone. But she knew she meant them.

Through her feet, she could hear the bongos beating in tandem. It was as if Genevieve's and her heart were doing the same.

"You better go," Genevieve said, giving Alissa a little squeeze. "Don't keep the bongo boys waiting. I'll be out in a bit."

Chapter Twelve

The "bongo boys" sat cross-legged on the patio behind their side of the duplex. Each wore a black beret, and with open palms, pounded his bongos. It wasn't as funny a sight as Alissa thought it would be. They looked kind of cute. If they each grew a thin black mustache, they could probably play at some Parisian, smoke-filled café and be a hit.

Here in their Pasadena backyard, Jake and Brad played to an audience of two: Fina, Genevieve's fourteen-year-old daughter, who was all eyes for the dynamic duo; and Steven, Genevieve's husband. He wasn't at all what Alissa had expected him to be like. She had pictured Genevieve married to a tall, muscular type of guy with a winning smile. Steven was medium height, medium build, nearly bald, with fair skin and a long nose positioned over his small round mouth like the top of an exclamation point.

He was reclining on the chaise lounge, eyes closed, absorbing the sound rather than participating in the music.

"Where, oh, where," Brad began in rhythm with the drum when he saw Alissa sit down in a patio chair next to Fina, "is your world-famous, ever-so-precious, not-to-be-slighted Chloe the cat?" It came out sounding like a poem, not like the subtle teasing Alissa supposed it was.

She had forgotten about her ultimatum that Chloe would have to be invited as well. She answered with the first thing that came to mind. "Hiding under the bed, most likely."

"The cat is smarter than any of us thought," Jake said in time to the beating of his bongo.

"So when does the concert begin?" Alissa asked.

"This is it!" Fina said, looking at Alissa with slight disdain. "This is what they do. They talk and play bongos at the same time. It's cool."

"Oh," Alissa said. The joke about walking and chewing gum at the same time came to mind, and she wondered if that was harder than talking and playing bongos. But she decided she should keep her lips sealed.

Jake gave a loud beat on his bongo and then broke into a fast roll with both hands flying first on the twin drums in his lap then over to the larger set in front of him. "Taco shell!" he announced loudly. Then softly he added, "Farmer in the dell."

Brad picked up the crazy beat and added to the poem, "Cat fell in the well."

Jake jumped in to finish the poetic masterpiece with "Eggplant pudding!"

A long roll followed on the largest set of bongos, and Alissa couldn't help herself. She burst out laughing. Fina looked at her as if she had defiled something sacred. Steven, eyes still closed, grinned from his reclining position on the lounge, and Genevieve stepped out of the shadows of the garden path to join them.

"Did I miss much?" she asked, sitting in the lounge next to Steven.

"It's sheer brilliance," Steven said, keeping his eyes closed.

Alissa was still laughing. "It's supposed to be funny, right?"

"Art," Jake said, straight-faced and in beat with the drums which Brad had taken down to a slower pace, "is in the mind of the beholder."

Brad took the lead and pounded faster, quoting a verse Alissa knew was at the end of the book of Psalms. "Let everything..." He thumped the smallest bongo. "That has breath..." Faster on the small bongo, faster still on the medium-sized one. Then, with a rolling beat on the largest, he finished with a loud voice, "Praise the Lord!"

Genevieve immediately burst into applause. Steven opened one eye and glanced over at his smiling wife. Alissa couldn't tell if he disapproved or was simply surprised at her response.

What surprised Alissa was that she had a response within herself as well. But she didn't let it out. She wanted to shout "Amen!" The impulse amazed her. It had been months, no, years since she had wanted to align herself with anything that came under the category of praising the Lord. That phrase had become sour to her.

For some reason she thought of Jake's comments about the way pickles ruin potato salad for him and how he thought there should be a law against them. Well, Alissa could relate. After the Phoenix disaster, the phrase, "praise the Lord," had become distasteful to her. She felt it was overused in a way that ruined Christianity. There ought to be a law against people flippantly tossing it out as a catchy slogan for believers.

But tonight something was happening inside Alissa. First Genevieve had reached out to her as a sister in Christ, and

Alissa had felt a connection with her. Now she was experiencing this reawakening of a feeling inside that said, "I agree. I think God should be praised." How could these two kooks with their berets and bongos—of all things, bongos—change something so deep inside her?

As the beat continued, Alissa looked up at the midnight sky. The moon hung overhead, shedding its soft radiance on the garden like a blessing. It was only a half-moon, a perfect, sliced-right-down-the-middle half-moon. But it was alive with light.

For the first time in a long time, Alissa felt as if God was near. And she wanted him to come closer.

The guys kept playing, the moon kept shining, and Alissa kept watching the sky. She thought of her parents and grandmother. They were all dead. Could they see her? Would she ever see any of them again?

The hardest truth Alissa had gleaned when she had read through the whole Bible years ago was the clear statement that anyone who had not called on the Lord for salvation was sentenced to eternal separation from God. She couldn't refute it. That's what the Bible said. And she believed every word.

Yet it broke her heart. Since that was true, it meant that every one in her family was now in hell. Even Shawn, the father of her baby. None of them had ever given any indication that they had surrendered their lives to God.

How could Alissa allow herself to fall into the arms of a God who was in so many ways a kind and loving Father yet who, at the same time, could condemn people like her mother and father to hell? She hadn't found a suitable answer. Perhaps that was why her zeal for Christ and the message of Christianity had waned. How could she promote the very same message of "good news" that had cursed her loved ones?

The bongos continued into the night. Alissa listened, not laughing, not commenting, only absorbing. Genevieve, Steven, and Fina headed back home after the first hour. Alissa didn't want to leave. She sat and listened, watching the sky.

"Coffee," Brad finally said after the moon had moved directly overhead. He padded softly on his drum. "The time has come for coffee."

"So be it," Jake said, thumping out a final roll. "I am a happy man. I have played the bongos and now…" His roll built to a crescendo. "Stick a fork in this turkey because, baby, he's done."

With a final "boom" Jake ended his portion of the bongo-fest. Brad followed behind with a slow tom-tom beat that ended in a strong "thwap." They performed some silly sort of handshake with their first two fingers and then tossed their berets into the air.

Alissa rose to go inside and said, "Thanks, guys. I have to admit, I really enjoyed it. Of course, if you try to get me to agree to that statement outside this little circle of friends, I might possibly deny it."

"She liked it," Brad said, giving Jake a half grin.

"Of course she liked it," Jake said, his dark hair still slicked back and in place even after the beret.

Brad, on the other hand, looked like a member of an alternative band. His long brown hair had lost its part long ago. The cocoa stubble across his chin shed a dark shadow in the weak glow of the patio light. But, as he hopped up and stretched his cramped legs, he looked at Alissa, and something in his summer green eyes caught her attention.

"Go to coffee with me?" He ended the statement so it at least sounded like an invitation.

"Is that a request or a command?" Alissa asked.

"Which do you respond best to?"

"Neither," she said. With a flip of her shoulder, she turned to walk away.

Jake scooped up his beret and bongos and was headed inside. In his Shakespearean voice, he called out, "Good night, fair Alissa. Parting is such sweet sorrow."

"Good night, Jake." Then, for good measure, she added, "Good night, Brad."

"No." Brad said. Another one of his statements.

Alissa turned and gave him a glance. Brad was standing his ground, face turned toward the heavens. She waited for him to speak. He didn't. He kept looking at the sky. Of course that made her want to look up, but she fought the urge and bored a hole into Brad with her stare.

"Can you tell me," Brad said slowly, tilting his head down and taking small steps toward Alissa, "why you pull away like that? Can't you just relax and be yourself? Be our friend?"

Alissa didn't have an answer. Brad seemed to slide past all her old, flirty ways and cut to the core of who she was, the way a brother would, if she had ever had a brother. Her instinct told her to run toward this relationship and embrace it. Something else told her to run away from it.

Alissa looked into his piercing green eyes and said, "I'm sure I don't know."

He waited, holding her gaze as if it were a light thing for him to bear and not heavy at all. Everything inside Alissa told her she could trust this man.

"What were you thinking?" he asked.

"When?"

"Now."

"Nothing."

"Then what were you thinking while we were playing?"

"Heaven and hell," Alissa answered truthfully to this man who seemed to look right through her.

He slowly nodded and rubbed the stubble on his chin. "Come on," he said, walking past her and heading into his side of the duplex. "That's too powerful a topic to walk away from. I'll make the coffee, and you talk. Better yet, I'll have Jake the gourmet make us a couple of cappuccinos, and we can both talk."

He was inside his back door before he stopped talking and turned to notice that she wasn't following. He stood there, without saying another word, his calm smile and stubbly face turned toward her, waiting.

What is your problem, Alissa? Can't you just put one foot in front of the other and go inside there? It isn't a date. This is your neighbor. And Jake's there. Just take the first step. Be friendly. You have to get over this aloofness if you want friends.

She looked down at her feet as if waiting to see what they would do. It didn't completely surprise her when the right one moved first, then the left, crossing the patio and delivering her at the back door of the bachelors' pad.

"Jake," Brad called out, "plug in the espresso machine. We have company."

Alissa didn't say anything as she entered their sparsely furnished living room. A light was on over an old television set, revealing a dark brown couch, floor-to-ceiling bookshelves along one wall, and an expensive looking stereo cabinet. Jake was in the kitchen with a bag of coffee beans in his hand.

"You like decaf or regular, Alissa?"

"Doesn't matter. Whatever is easiest." She felt sheepish, as if she had walked into a trap. For so many months she had kept to herself, and now she was interacting with people she might actually refer to as friends. The only thing was, she hadn't decided if she wanted to stop being an island yet.

Jake ground up the coffee beans and spooned them into the filter of his espresso machine. Brad kicked back in the one easy chair in their living room and motioned for Alissa to take the whole sofa.

"Heaven and hell, huh?" Brad began. "So what are your thoughts on the subject? Wait. Before you answer you should know that Jake and I are God lovers so that's the direction our thoughts are slanted."

Alissa tried to remember where she had heard that term before. Not in Phoenix, not in Boston. Maybe it was Atlanta. Or California with her beach friends.

"I'd say that's the point of view I'd be coming from, too," Alissa said. Then, as if she were fed up with her reserved approach to everything, she let go with her double-barreled question. "But answer me this: how can you love God when he sends people to hell?"

"He doesn't send them," Jake said quickly. "They choose to go there by not accepting Christ."

"My parents didn't choose to go to hell," Alissa said fiercely. "Neither did my grandmother and neither did…another friend of mine."

"But if they rejected Christ," Jake continued, "it's the same as choosing to be separated from God for eternity."

"They didn't choose that," Alissa argued. "They didn't make any choice for or against God."

"Same thing. To not decide is to decide. By not receiving God's gift of salvation through Christ, they rejected him." Jake pulled a coffee mug from the cupboard and seemed to be scrounging for two more. "I'm sorry, but that's what the Bible says."

"I know what the Bible says," Alissa muttered. She wondered why she had ever agreed to come in and talk to these guys. If there was one thing she couldn't stand it was a know-it-all, especially one who acted like he had the Bible all figured out. She never would have guessed Jake would be so dogmatic.

Alissa felt a gentle tap on her arm. It was Brad. He had moved from the easy chair and was now sitting next to her on the couch. "When did your parents pass away?" he asked softly.

"My dad when I was in high school and my mom a few years ago. Then my grandma."

"Any brothers or sisters?" he asked. She noticed his T-shirt was torn at the ribbing around the neck. This guy needed a few tips in grooming. But he had managed to look fantastic at Chet and Rosie's wedding.

"Ah, no. Just me." Alissa's mind quickly sprinted away from his question.

A kind smile spread across Brad's unshaven face. "You're a strong woman," he stated. "My dad left before I was born. I mean, it's nothing like what you've been through. But it made my sister and me really close. I told you about her. Lauren. The one with the cat. Anyway, sometimes I wonder if he's dead, my dad. He just vanished. Is he in hell? Or did he turn to the Lord?"

"There's no way of knowing," Alissa said, feeling the pain of the words as she said them.

"Sugar?" Jake called from the kitchen.

Alissa looked over her shoulder at Jake, holding up a pink and white box of granulated sugar. "Yes. I mean no. Or, well, how about half a teaspoon. Thanks, Jake."

She could hear him fumbling in the drawer for a teaspoon as she turned her attention back to Brad.

"I may be all wrong on this," Brad said, using both his hands to smooth his hair back off his face, "but I hold on to the hope of the fifty-fifty thief principle."

"Which is..."

"When Christ hung on the cross, two thieves were beside him, right? One on either side. And one of them, the guy on the right, I think, said, 'Remember me.' That was it. Nothing else. And Jesus himself promised the thief he would be with him that day in paradise."

Brad got up and went to the kitchen counter to pick up the full cups of coffee. "This may sound crazy, but I wonder how many people in that final breath turn to Christ. How many people will we be shocked to see in heaven? It could be a fifty-fifty thing. Half are stubborn until the very end. Half turn in that last moment. That's why I think there's a fifty-fifty chance I may see my birth father some day."

Jake joined them as Brad offered Alissa the cup of aromatic java and sat down again beside her.

"Your theology is pretty shaky," Jake said. "I could shoot it full of holes in a second. But I won't in front of our company."

"Don't start acting polite on my account," Alissa said, taking a cautious sip of the frothy layer floating on top of Jake's gourmet brew. A sip of the cappuccino came next. "This is good, Jake."

"My years as a waiter have paid off," he said. "Now, if we could only find a useful trade for brain-boy, here."

They both turned to look at Brad. "So," Alissa asked cautiously, "what do you want to be when you grow up?"

Chapter Thirteen

I think I want to be a teacher this week," Brad said, taking a quick drink from his mug. "Or maybe a counselor. Stick around. It changes each semester."

"I'm just glad we got past the firefighter and train engineer phases," Jake said with a tip of his mug to his roommate.

"How did you two meet?" Alissa asked.

"In college. At the Christian club on campus. Neither of us was much interested in the frat route or apartment life. We were pretty stoked when we found this place." Jake pulled the lever on the side of the brown recliner where he sat. With a jerk, the footrest popped up.

"Are you still in school?" she asked.

"Sort of," Brad said.

"I'm long done," Jake said. "But Bradley here thinks he needs a master's in psychology. I told him he's already a master psycho in my book."

Alissa drew her cup to her lips to hide her telltale smile.

She wondered if Brad analyzed Jake the way Brad had analyzed her the night he had helped her move from the condo.

"What about you?" Jake said, turning his perfectly chiseled face toward Alissa. "Where did you go to college?"

"In Boston. No place you ever heard of."

"I'm sorry about your parents and grandmother," Brad said. "That they're gone, I mean. I can't imagine what that would be like."

Alissa started to feel uncomfortable again. While they were talking about Jake and Brad, she felt fine, comfortable, and like one of the gang. But when the conversation turned to her, especially her personal tragedies, she felt like running away. It was an old habit, and one she didn't know if she could break.

"Tell me about your acting, Jake," Alissa said, changing the subject as quickly and smoothly as she could. "I hear you were in an aspirin commercial."

"Please. It's not aspirin. It's a pain reliever. There is a difference, you know." He described his adventures during the three days the sixty-second spot was shot with his posing as a mechanic. It sounded like a lot of tedious work. "Then in April I did one for toothpaste, but it hasn't aired yet as far as I know."

"Like we would know," Brad said. "We're never home long enough to watch TV."

"I have an audition next week for a part in a made-for-television movie. That would be a great foot in the door."

"When I was little we lived in Argentina, and there was this guy who did gardening for us," Alissa said. She rested her cup in her lap and continued her story. "He was on the news one night because at another house where he did yard work he helped stop a robber with his rake. I remember asking for his autograph the next time he came to work for us. He was so shy. That was my first brush with a movie star. And now you!"

Jake smiled his appreciation for her gentle ribbing. "One day," he said, "you'll say you knew me when."

"And then I'll be his agent," Brad said. "Or maybe his stockbroker, if he makes it really big."

They talked until after three in the morning. Alissa probably could have kept going until the sun came up. The guys seemed wide awake, too. But she needed to use the restroom. When she thought of how Jake had searched for a cup and a spoon, it made her leery of using their facilities. Besides, she had to work in the morning. She needed at least a few hours of sleep.

Both men walked with her out their back door and over to her back door. "Not locked," Jake said with a wink for Alissa alone. "That's a good thing. We'd probably have to break in through a window or something."

"Good night, you guys, and thanks a lot for everything. I..." she felt all choked up and ready to cry. "This was a good night for me. I've needed friends for a long time. I'm glad I moved in here."

"And who do you have to thank for that?" Brad teased.

"Oh, brother!" Alissa said. Turning to Jake she asked, "How do you put up with his need to be thanked all the time?"

"Same way I've put up with everything else. I ignore it."

Alissa shook her head, laughing instead of crying, as she thought she might a few seconds before. "See you later." She opened the door and slipped into the solitude of her comfortable home.

Home. That's what this feels like. What a night. What a day and night! I have so many thoughts and feelings I'm processing in such a short time.

She thought about Brad's fifty-fifty theory as she got ready for bed. Even if the odds weren't fifty-fifty, a possibility still existed, be it ever so slight, that one of her parents or her grandmother might be in heaven. Might. It was a big might. The harder reality was that as much as heaven was real, so was hell. And people really went there. And somehow that still felt unfair, even though she knew all the logical reasons God created a place where souls would be eternally separated from him.

Alissa pulled up the sheet to her chin and rolled over on her side. "There's so much more I don't understand, God," she whispered into the still of the night. "So much I don't know. I stopped learning about you somewhere along the way. And when I did, I think I stopped trusting you, too. I'm sorry. I want to move forward. I feel as if you broke up a big hunk of ice in my life today. Now keep it moving, flowing. Let it turn into a river of life."

As Alissa drifted off to sleep, she thought of a song the congregation used to sing at one of her churches. The words went on about some "river of life flowing out of me."

The song was still on her mind when her alarm jolted her from bed at 7:30. It was maddening to only remember part of a song. She tried to brush it from her thoughts at work that day, without much success.

When she got home, she went right to the bookshelf in the living room where Shelly kept all her books. Alissa scanned the titles until she found the one she was searching for, a hymn book.

After changing from her work clothes and popping in a microwave dinner, Alissa made herself comfortable on her wicker love seat and patted the cushion for Chloe to hop up and join her. With her steaming hot halibut cooling on a plate and a purring Chloe by her side, Alissa began to scan Shelly's old hymn book for the river of life song. It didn't seem to be there. However, another hymn caught Alissa's eye. Then another. And another.

She spent the evening, oblivious to the time, reading each stanza of each song and finding herself astounded that she had never heard these songs before. In all her church experiences, the songs had been choruses. The words appeared on the wall of the church, shot there by an overhead projector.

They were nice songs. She loved them, in fact. They were cheerful and easy to remember. But these hymns were so much deeper.

Brad tapped on her back door sometime after sunset, and she nearly jumped off the love seat.

"Sorry," he called out through the open door. "I saw the light on and wondered how you were doing. Were you dragging this morning?"

"No, not too bad. How about you?" Alissa went over and opened the door, welcoming Brad in for the first time. It felt natural. None of the tension that had sparked them both off when they first met was present now.

"Do you know a lot of old hymns?" Alissa asked.

"Some. Why?"

"Listen to this." She read the words to a hymn written by Samuel Wesley in 1864:

"The Church's one foundation is Jesus Christ, her Lord,
She is His new creation, by water and the Word
From Heav'n He came and sought her, To be His holy
   bride
With His own blood He bought her, And for her life He
   died.
"Though with a scornful wonder, men see her sore
   oppressed
By schisms rent asunder, by heresies distressed,
Yet saints their watch are keeping;
Their cry goes up, 'How long?'

And soon the night of weeping, shall be the morn of
   song.

"Mid toil and tribulation, and tumult of her war
She waits the consummation of peace forevermore
Til with the vision glorious her longing eyes are blest
And the great Church victorious shall be the Church at
   rest."

Alissa put the hymn book down and looked at Brad. "Who
does that make you think of?"

"Mildred Stanislav," he said without blinking.

"No," Alissa said. "Think about it."

Brad thought a half a second and with a shrug said,
"Mildred Stanislav. She used to play the organ at the church I
grew up in. I know she played that one. She would play real
loud on the last verse."

Alissa tilted her head back and said, "Never mind."

"Why?" Brad asked, making himself at home in the wicker
chair next to Alissa. "Who does it remind you of?"

"Rosie, of course. She was a vision glorious at their wedding. And she's gone through so much trial and tribulation, but
she's prevailed."

Brad seemed to consider her observation for a while before
saying, "You know the hymn isn't talking about a bride-bride.
It's about the Church. The Church is called the Bride of Christ.
You've read that, haven't you?"

"I suppose I have, but it never hit me before." Suddenly an
even stronger image came to Alissa's mind. For so long she had
stayed away from churches of any kind, saying they were all
messed up. But that wasn't the Church's fault, the Church in
the universal, biblical sense, at any rate. The Church was the
Bride, and she was promised to Christ. He was coming back

for her, no matter how long it took. Just like Chet and Rosie.

"I never saw this before," Alissa said. "Look at the terrible stuff that happens to churches and in churches, just like this hymn says. But even though she's been abused and deeply wounded, she's still his bride. He loves her."

Brad tried to make eye contact with Alissa. "Are you talking about Rosie now? Or the church? I lost you."

Alissa broke into a gigantic smile. "It's the same picture in my mind. Rosie making her way toward Chet in that beautiful white gown, those flowers in her hair. That woman has endured horrible things over the last fifty years, but she's not bitter." Alissa looked over at Brad and took pity on him for his confusion.

"I don't expect you to understand," she said, feeling a puddle of tears forming in her lower eyelids. "This is just for me. I had to see this."

"See what?" Brad asked.

"That you don't turn away from the bride. You don't speak badly about her or act like you don't know her. As imperfect and battered as she is, she's still his bride, he loves her, and he's coming back for her." Alissa took a breath and blinked away her tears. "What I'm saying is that I want to go back to church."

Brad paused a moment, taking in her words. Then he said, "So, what took you so long?" Alissa realized he had used that same phrase on her at Starbucks when she had hesitated before placing her order. Perhaps Brad thought of this as some kind of friendly phrase. But to her it sounded rude.

Alissa wasn't sure if he meant what took her so long to explain her conclusion or why did it take her so long to decide to go back to church. She wisely decided not to push it. "Can you recommend a good church around here?"

"I'm kind of partial to the one I've been going to for the last four years. Genevieve and the girls go there, too."

"Steven doesn't go?"

Brad shook his head. "No, but we're working on him."

"What time Sunday? I definitely am going with you guys."

"You can catch a ride with me at nine, if you want. I teach junior high guys' Sunday school the first hour, then I go to the worship service."

"Junior high guys, huh?" Alissa said, making a face. "Maybe I'll check with Genevieve and see if I can go with her."

"Sounds good," Brad rose to leave. "Oh, hey, next week when Shelly's home let's all get together and do something, okay?"

"Sure. Like what?"

"Doesn't matter. You nice girls can fix dinner for us or something." Brad stood by the back door, leaning against the door jam and looking an awful lot like a junior high boy himself.

"Guess again," Alissa said. "My days of fixing dinner to impress a man ended quite some time ago."

"You don't have to impress us," Brad said. "You can just feed us, and we'll be happy."

Alissa picked up a pillow from the love seat and tossed it at Brad. He ducked, and it bounced off the window. "I'll ask Shelly when she gets back. I think she's home Monday."

By the time Shelly did arrive on Monday, Alissa had a lot of news for her. "I went to church yesterday," she told Shelly. They were both in the kitchen putting together a salad for dinner. "With Genevieve and the girls. The church was a little different from what I'm used to, but I liked it. So much is happening inside of me. I don't know what triggered it, but I'm doing better than I have in years."

"That's terrific," Shelly said. When she had walked in the door half an hour earlier, she had told Alissa she had big news but wanted to wait until they sat down to eat.

"And you'll never guess what I've been reading," Alissa said. "Your old hymnal."

"Really?"

"So much stuff is in there that I've never learned about Christianity."

"You mean like the Apostle's Creed?" Shelly asked.

"What's that?"

"You know, 'I believe in God the Father Almighty, Maker of heaven and earth. And in Jesus Christ his only Son, our Lord.' You don't know this?"

Alissa shook her head. "That is so amazing. You can just rattle off what you believe like that. How did I miss all these basics?"

"You obviously didn't go to confirmation class when you grew up."

"I want to learn this now. I want to know what I believe. I want it to be so much more than an emotional high from Sunday to Sunday."

"That's funny," Shelly said, carrying the salad dressing bottles over to the table. "I've been drilled in the basics my whole life. What I want is more emotion. More pizzazz in my faith."

"Sounds like we're a good match," Alissa said, following her with bowls, forks, and napkins.

"Well, whatever happened to you while I was gone is great. You seem really refreshed. I'm happy for you."

They sat down and scooped up the salad. "You want to pray for us?" Shelly asked.

"Okay," Alissa said. Praying aloud had never been her favorite activity. As a matter of fact, she could only remember praying aloud a few times in her life. With calm determination, she closed her eyes and reverently formed her words of thankfulness to her heavenly Father. She thanked him for this new home, her new friends, for all he had provided. Then she especially thanked God for allowing her to move in with Shelly. She closed with "Amen" and looked up with a feeling of victory. She had prayed aloud, and it hadn't been awkward at all.

Shelly, however, didn't have the same look of satisfaction on her face. She actually looked as if she were in pain.

"Are you okay?" Alissa asked.

Shelly quietly nodded.

"Didn't you have some big news to tell me?" Alissa prodded as she scooped the salad from the bowl.

Shelly took a deep breath. "The airline has transferred me to Seattle."

Chapter Fourteen

Alissa put down the salad tongs and looked hard at her new friend, hoping for some hint that this was a joke. "Seattle?" Alissa repeated.

Shelly nodded. Her jaw seemed to clench and unclench. She slowly said, "When I was having a hard time finding a roommate a few months ago, I put in for a transfer to Seattle because a lot of my family lives there. I grew up there. When it was denied, I forgot about it. Then you moved in, and my financial situation was straightening itself out."

"Can't you turn it down?" Alissa asked.

"It's a little more complicated than that. I'm due for a pay raise, and I'd definitely get it if I transferred to Seattle. I might not get it for another six months if I stay here. Plus I'd have a new flight schedule with weekends off, which would be a first in my career." Shelly leaned back in her chair. "And I'd be near family. I have friends here, but it's not the same. You know."

"Well, I don't exactly," Alissa said. "But I think I know what you're feeling. It sounds like you need to take the transfer before they change their minds."

"But I feel so bad," Shelly said. "You just moved in, and we're barely starting to know each other."

"Don't worry about that," Alissa said. "I know what jobs are like in the travel industry. You have to take any advancement you can when it comes to you. I think it's great you'll be near your family again."

"What about you? Can you handle the payments here by yourself?"

"I'm sure I can for awhile. I may need to look for a room-mate, but not right away. When do you leave?" Alissa pushed the salad closer to Shelly, encouraging her to dish some up for herself.

"Two weeks," Shelly said.

"They don't waste any time, do they?"

"Not in the summer. Would you pass me the salad dressing, please?"

Alissa took a bite of salad and hoped the chewing sound would dull the pounding that had started in her head. She knew Shelly's move wasn't a decision she should take personally. Yet she couldn't help but feel a sense of loss already. Loss was a feeling she was familiar with. In her earlier years, she had been the one to leave people and places. Then important people in her life started to die, and they all left her.

Without expecting it, Alissa felt a salty tear slip from her tear duct to land in her salad. She hoped Shelly hadn't seen it. She didn't want to make Shelly feel bad.

But Alissa couldn't help it. The tears started to come. And she couldn't stop them. This was so unlike her. She had barely cried when she experienced big losses in her life. She was always strong and immovable. This was only a roommate, someone she had known less than a month. Why should so many tears come now?

"Excuse me," she said once she could find her voice. "This isn't about you. I just need to have a good cry." Alissa got up from the table and slipped into her bedroom. Once the door was closed, she really began to cry. So many tears. So much loss and injustice over the last ten years of her life.

As she pulled the last tissue from the box and dabbed at her red eyes, Alissa chided herself for crying a river of tears. The thought brought back the memory of that song she had tried to find in the hymn book the previous week, "I've got a river of life flowing out of me." Tonight she had a river of tears, not life, flowing from her. She had held on to her sorrow for too long, secretly questioning God and feeling bitterly betrayed by his insensitivity to her needs.

Those long stored-up grievances against God were pouring themselves out. She was beginning to see things differently. God was God. God could do whatever he wanted. He didn't have to answer to Alissa for what happened in her life. Instead, she was the one who would one day stand before him and give an account of what she had done with all he had given her.

There was a gentle tap on her door followed by Shelly asking if she could come in. Alissa sat up in bed, embarrassed for losing control in front of Shelly. "Come in."

Shelly opened the door with the newspaper in her hand. "How are you doing?"

"Better. I'm sorry."

"No need to apologize. I was noticing a good movie is on television tonight. Why don't you watch it with me? I made some popcorn."

Alissa didn't hesitate. "I'd like that. I have to be honest and tell you I'm really bummed you're moving. But I think it's the right thing for you."

"Thanks," Shelly said. Her clean, scrubbed face caused her to look open, sweet, and happy. "We can still get together sometimes, with the way we both travel. Maybe we could plan a vacation somewhere. With your travel discounts and my airline discounts, it could be an inexpensive trip."

"That sounds like a great idea," Alissa said. "I'm going to change, and then I'll join you for the movie."

"Okay. I'll grab a drink for you. What do you want?"

"Water is fine," Alissa said. "With some ice."

The next morning at work Alissa was thinking about how the "pajama party" had turned out to be the best thing the two friends could have done. It helped her move past her grief.

It occurred to Alissa that she could also raise her spirits by spending time with Rosie. On a lark, she called Rosie, who answered on the third ring.

"Why, hello!" she said. "How are you, Alissa? I was just about to go out. I'm glad you caught me."

"Oh, too bad. I was calling to invite you to lunch today."

"Well, it's just a doctor's appointment. His office isn't far from your agency. Why don't you join Chet and me for lunch? We're going to Green Street. That Diane Salad is my favorite. It'll probably be too hot to eat out on their patio, but we do like the menu."

"I would love that," Alissa said.

"Is 11:30 too early?"

"No," Alissa said. "That's perfect. I'll see you then."

She returned to the tedious job of cataloging the new travel package brochures while Cheri caught all the incoming phone calls. Renée came in around eleven, and since no customers were in the agency at that moment, she stood between Alissa and Cheri's desks. She smoothed back her fluffy red hair and made an announcement.

"We did record sales in June," she said, lifting her hands in the air, "and you both get raises! I was just at the accountant's, and your raises will begin with your August 1 paycheck. Don't all thank me at once."

"You should thank us," Cheri said with a half smile, which meant that, even though she was going to present this as a joke, she was serious. "Alissa and I have been doing the work of three employees. Have you thought any more about hiring someone else, even if the person is only part-time?"

"What do you want," Renée said, placing a hand on her broad hips, "a raise or another employee?"

Alissa and Cheri looked at each other. "Both," they said in unison.

"You two are impossible," Renée said good-naturedly. She wasn't the best of bosses, but at least she rolled with the punches. "This month you get the raises. Next month, we'll talk about another employee."

Alissa left to meet Rosie for lunch and felt as if she were walking on the clouds. A raise, right when she needed the extra income to cover the soon-to-be increased rent on her duplex.

"Why are you doing this, God?" she whispered as she walked the four short blocks to the Green Street Restaurant. "You just keep doing more good stuff in my life. Thank you."

It struck her that only last night she had been dragging before God all the things he had taken away from her, and she had complained much louder than she was thanking him now. She recalled a verse in Job that seemed like a good one to help her keep her perspective in balance. "The Lord gave, and the Lord has taken away; Blessed be the name of the Lord."

As she hoofed it past the flower shop and stationery store, Alissa wished she could grasp the eternal truth that was wrapped up in Job's statement. God does give. And he does take away. He's God. He can do whatever he wants. Alissa realized she was supposed to thank him, to bless him no matter what, in good times as well as bad.

She was less than a block from Green Street when she strode past The Computer Wiz. As always, she looked in the window on the off chance she might see Brad working there. She never had seen him. But then, she didn't know his hours or where he worked in the shop.

Today, however, she did see him. He was walking out the front door just as she was going by. He had on tan shorts and a long-sleeved denim shirt with the sleeves rolled up. His hair was pulled back in a short ponytail, and his face was shaved. He looked a lot different than he had on Friday night when he showed up at her back door and listened to her go on about the hymn she had discovered.

"What took you so long?" Brad said, and then fell in stride alongside her.

Alissa stopped to look at him incredulously.

"Come on. We're going to be late for lunch," he said.

"I don't remember inviting you to go to lunch with me."

"You didn't. Chet did." Brad gestured with his hand that she should step it up.

This was supposed to be my time with Rosie!

Alissa slowly took a step, a scowl on her face. "I didn't know you were coming."

"We didn't know you ladies had made plans that overlapped ours."

"Overlapped yours. When did you and Chet make your plans?" Alissa asked, now in step with Brad.

"Last Friday. I called him to see if he wanted to go for another milk shake, and he suggested we get together today since Rosie had a doctor's appointment. Only you called Rosie this morning and goofed up everything."

"I didn't goof up anything!" They were at Green Street's

door, and Alissa felt like punching Brad in the stomach. He could be so rude sometimes.

Brad reached over her head to open the door for her. With his arm still shadowing her like a canopy he leaned forward and said in her ear, "Hey, listen, you can be mad at me later, but do me a favor and be nice to me in front of my friends. I like these guys."

Alissa couldn't help herself. With both hands, she pushed Brad away from the door and against the wall where no one inside could see her give him a piece of her mind.

"Hey, you listen," she said. "These guys are my friends, too. I don't like it when you talk down to me. And I don't like it when you're rude."

"How am I rude?" Brad said, his arms folded across his chest.

"You're so blunt. I don't like it. Like your little line, 'What took you so long?' That's rude. Blunt and abrasive and rude."

"Maybe you're just sensitive because you're used to people treating you like a little princess."

Alissa felt the blood rush to her face. If they hadn't been about to meet Chet and Rosie, Alissa would have slapped Brad for saying that and then marched away. She had never slapped a guy before, but she sure felt like it now.

"You know," Brad said, shaking his head, "I thought we were doing so well. Last Thursday, the bongo-fest and our great conversation afterwards. What's going on with you?"

Alissa had been so up and down emotionally the past few days she didn't know where she was now. The last person she wanted to confide in regarding her spin-cycle feelings was Brad. Yet at the same time, she had this strange feeling that he—of all people—might actually understand what she was going through and have some worthwhile advice.

Drawing in a deep breath, Alissa said, "Okay, Brad, look.

Let's not go ballistic over this. I'm fine. Really. You might want to consider my advice that occasionally you could practice using some manners. It wouldn't hurt. And I'll take your caution to heart and not be overly sensitive. Now, can we go have lunch with our mutual friends and not be at each other's throats?"

Brad looked as if he had a pithy comeback ready to whip out, but he pressed his lips together and answered, "Sure. Okay. Let's go." As a gesture of his attempt to be more mannerly, he held out his bent arm, offering to usher her in like a queen.

"Don't overdo it," Alissa muttered, without taking his arm. They walked in tandem to the front door where Brad reached for the handle first and opened the door for her.

They both spotted Chet and Rosie at a corner table. Brad stepped back, inviting Alissa to go first. He shook hands with Chet and placed a kiss on Rosie's cheek. Alissa slid onto the chair next to Rosie and glanced at Brad. He was looking at Alissa. It was as if each of them was wondering if the other would keep the peace.

"They've just added a barbecue buffet," Rosie said. "Looks wonderful. That's what I'm going to have. But everything on the menu is good."

Chet gave Alissa a big smile. "So nice the way it worked out for the four of us to meet up like this. Rosie was real glad you called this morning."

Alissa couldn't help but flash an ever-so-subtle "so there" look at Brad. His steady green eyes were watching her, almost daring her to make one false move so he could have an excuse to stop being polite.

Alissa carefully did not make any false moves. She ordered the barbecue along with Rosie, and as they went over to the buffet, Alissa said, "I still would like to have lunch with you sometime when it's just the two of us."

"I'd like that, too," Rosie said. "One can never have too many friends."

"I didn't tell you," Alissa said, holding out her plate to the carver for some of the sliced beef, "but I met Meg at your wedding. I think she's adorable. She told me more of your story, but she only got to the part about some woman named Hannah who took Chet away."

"Oh, Hannah didn't take Chet away. She was married to Elton, you know. They were missionaries in Brazil, back in the '50s. They actually lived in a tree house. Can you imagine that?" Rosie reached for a scoop of potatoes. "Oh, look at that, will you? They have corn on the cob. I do enjoy fresh corn."

Alissa put a piece of corn on her plate as well. It might as well have been a banana fresh from the Brazilian jungle because, whenever she started to listen to Chet and Rosie's story, it was as if she had been transported there.

"What happened?"

"Hmm?" Rosie said, looking up from the zucchini bread basket at the end of the buffet. "Oh, yes, Hannah. She developed cerebral palsy. She and Elton returned to England after only three years on the field."

"How sad."

"Oh, it was," Rosie said, returning to the table and sliding her chair forward as Chet rose to help seat her. "But Chet saw the need for someone to assist the missionaries who were going into the jungles. You know, in all the practical ways. Building things for them. Taking in supplies. He earned his pilot's license in Brazil, and when he wasn't working for the government, he was helping the missionaries."

"The government position only lasted until '78," Chet added. "But I stayed on another fifteen years or so. Couldn't leave my friends. There was always a missionary who needed something."

"They must have viewed you as a blessing sent from heaven," Alissa said.

"Or a critter from the earth," Chet said. "I guess that's why they all called me 'Gopher.'"

Brad laughed softly.

The waitress stepped up to serve Brad his hamburger and Chet his club sandwich with a glass of milk. Chet offered to pray, and then they all dug in.

"What I want to know is how you and Rosie ended up together," Alissa said. "I mean, you were in Brazil, and Rosie was in Redlands."

"Actually, she moved to Altadena in '86," Chet said.

"It was '87, but that doesn't really matter. I'd still be on the ranch if it weren't for Walter's brother, Martin. He showed up only days after I'd gotten the last child through college and presented me with some legal documents proving the ranch was his. I hired a lawyer and tried to fight it, but Martin won. He was the blood relative listed in the will. Even above Walter's own children. I still think it was terribly unfair."

"You see," Chet said, waving a french fry at them, "Walter had signed over the ranch to Martin the day he bought the land, before he was even married. And then the man never drew up another will."

Rosie shook her head. "And, of course, since I never married Walter, I wasn't even a legal guardian to those five children. But Martin conveniently waited until they were all grown and out of the house before presenting his documents, just to be sure the court didn't saddle him with the kids, too."

Putting down her fork, Rosie said, "Oh, let's not talk about it. I always feel my blood pressure go up when I think of Martin."

"Her kids moved her to the house we're in now. It was Amelio's, and he lived with her for a few years," Chet explained. "When I left Brazil, I stayed with an old army buddy who lived up in Santa Barbara. His wife had passed on, and he didn't mind my company."

Rosie chuckled. "I guess not. You turned into a five-year house guest."

"It was a big house," Chet said. "Needed lots of repair work, which had become my specialty. Then I lived in a trailer on the beach for awhile. Sort of a bum, you might say. It was awful hard for me to adjust to all the comforts and advancements of life in the States after having been gone so long."

Alissa looked over at Brad. She was engrossed in the story. Brad had a vague look in his eye, as if he were wondering what the point was to all this.

"We should get to the point," Rosie said gently, as if reading Brad's mind. "These two have been such patient listeners."

Chet drew himself up to full posture, and with his head held high, he announced, "Then the mailbag arrived. My buddy in Santa Barbara received a stack of mail for me that had been forwarded from the last government office where I'd served in Brazil. One of the letters was a notice about our high school class reunion."

"Did you go?" Alissa said eagerly. "Is that where you two found each other?"

"Couldn't," Chet said flatly. "The announcement arrived two years after the reunion." His eyes lit up, and he reached over for Rosie's hand. "But my Rosie's name was on the list. I nearly died and went to heaven right then and there. And the best part was, her address was listed right there by her name."

Chapter Fifteen

Alissa's eyes moved from Chet to Rosie, over to Brad, and then back to Chet. "Wait a minute. Wasn't Chet's name on the reunion list, too? Why didn't you write to him, Rosie?"

"She did," Chet answered. "Her letter went to Brazil, too. It was in the stack of mail I received that day."

"It was such a formal letter," Rosie said with a chuckle. "I had mixed feelings, you see. He had never answered any of my past letters. I assumed he had forgotten about me and married someone else. All my years of hoping and dreaming seemed to have been for nothing."

"Then what happened, Chet?" Alissa asked. "After you received the list and the letter from Rosie."

"I'll tell you what happened," Rosie spoke up. "He went broke on flowers! They started to arrive at nine o'clock on a Tuesday morning. No card, just flowers. First daisies, then mums. By noon I had four bouquets all over my living room and no idea who they were from."

"I wanted to spice things up a little," Chet said. "Women like that kind of romantic mystery. Keep that in mind, Brad."

Alissa chanced another glance at Brad. He didn't act as if he thought this were the kind of advice he would ever need.

"At four o'clock the largest bouquet arrived," Rosie said. "Five dozen red roses. Absolutely breathtaking. And this time there was a note. 'Roses for my Rosie,' it said. He signed it, 'The man of your dreams.' That was my secret name for him in high school."

"You must have been pretty overwhelmed," Brad said.

"I couldn't figure it out," Rosie admitted. "At first I thought it was a mistake, and all these flowers were for a neighbor or something. But the card said Rosie, and I knew Chet was the man of my dreams.... It was all so much to process. I thought I was the one dreaming."

"Then I rang her doorbell," Chet said proudly. "She opened that door, and neither of us said a word. We must have stared at each other for a full two minutes."

Alissa could just see them, frozen there, the two ageless lovers, suspended in time and space. "So what happened?" she asked cautiously.

"I kissed her."

Rosie blushed. "He certainly did."

Brad was the only one who had been eating during the unfolding of the story, and his hamburger was gone. "I hate to jam without hearing the rest," Brad said, checking his watch, "but I have an appointment with a frantic client. He's a scriptwriter, and his hard drive crashed when he was on the last scene of some film script. He didn't back up on a disk, so if I can't reconstruct the file for him, he's going to be hurting."

Rosie turned to Alissa and said, "I think that was all in English, but I have no idea what he just said."

"He has to leave," Alissa summarized.

"Oh, dear," Rosie said, turning her apology toward Brad. "I'm afraid I monopolized the entire conversation. Let's do get together again soon, and I'll keep my lips sealed."

Alissa watched Rosie's firecracker red lips as she spoke, picturing what they would look like when "sealed." Alissa was thankful Rosie had finished her story before she realized she had been doing most of the talking.

"I'll look forward to it," Brad said, pulling a twenty-dollar bill from his pocket and slapping it down on the table. "This is for mine and Alissa's. Leave the rest for a tip. That way we'll be even next time we meet for lunch. None of this, my-turn-your-turn stuff."

"Brad," Alissa began. His paying for her lunch caught her off guard. That made the lunch almost like a date. His intense look silenced her. This was an argument they could have later, away from Chet and Rosie, he seemed to be saying.

With all the strength she could muster, Alissa said, "Thanks, Brad. It'll be my turn to treat you next time."

Brad looked at her another lingering moment, as if he were trying to make sure she didn't have any other little stingers to add. Alissa knew that look. She had seen it enough during the past few weeks. It was a look that said, "You intrigue me and infuriate me at the same time. If I could get you out of my head, I would. But I can't."

"You're welcome," Brad said with a smile. He nodded to Chet and Rosie and strode out of the restaurant.

"We certainly like Brad," Rosie said as she picked up her fork and broke off a dainty corner of zucchini bread. "Are you two getting serious about each other?"

"Brad and me?" Alissa quickly swallowed the bite of corn in her mouth. "No! Not now, not ever. Never!"

Chet laughed at her strong reaction. "I suggest you carry around a packet of salt, my dear girl. You may end up eating those words one day, and I'm sure they'll go down easier with a little seasoning."

Alissa carried around Chet's words all day. How could anyone think a relationship was brewing between Brad and her? Especially someone like Chet, who had seen it all. Nothing hinted that Brad and she were in love. Nothing.

To prove it to herself, Alissa stayed away from Brad for days. She heard him in the living room one evening talking with Shelly and Jake. Alissa pretended to be asleep and didn't venture from her room to join them. She heard Jake asking when the four of them could get together as a good-bye for Shelly. As it turned out, between their busy schedules they couldn't find a free evening, so that was the end of their planning.

Shelly's two weeks zoomed past. She packed in a day and a half, leaving a lot of her furniture and kitchenware as a gift for Alissa.

"Whatever you don't want just add to the garage sale bin. I'm moving in with my parents for the first few months, and I don't want to pay to have this stuff stored," Shelly said.

"Are you sure?" Alissa looked appreciatively at the wicker couch and coffee table. Shelly was planning to take the kitchen table she had made with the clever tree-like base. "I should pay you for your furniture."

"It's okay," Shelly said. "Besides, you'll have to buy a new table now, and that won't be cheap."

The day Shelly moved, Brad, Jake, and Alissa all helped her. Shelly had rented a small trailer, which Brad had hooked up to her Firebird. Everything fit surprisingly well since the only large pieces were her bed, the table, and her dresser. With the back of her car jammed full and the trailer safely locked,

Shelly stood on the front lawn and started to cry as she told her friends good-bye.

Jake kissed her. Brad gave her a hug, and Alissa found herself crying as she gave Shelly a hug and a kiss. Genevieve and the girls were there, too, and they all started to cry when they said good-bye.

"I better get out of here," Shelly said, "or we're going to soak the grass."

"It could use a good soaking," Genevieve said, handing Shelly a small wicker basket with a bright blue cloth tucked in the sides. "This is a snack for you. Anna convinced me to make your favorite snickerdoodles."

"This is great. Thanks, you guys. I'm really, really going to miss all of you. Come see me in Seattle."

As she drove off, they all waved until the car turned a corner and disappeared.

"What are you going to do now, Alissa?" Anna asked, slipping her hand into Alissa's.

"I don't know. Do you have any good ideas?"

"You could take me swimming," she said coyly.

"Oh, I could, could I?"

"She means at the athletic club," Genevieve explained. "You're welcome to go there as our guest any time, but you don't have to take Anna."

"I'd love to take Anna," Alissa said, "and Fina and Mallory, too, if they want to come."

"Why don't we all go?" Genevieve suggested. "You guys want to come?"

"Another time," Jake said.

"I'll take a rain check," Brad responded.

"Looks like it's girls' afternoon at the pool," Genevieve said.

"I wish Shelly didn't have to leave," Fina said.

"I know," Genevieve agreed. "We're all going to miss her."

Alissa spent the afternoon in quiet thought at the pool, as she watched Genevieve slip down the pool slide laughing all the way, with Mallory in her lap. Alissa realized how much she admired Genevieve. She was a patient mother and a kind-hearted friend.

It turned out to be a relaxing afternoon. When Alissa got home, she opened the front door and automatically took off her shoes. Then she paused. A smile crossed her lips. Shelly wasn't here anymore. She didn't have to take off her shoes. But she still wanted to; it felt natural. She would probably continue this new custom for a long time.

With bare feet moving noiselessly across the floor toward her room, Alissa thought the duplex felt empty. Most of the same furniture was there, and Shelly had rarely been home. But tonight it felt different. There was a definite loss. It wasn't just because Shelly was gone. Being around Genevieve and the girls all afternoon had made Alissa feel a loss over her own life. She wanted Genevieve's life. Was that coveting?

The next morning when she sat next to Genevieve at church, Alissa realized maybe Genevieve didn't have the perfect life after all. She had a husband who was gone more than he was home, and the worst part was he didn't share in her spiritual interests.

Alissa loved the little church. She loved being back in a consistent time of worship each week. If she were ever to marry, she would want to share this with her husband.

If only I could go back to my high school days, back to my junior high days, and start all over again. I'd be a different person today.

Genevieve invited Alissa to go with her and the girls to the pool again that afternoon, but Alissa decided not to. She needed to be somewhere else. So she headed home, changed into her bathing suit, collected a few things in a big straw bag, and drove to the beach—Newport Beach—where she had spent two of her high school summers.

The freeways were uncluttered until she got closer to the coast. It seemed, as she took the interchange on to the 55 Freeway, that everyone in Orange County had realized at the same time that today was a perfect beach day. She pulled into the fast lane and cranked her air conditioning up a notch as the traffic slowed. Alissa couldn't explain the urgency she felt as she raced toward the water and the sand. But something was waiting for her there, and she didn't want to miss it, whatever it was.

The first place she drove to once she entered the Newport Beach area was the rental house where her mother and she had spent their first summer. Alissa still didn't know why her mother had decided Newport was the place to go except maybe that it was so far from Boston. And being far from Boston meant being far from Alissa's grandmother, who always had frowned whenever Alissa's mom entered the room or spoke up. Alissa didn't blame her mom for wanting to get away.

She couldn't find a place to park, so she kept driving until she spotted a metered parking place she could back into. Alissa fed the meter six quarters, then slung the straw bag over her shoulder, and with determined steps headed to the second place she wanted to see. The house looked the same as she remembered it: clean, white trim on the two-story modern, beach-front home; potted flowers along the walkway; curtains open, displaying the expensive white living room furniture; and a welcome mat at the front door.

Slipping her sunglasses to the top of her head, Alissa rang the doorbell. She pursed her lips together and waited, not sure what she would say if anyone actually answered. No one came, so she rang again.

The first time she had come to this door was to pick up a younger girl she had met on the beach. It was Christy, the friend who had led Alissa to Christ her second summer at Newport. Christy's aunt and uncle lived here. It had been a long time, but Alissa thought Aunt Marti might remember her. She hadn't kept in contact with Christy, so she didn't know if Christy still lived in Escondido or if her aunt and uncle still lived in this house.

Alissa rang the doorbell a third time. No answer. She turned to go, sad that she wouldn't be able to solve the mystery of what had happened to her friend.

She knew the next doorbell she needed to ring. It was several long blocks to her previous boyfriend's house, and Alissa felt nervous. What was she trying to prove? What in the world would she say? "Hi, remember Shawn, your son who died in high school? Well, you never knew this, but I had his baby. You're grandparents; only she was adopted, and you can never see her."

Alissa's stomach twisted into a huge knot. Why was she doing this? Was she trying to purge herself of the painful memories by dumping them on someone else? No, she couldn't do that. But she could at least meet Shawn's parents and tell them she knew their son and she was sorry he had died such a tragic death. No, she couldn't do that either.

Before she could decide what she was doing, Alissa was at the front door. She stood silently, commanding her heart to stop pounding so fiercely. The last time she had walked through this door was the night Shawn had died in a surfing accident. His parents had been out of town that night, which was why Shawn had decided to throw a wild party. And she never had met his parents afterward because she didn't go to his funeral.

How could I have been so foolish? So blind and insensitive?

Tears of regret began to well up in her eyes. She blinked quickly as the front door opened before her. She hadn't even rung the bell, but now she was caught.

"May I help you?" a young woman with white-blond hair asked.

"I was wondering if this is where Mr. and Mrs. Russell live."

The woman shook her head. "We've lived here three years. The people before us were the Bostellers. I don't know the Russells. Maybe they lived here before the Bostellers."

"Probably," Alissa said, trying to force the lump in her throat to go back down. She should have visited Shawn's parents eight years ago. Now it was too late. "Sorry to bother you."

"Sure. No problem."

Her heart still pounding, Alissa turned to walk quickly down the street, heading for the only other house she knew in this neighborhood. Another Christian girl had lived there and had hosted a party that Alissa went to her second summer.

Alissa knocked on the door, and a gray-haired man answered.

"Does Tracy still live here?"

"Tracy?" the man said, looking confused. "Here?"

An older woman wearing glasses appeared behind him. "Hello," she said cheerfully.

"I was trying to track down Tracy. I'm sorry if I've disturbed you."

"Well, she's married, dear. She doesn't live here anymore. We're house-sitting for her parents. I don't know that I could even find her phone number for you."

"Oh, that's okay. That's wonderful that she got married."

"Yes," the woman agreed. "Lovely wedding. She and Doug were a charming couple."

"Doug?" Alissa repeated. Doug had to be the most sincere, solid guy of the beach gang. Alissa remembered how he had called himself a God lover once. Now where had she heard that phrase before? Just recently, wasn't it?

"That's wonderful!" Alissa said. "I think that match was made in heaven."

"Yes, it was. They're doing just fine. Would you like to leave a message for Tracy's folks? They'll be back from their trip in a week."

"No, that's okay. I'll stop by another time. Thank you."

Something inside Alissa felt soothed. Doug and Tracy were married. There was some justice in the world. They deserved each other. Alissa wished she could have been at their wedding. She wished she had kept in contact with all these people. They were the truest friends she had ever had. Only at the time, she hadn't known how to be a friend back.

Still not knowing what she was searching for, Alissa turned west and didn't stop until she came to the edge of the beach. Then, slipping off her shoes, she walked barefoot to the shore and stopped where the blue Pacific raced to kiss her hot feet.

"I'm here," she whispered. "I'm back." In her heart she knew she meant more than just being back at Newport Beach. She was back in her relationship with God.

Chapter Sixteen

The memories that came rushing to Alissa on the ocean's misty breath were sweet ones. The best memory was of the day she had prayed with Christy on this beach and given her heart to the Lord. Christy and Alissa had run together into the water, laughing like little girls on the first day of summer vacation. In many ways, Alissa had become a little girl that day. It was a brand new start for her. She remembered feeling full of joy and an immense sense of release. She was sure no other feeling in the world could be more wonderful. She certainly hadn't experienced any to rival it before or since that day. It was a sacred corner of her life.

Today she longed to go back and feel that fresh baptism of her spirit again. She wanted to be free.

"Make me free, God," she whispered as the waves buried her feet in the wet sand. "Why can't I live free and unburdened like I felt that day?"

Alissa wiggled her feet free and went up to the dry sand.

She rummaged through her straw bag and pulled out her beach towel. For a long time, she sat, staring at the sea, listening to all the people around her. Images danced through her mind of mistakes she had made, pain she had felt, injustices that had happened to her. The seemingly endless parade exhausted her.

At last she lay on her stomach and tried to sleep. She thought of how God wanted her to come to him. She knew that. It wasn't easy, but she longed to once again feel forgiven and free-spirited like she had that summer day long ago on this same beach.

It was too hot to lie there. She pulled off her T-shirt cover-up, strolled down to the water, and dove in. She didn't splash and scream like she had with Christy. This time she entered slowly, solemnly. It felt as if God's favor were washing over her as she bobbed under the oncoming wave.

This was definitely a sacred spot in her life. Now she understood more clearly that God loved her and wanted her to be close to him, in the same way a groom desires his bride. It didn't matter how much had happened or how battered she might feel.

God had sought out Alissa. She had promised herself to him. It was time to live as if she really believed that.

It occurred to Alissa that she was God's beloved. "God loves me," she declared to the next wave as it was about to wash over her. She came up on the other side, refreshed and more clear-minded than she had felt in a long time.

But he more than loves me, she thought, as the image of Chet and Rosie, groom and bride, loomed before her. *God* wants *me. And I want him. Nothing can keep us apart.*

To her surprise, the next thought that came to her was, *What took you so long?*

What am I doing thinking about Brad's rude line at a time like this? Then Alissa wondered if by some really freaky chance that thought had come to mind because God had put it there. Perhaps he was trying to say to her, "What took you so long to recognize my eternal, unconditional love for you?"

Alissa contemplated these thoughts for days after her visit to the beach. She felt as if she were coming to understand the deeper mystery of love, the pleasure of being desired, of knowing someone wanted to be with her and share her every thought. And truly, God was there. The choice was hers to ignore him or to receive his love.

She was writing these thoughts in her journal after work Thursday evening when Brad knocked on her front door. The top portion was open, and she smiled when she saw him and welcomed him in. Out of habit, Brad slipped out of his Birkenstocks and left them by the door.

"Pretty hot tonight," Alissa said. "You want something to drink?" She went over to the refrigerator and had a look.

"Sure. Whatever you have."

Alissa thought that was a good, safe beginning for them. They hadn't talked in quite a while, and she never knew with Brad if she was going to turn defensive or roll with his directness. Tonight she felt so at peace and so settled inside her spirit with God that it seemed no one—not even Brad—could rile her up.

With two large glasses of ice water, she joined Brad in the living room and sat down across from him. He eyed the water and then looked at her bare legs in her shorts and said, "How much have you lost so far?"

Alissa took off her glasses and said, "Excuse me?"

"How much weight have you lost? I know you've lost weight."

She wasn't sure if she should be flattered that he had noticed or offended that he had brought it up. Tonight, she wasn't going to let it bother her. "Just six pounds," she said calmly.

"Good for you!" Brad said, lifting his glass in his favorite gesture of a good-will toast. He took a sip of water, and his eyes rested on her closed journal and the old hymnal on the coffee table. "Find any more great hymns?"

"A lot," Alissa said, deciding not to camp on his rude comment about her weight. "Shelly left me her hymnal. She said she had the main ones memorized. I think she had a hard time believing I didn't know all these songs. Have you ever heard this one?" She flipped through the book to where she had marked page 381. "Listen:

"Renew me, O Eternal Light,
And let my heart and soul be bright,
Illumined with the light of grace
That issues from Thy holy face.

"Destroy in me the lust of sin,
From all impureness make me clean.
Oh, grant me power and strength, my God,
To strive against my flesh and blood.

"Create in me a new heart, Lord.
That gladly I obey Thy Word
And naught but what Thou wilt, desire;
With such new life my soul inspire.

"Grant that I only Thee may love
And seek those things which are above.
Till I behold Thee face to face,
O Light eternal, through thy grace."

"I've never heard that one," Brad said. "The thees and thous always throw me off track."

"I think it makes it more holy or something. I've been reading through the whole hymnal," Alissa said, laughing a little at her own obsession. "Is that crazy or what? I just never heard this stuff before. Like the Apostle's Creed. I almost have it memorized."

"Prove it," Brad said.

Alissa took his challenge, and sitting up a little straighter, she recited, "'I believe in God, the Father Almighty, Maker of heaven and earth; And in Jesus Christ, his only Son, our Lord; who was conceived by the Holy Ghost, born of the Virgin Mary; suffered under Pontius Pilate, was crucified, dead, and buried; He descended into hell; the third day he rose from the dead; He ascended into heaven, and sitteth on the right hand of God the Father Almighty; from thence he shall come to judge the quick and the dead…'"

She hesitated, and Brad spoke up. "'I believe in the Holy Spirit…'"

"Oh, right. Only in this version it says Holy Ghost. 'I believe in the Holy Ghost; the holy Catholic Church; the communion of saints; the forgiveness of sins; the resurrection of the body; and the life everlasting. Amen.'"

A smile flashed across Brad's handsome face. "Good for you," he said. Then, taking his clear green eyes off of her, he added, "That's something I admire about you, Alissa." He glanced up again, the smile playing across his lips. "You go after the answers."

She wasn't sure what he meant, but she took it as a compliment. "Thanks," she said quickly, remembering how Brad had a thing about being thanked.

"Hey," he said, shifting in the chair and placing his empty glass on the floor, "I have a favor to ask you."

Alissa brushed her blond hair off her shoulder and said, "I should have known you came knocking on my door for a reason."

Brad didn't bristle but calmly went on. "My sister's coming this weekend. Would it be okay if she stayed with you? She's going to a wedding."

"Sure. I'd love to have some company. I'd have to get an air mattress or something to put in Shelly's room for her."

"I think Genevieve has one," Brad said. "Shelly borrowed it once. I don't remember what time Lauren gets in, but I'll let you know."

"Great," Alissa said. "She's welcome here."

"Thanks." He rose to leave, and Alissa felt an impulse to say something quick to make him stay.

"I'll let you know, then," Brad said. "Thanks for the water."

"I'll have something a little nicer to drink on Friday."

"Lauren likes tea," he said. "Some kind of Irish tea. But don't worry about it. She's easy to please. I'll see you later."

He let himself out as she followed him to the door. Alissa wished she could pull her thoughts together and make them form the words that were shouting in her heart. *Stay. Talk to me. I want to be with you.* The thoughts surprised her. She must be feeling lonely with Shelly gone, she decided. It would be good to have Lauren as a weekend guest.

Friday evening arrived, but Brad hadn't told Alissa what time Lauren was coming. Alissa changed into shorts and a T-shirt when she got home from work and then went into the kitchen to unload the groceries she had stopped for. Reaching into the plastic bag, she pulled out a package of Pepperidge Farm Mint Milano cookies. She used to eat them by the bagful, but it had been a long time since she had bought them. Tonight, the thought of needing something nice to serve company had prompted her to buy a lot of things she hadn't splurged on in a long time.

The last goodie she pulled from the bag was a green box of Irish Breakfast tea. She didn't know if it was the kind of tea Brad meant when he said his sister liked Irish tea, but it was the only one that had caught her eye on the grocery shelf. It seemed like a nice gesture to have it ready.

With the groceries put away and the kitchen picked up, Alissa slipped on her sandals and went next door. Brad answered her knock and invited her in. As he stood back, she brushed past him and looked up into his summer green eyes. She felt as if something had hit her in the middle of her chest. Stopping in the entryway, she tried to catch her breath.

She felt her cheeks beginning to blush. She couldn't deny that she was having an emotional response to Brad. But why hadn't she felt overpowered by him before? Or maybe she had but had just plowed her feelings under with feistiness.

Alissa realized that, since her soul-cleansing time at the beach on Sunday, she had been feeling more alive emotionally. She had cried over a telephone commercial on Tuesday night, and then she had cried again at work on Thursday when Renée handed her a bonus check she hadn't planned on. She was overcome with joy.

Because of Sunday, she had become more alive. All her feelings were out in the open, not covered with layers of complications and hurts.

"Is your sister here yet?" Alissa asked

"I haven't heard from her," Brad said. He sat down in the recliner, and Alissa sat on the couch across from him.

"Do you have plans for the evening, or do you want to stick around with me and wait?"

"I don't have any plans," Alissa said. "Is Jake here?"

"No, he's working. The best tips are Friday and Saturday nights."

"Have you eaten yet?" Alissa asked.

"No. I was thinking of making a run for some Chinese. You want to go with me?"

"Sure. Or I could go, and you could wait here in case she calls. What do you like?"

"Go to The Imperial Palace. They have the fastest takeout. Can you get me a general's chicken and sweet and sour pork? Here's some money."

Alissa wouldn't take it. "It's my treat. Remember? You bought lunch."

"See, that's what I don't like," Brad said. "It becomes a back and forth ping-pong contest of who's going to pay."

"Okay," Alissa said holding out her hand. "Then you can pay again." She wiggled her fingers, prodding him to hand over the cash.

"Why should I pay again?"

"Then don't," Alissa said. She shook her head and gave Brad half a smile. "Do you just live to be ornery? I mean, have you ever gone an entire day without picking a fight with someone?"

"Of course I have. It's just you."

"It's me?" Alissa put her hand on her hip and looked at him in disbelief. "How in the world can you say that? I'm not the one who's easily irritated."

"You look pretty irritated right now."

She slid her hand off her hip and turned to go to the door. "I am not irritated. I'm going to get Chinese food. General's chicken and sweet and sour pork." Alissa turned the doorknob and tossed over her shoulder, "But I'm going to the Red Dragon, not the Imperial Palace."

She shut the door behind her, but it swung open and Brad said, "Why?"

Without turning around to look at him, she said, "Because the Red Dragon has better food, and don't you even try to argue with me on this one."

Brad didn't. He went back inside, and she went to the Red Dragon. She returned nearly fifty minutes later with two large white bags full of delicious smelling food. Brad was probably right about the Imperial Palace having faster takeout.

The sweet and sour pork was on top of the bag. Alissa drew in a deep whiff, and suddenly a memory of Chang's Chinese Restaurant in Phoenix and Thomas Avery sprang to her mind. Instead of the usual cloud of depression that settled on her when such thoughts came back, Alissa tried a new approach. She had read in a devotional book that week, "When the devil comes knocking on your door simply say, 'Jesus? It's for you.'"

Alissa mouthed the words, "Lord, I turn this over to you." It was as if the black cloud stopped in midair and then evaporated.

With a spring in her step and a smile on her lips, Alissa rang Brad's doorbell with her elbow. He opened the door and started to say, "What took you so…," but then he caught himself, apparently remembering how Alissa didn't like that line. Pressing his lips together, Brad stood back and let Alissa step inside.

"Feel free to pitch in here and take one of these bags," Alissa said. "And just so you know, I'm sure the Imperial Palace does have faster takeout, but this will be higher quality food than you're used to."

"Fine with me," Brad said, taking one of the bags from her and carrying it over to the kitchen counter. "You paid for it."

Chapter Seventeen

$\mathcal{B}$rad and Alissa ate and talked and then discussed and ate
some more. The conversation was lively and enjoyable, Alissa
decided. Brad was a man who spoke his mind, with nothing
hidden or unsettled.

Alissa realized that was good for her. She needed honesty
and openness in her life, which meant that developing a friendship with Brad could be a good thing. She decided to write off
as a fluke the emotional impact he seemed to have had on her
earlier. What she needed was a good, solid friendship.
Certainly Brad and Jake were the perfect source.

A few minutes after eleven Alissa asked if they should start
to worry about Lauren, who had neither called nor shown up.

"She'll call," Brad said.

"Is the wedding around here?"

"It's in Escondido. You want something more to drink?"

"No, thanks," Alissa said, holding up her hand. Then, for
some reason she couldn't explain, Alissa opened up to Brad

more than she expected to. Their evening together had been full of openness, and her confession seemed to fit in. "When I was in high school, I was pretty wild. I've changed a lot."

"I was a nerd in high school," Brad stated. "Girls scared me."

"They don't any more?"

"Only sometimes," he said, getting up and going to the refrigerator for something to drink.

"You had lots of boyfriends." He seemed to surmise this statement rather than ask it.

Alissa nodded.

He leaned across the counter and looked at her with a tender seriousness. "Did you get pregnant?"

Alissa was shocked. "Why would you ask me a thing like that?"

"Because you seemed to want to talk about it. You just admitted to being wild and having lots of boyfriends. A lot of the girls I knew in high school who were wild and had lots of boyfriends got pregnant."

Alissa turned away.

"If you want to talk about it, I'm open. Believe me, I don't judge you. I think you know that. I think you also know you can trust me. And you do know, don't you, that I can read your face? It's becoming a lot more decipherable than when I first met you."

Alissa was still in shock over his blunt question. It was as if she had kept this secret all covered up and tucked away in a corner of her life, but he had just marched in, swooped off the blanket, and exposed what she had worked so hard to hide.

She hesitated, pushing the white box of leftover rice to the side of the counter and flicking away a few stray grains. Then, looking up at Brad's steady gaze, she asked, "Why do you want to know?"

He paused before shrugging and saying, "I honestly don't know. Maybe it's something I picked up from Shelly. One of the first things she said when she met Jake and me was that she wanted to get to know us. I like that. People don't communicate like that anymore. They're not transparent enough. I guess what I'm saying is that I want to know you."

Alissa drew in a deep breath. "How much do you want to know?"

"Whatever you want to tell me," Brad said. He tilted his head and waited.

Alissa told Brad her story. He didn't interrupt. He didn't show disapproval of anything she said. He just listened. At one point he tore off a paper towel and handed it to her when she started to cry. She even told him about her day of cleansing and release at Newport Beach. When she finished, she felt lighter, calmer than ever.

"So that's it," Alissa said. "Now you know."

"You don't know this, of course," Brad said after a slight pause, "but you just gave me a really healthy response. I didn't hear you blaming anyone, not even yourself." He smiled at her and said, "Cool."

Cool? I just pour out my heart to this guy and he says "cool"? What Alissa didn't want to admit to herself was that his response was freeing. She felt safe.

Alissa glanced at the clock. "You don't have any idea what time your sister is getting in?"

Just then the phone rang.

"I'd say she's getting in right about now." Brad reached for the phone and answered with, "Hi, Wren. Where are you?" There was a pause, and then he said. "Really?... Okay... Sure... No, don't worry about it. When are you going home?... Okay... Well, next time, then. Eat some salmon for me. Bye."

Alissa had moved over to the couch and stretched out her cramped legs. "Well?"

Brad hung up the phone, went over to the recliner, pulled up the side lever, and leaned back with his feet up. A smile inched across his lips, and he began to chuckle softly.

Alissa waited for him to share the joke.

"She's in Alaska," he said, a chuckle leaking out. "Things like this happen to my sister all the time. She caught a plane in Nashville, thinking she was going to Burbank, and she ended up in Fairbanks." He laughed aloud.

Alissa laughed with him. His sister must be quite a person. Alissa had a feeling that if she ever met Lauren, she would like her immediately. "She's going to miss the wedding then. I don't know any airline that flies out of there so late at night that could get her down here in time. When is the wedding?"

"I don't know. All I know is that they're feeding her smoked salmon and sending her back to Nashville tomorrow."

"As long as she's there, she should stick around for the weekend and see the sights. It's a beautiful time of year. There are some fantastic state parks. She could rent a car and make an adventure of it."

Brad laughed some more. "If she got lost coming from Nashville to Burbank, would you really want this woman to be alone, loose in a rental car in the middle of Alaska?"

"I see your point," Alissa said.

The front door opened, and Jake stepped in, wearing his waiter uniform. He spotted Alissa and said hi, then he looked around and said to Brad, "Where's your sister?"

"Alaska," Alissa and Brad answered in unison.

Jake pulled off his bow tie and plopped down next to Alissa. "Alaska?"

"She got lost," Brad said. "She won't be joining us this weekend."

"Bummer. I was looking forward to meeting her," Jake said. "Have you seen her pictures?" he asked Alissa.

She shook her head.

"Come here." Jake rose and led Alissa into Brad's bedroom. It was surprisingly tidy. Alissa wondered if that was in honor of Lauren's coming. One side of the room was set up with a long table. A computer with an extra large screen, a printer, and a variety of electronic gizmos with long cords covered the table.

"Brad," Alissa called out in a teasing voice, "I found where you left your brain. It's in here."

"Don't touch anything," he hollered back.

"Here she is," Jake said, lifting a picture in a brass frame from Brad's desk. It was an informal shot with a volleyball net in the background. In the forefront, Brad and Lauren stood with their arms around each other, both laughing wildly. Lauren wore a white visor and had blond hair that continued down her side, past the frame of the photo. Her face was delicate. She was a classic beauty. Alissa could see why Lauren had caught Jake's eye.

"Look how short Brad's hair is," Alissa remarked to Jake. It was shaved on the sides and clipped short on top. He looked young and had a hint of nerdiness to his appearance. "Hey, Brad, how long ago was this picture taken?" Alissa called out.

"Three years ago," he said calmly. He was standing right behind her.

"Oh!" Alissa jumped. "I didn't see you come in."

"This one was two Christmases ago." He handed her another framed print. Lauren, Brad, and a woman who had to be their mother were sitting on the floor in front of a huge Christmas tree.

"Your mom?" Alissa asked.

Brad nodded. "Stan took the picture. He's our stepdad, but the only dad I've ever known."

Brad's admission caused Alissa to feel something soft inside. She had forgotten that Brad had lost his father, too. Someday she wanted to hear the whole story. He didn't seem to have any problem inviting himself into other people's private lives, but Alissa wondered if he were as open with his own intimate hurts.

"You guys want to watch a movie?" Brad asked.

"It's almost one in the morning!" Alissa said.

"So? I'm not tired. Are you?"

"I'm up for it," Jake said. "Do we have anything around here?"

"Yeah," Brad said, leading them back to the living room. "I rented some foreign films today." He picked up a stack of three videos from the floor by the TV. "This one isn't exactly foreign. It's an Australian surf film. This is French with subtitles, and I think this one is Italian."

"Let's do the Australian one," Jake said. "I'm up for watching a movie, but I'm not up for reading one."

"Aussie it is. You're staying?" Brad asked Alissa.

She was wide awake. The thought of going home to Chloe didn't sound half as fun as watching a surfing film. "Sure. I have a bunch of junk food. I'll go get it because I don't want it sitting around my place all weekend."

"Cool," Brad said. "I'll run the head cleaner while you get the food."

"I'm going to change," Jake said. "Anyone else want a coffee?"

"No thanks," Alissa said as she scooted out the door. She smiled to think of Brad conscientiously running the head cleaner through the video machine. She didn't know any guy who did that.

Armed with cookies, candy, and microwave popcorn, Alissa returned to watch the video. The guys appreciatively helped themselves to all the goodies. Within the first two minutes of the video, Alissa could see what kind of experience this was going to be. These guys didn't watch movies; they participated in them.

Her first clue was when Jake started to talk back to one of the characters. The film started with a surfer jogging out of a beach shack at dawn with a surfboard under his arm. He checked out the waves and called over his shoulder, "Today's the day, mates!" Jake imitated his accent perfectly and quickly added, "Let's take this wave all the way to Fairbanks."

Brad added in a poorly executed accent, "Wait for me!" as a bushy haired, groggy companion came stumbling out of the shack.

The movie was nothing more than a springboard for Jake and Brad to launch their own brand of humor. Any film was a sort of electronic, visual fencing partner for their wits. Alissa watched, listened, and then found herself laughing all the way through.

"Ready for the next one?" Brad asked when all that filled the TV screen was a hot orange Australian sunset. "French or Italian?"

Alissa didn't want to leave. Her better sense told her it must be after three and this was ridiculous. She should be mature and responsible. She should treat her body with respect and get some sleep. But one look at Brad, and Alissa heard herself say, "Italian. Definitely Italian."

This film had a slow start. The jokes were limited because a lot of the film was silent with extensive scenery of the wine country. A long table was set outside on the pinnacle of a vineyard. Dozens of mismatched, high-back chairs surrounded the table. Covering the table was an exquisite, white linen tablecloth on which a feast was set. Only one old man sat at the table, leaning on a gnarled cane and mumbling to himself.

Jake tried to make a joke of the old man saying, "Is my athlete's foot really that bad?" But it fell flat. The bitter old man had spent his life repelling people, and now he was befuddled as to why his family and neighbors didn't show up when he threw a party.

Alissa started to think about her own life. She hadn't rejected people, but she certainly hadn't held tightly to any of her relationships. Yet in a few short months, God had brought some incredible people into her life. She wanted to hold on to their friendships and nurture them.

She had her first opportunity to make good on that decision at dawn. Once the complicated Italian film was over, Alissa was ready to get some sleep. "Good night, you guys. Or I guess I should say, good morning. Thanks for a very, very fun night. I'm sorry Lauren didn't make it. Maybe another time. She's always welcome to stay with me."

"I'll be sure to tell her what a great time she missed," Brad said. He walked Alissa to her front door. A family of birds was awake and chirping brightly in the tree overhead. The early morning light made everything—the grass, the narrow walkway, the lace curtains on Alissa's window, and the place by the door handle where the paint was beginning to chip—appear dreamy, soft and hazy, too sweet and rich to be real. She felt content.

"I want you to know," Brad said, standing close to Alissa as she put her key in the lock, "I think you're something."

Alissa tried to chase the blush away from her cheeks by softly laughing at his comment. "Something?" she repeated. "Well, I must say, Mr. Phillips, you certainly have a way with words."

For the first time she thought Brad looked a pinch shy. He glanced past her, his summer green eyes looking bloodshot and hazy, just like the rest of the morning around them.

"I appreciate your telling me about Shawna and everything. I think you've come a long way."

Alissa's protective instinct told her to thank him for his compliment and move on. Instead, she said, "I know. God's doing something in my life. It's cool, huh?"

Brad nodded and smiled.

Everything within Alissa told her to lean forward and tilt her chin toward his strong face. She wanted to invite him to kiss her. How long had it been since she had felt that way? Never had her motive seemed so pure and sincere. It was as if she felt full of life and wanted to give a bit—a kiss—of that rich life to Brad. Always in the past, her soul had felt parched, not full. She had turned to men with the hope that they might touch their lips to hers, and in the mingling, she might snatch a bit of life from them to fill the longings inside herself.

Without a word, Alissa turned her mouth away from his. She looked down, her lips pursed together. Pushing open the front door, she said, "I'll see you later, Brad."

"Take care," he said and turned to go.

Alissa closed the front door and leaned her back against it. "What was that?" she whispered to God. "Am I supposed to be feeling these things? It's so different. What's going on?" Her heart thumped softly. She drew in a deep breath. Then the prayer that had been on her lips daily for the past week came back to her. "Father, I surrender all this to you. Have your way."

The words to one of her treasured hymns came to her, and as she slipped off her sandals and sauntered to the bedroom, Alissa prayed aloud, "Destroy in me the lust of sin, from all impureness make me clean. Oh, grant me power and strength, my God, to strive against my flesh and blood."

Dropping into bed without even changing her clothes or brushing her teeth, Alissa repeated the next verse in a final petition. "Create in me a new heart, Lord, that gladly I obey Thy Word, and naught but what Thou wilt, desire; with such new life my soul inspire."

Eyes closed, heart at rest, lips curled in a smile, Alissa whispered, "Amen," and fell into a deep, cradled sleep. The sleep of innocence.

Chapter Eighteen

efinite changes had taken place in Alissa's life. She couldn't accurately describe them in her journal or to herself when she tried to explain why she felt different. Certainly her soul-searching day at Newport had made a difference. But so also had the daily newness of communicating with the Lord. She went to him with everything, not just when she was stuck or depressed.

If she had to define the transformation, she would have said she was in love, in love with God. He dominated her thoughts, filled her longings, and daily gave her a sense of his presence. This is how she always had wanted to live. Too many years had been lost to critical introspection. God knew her thoroughly, yet he loved her. Better still, he wanted her, and she wanted him.

The effect that had on her feelings for Brad continued to surprise her. Inside, she was a shy young heart fumbling through her first crush as if all the years of sophisticated affairs had never taken place. Those relationships had begun with her imagination ignited through steamy scenes she had read in romance novels. She had played them out with different guys, as an actress would. But her heart and soul had not participated.

That was all past and forgiven by the Father. She was, in every way, starting over.

Cheri noticed the change in her at work. Each morning Cheri would comment on Alissa's appearance and the cheerfulness she brought with her. Alissa told her in a whisper, as if it were a great secret, "It's God. He's doing something in me."

Cheri didn't hold the same religious views as Alissa, but she did start to ask questions and even willingly accepted a Christian novel Alissa brought her one morning.

Alissa hung around her little nest on the weekends. She spent lots of time with Genevieve and even took Anna to lunch one Saturday afternoon, just the two of them.

Brad ran on his own sporadic schedule, balancing work and summer school classes, as well as his weekly involvement with the junior high guys at church. One Friday night Brad had seven of the guys over, and they slept outside under the stars. They were supposed to go to Mexico on an outreach trip, but when that didn't work out, Brad had invited them over for a camp out instead.

Alissa had her bedroom window cracked open, and she lay in bed smiling, as Brad allowed the pubescent bunch access to his wisdom. "Take it slow when it comes to girls," Alissa heard him say. "Don't ever rush into anything, but get to be really good friends first. You have plenty of time. Don't rob yourself of God's best, which is entering into marriage pure."

"Do you have a girlfriend?" one of the high-pitched voices asked from somewhere on the lawn.

"No."

"Have you ever?"

"Yes."

"Is that all you're going to tell us?" another falsetto voice asked.

"I went out with one girl in high school," Brad offered. "But that didn't last long."

"Don't you want to get married?"

"Yes, I do."

"Well, you're getting kind of old," one of the boys said. "Don't you think you better hurry up? Nobody is going to want you if you're bald and your teeth fall out."

The other boys laughed, and inside her room Alissa smiled. She thought of how bald Chet was, and yet how badly Rosie had wanted him.

Young people just don't understand. With true love it doesn't matter. True love is blind and kind.

"I'm not in any hurry," Brad said. "Hey, did you see that shooting star?"

The next morning after all the boys had gone, Brad went out back to clean up the residue. Alissa stepped into the sunshine and joined him. She had gone walking with Genevieve earlier that morning and then vigorously cleaned her floors. Her hair was pulled back in a high ponytail, and blotches of water were streaked down the front of her T-shirt.

"You need any help?"

"I think I'm about done," Brad said, stuffing an empty Cheetos bag into the black trash bag in his hand. "Hope my guys didn't keep you up last night."

"Nope. Did you have a good time?"

"I think they did. Hey, are you doing anything over Labor Day weekend?"

"No."

"You want to go on a road trip with Jake and me?"

Alissa was surprised at the offer. "Where you going?"

"Oregon." Brad sat down in a lounge chair in the shade, and Alissa settled in the one next to him. "You won't believe this, but my sister is moving to some tiny town in Oregon."

"What's wrong with that?"

"She met a guy, and she thinks she's in love. She's following him there."

"Good for her," Alissa said. "By any chance did they meet in Fairbanks?"

Brad ran his fingers through his unkempt brown hair and said, "Actually, I introduced them." He didn't look too happy about the admission, which surprised Alissa. Brad seemed to enjoy taking credit for things such as Chet and Rosie's choice of Italy for their honeymoon.

"You sound less than thrilled. Don't you like the guy?"

"I don't know him. See, I found him on the internet more than a year ago when I was at Wren's place in Nashville. They started an e-mail correspondence, and then they met in Hawaii a couple of weeks ago. Now she's rearranging her whole life to be near him."

"Hawaii?" Alissa repeated. "Was that before or after Alaska?"

"It's a long story. Something like this could only happen to my sister. The airline that flew her to Fairbanks gave her a free ticket. So she went to see her friends in Oregon. They invited her to go with them to Hawaii. Then it turned out Lauren's new boyfriend was the brother of the people she stayed with in Oregon."

Alissa smiled. "Sounds like God was involved, don't you think?"

"I don't know." Brad looked tired. The cocoa stubble across

his chin was approaching the beard stage. His eyelids drooped. This shady spot was the perfect place for a morning nap. "How can she know in two weeks that she wants to be with this guy? Relationships take years and years."

"I thought you said they had been writing to each other for more than a year."

"They have," Brad said. "But that's different."

"It can be a lot more intimate," Alissa said. "You get to know someone more deeply when you commit your thoughts to paper."

"I don't know," Brad said, looking like he might doze off.

Alissa closed her eyes and listened to the gentle fht-fht-fht of the lawn sprinklers that had turned on automatically. Down the street a lawn mower whirred, lulling them both to sleep.

Alissa was the first to wake up. She looked over at Brad, who was sound asleep, his hands folded across his chest. His mouth was open slightly, and his hair stuck up on the right side. She wondered if Adam looked that cute while he slept and God took his rib. If so, Eve would have definitely been at a disadvantage. Who could resist a man when he was sleeping?

Noiselessly rising, she tiptoed back inside where she checked the clock. She had only snoozed for twenty minutes, but she felt as refreshed as if she had slept a couple of hours. The floor had dried, and her little house looked and smelled clean and inviting. All that was missing was a table and chairs in the big open space where Shelly's had been.

Alissa decided to shower and dress and see if Genevieve or the girls would like to go table hunting with her. She had been wanting an excuse to poke around in some of the antique stores in the funky part of downtown Pasadena. If she could actually find a table there, it would be especially memorable.

Dialing Genevieve's number, Alissa peeked in on Sleeping Brawny on the patio. He was still in slumberland. Alissa wondered what it would be like to go antique shopping with Brad. Was he that kind of guy?

Genevieve's voice mail answered the phone, and Alissa remembered that Genevieve had promised the girls a trek to the pool. Alissa decided she would have to go on this adventure alone. Out on the patio she heard Jake's voice rousing Brad. "Did I get any calls while I was gone?"

Alissa went over to the back door and stepped into the brightness of the afternoon sun. "Hi, guys."

Brad sat up, and with a big stretch he asked, "Did I fall asleep on you?"

"That's okay," Alissa said. "I fell asleep, too."

"I can't believe this!" Jake said, transforming himself into a soap opera star. "I turn my back on you two for one minute, and when I come back, you hit me with this announcement." He took a melodramatic stance. "How could you do it? How could you two sleep together?"

Neither Brad nor Alissa showed any hint of appreciating his rank humor.

"Keep your day job," Alissa muttered.

"Okay, that was bad. I'm sorry. I do have news for you guys. I landed another commercial. This one's for Jeep. I get to swerve so I won't hit a moose. You want to see the surprised look that won me the part?" Jake pretended to turn an invisible steering wheel, then a startled expression lit up his face.

Alissa clapped. "Brilliant. A masterpiece. Two thumbs up. And to think, you get paid for that."

"Paid rather well, thank you very much. Are you going somewhere?"

"I'm going to look for a table. You guys want to come with me?"

"Pass," Jake said.

Brad stretched again and stood up. "I'll go if you buy me

lunch at Market City Caffe first."

"Oh, well, you didn't say we were doing food," Jake said. "I'm in."

"Give me ten minutes," Brad said. "I have to take a shower."

"Well, well," Jake said, "the Beav discovers personal hygiene is important to his social life. And just think, June," Jake took on his best Ward Cleaver voice and wrapped his arm around Alissa's shoulder. "We were there to witness it."

Brad brushed past him and mumbled, "It's a good thing I love you, man. Otherwise..." Brad stopped and turned to face Alissa and Jake. He changed his posture into a Jackie Gleason pose, and as if he were in competition with his roommate, Brad spouted with a clenched fist, "One of these days, Alice. POW! To the moon."

Jake burst out laughing. "That wasn't bad. Who says I haven't had a positive influence on you?"

Alissa only vaguely recognized the impersonation. She still thought it was funny to see the way Brad and Jake interacted with each other. And she liked being a part of their friendship, one of the "guys." That was something she had missed as an only child who never had boys for friends while she was growing up. Once again it seemed to her that God was giving her back the childhood she had forfeited by losing her innocence so fast.

Brad's shower took more like twenty minutes, but it was worth it when he showed up shaved and smelling like a combination between moss and wood fire. Jake accused him of stealing his aftershave, and Brad ignored him, insisting that he drive his truck.

Alissa was pleasantly surprised to see that Brad had done away with his collection of empty fast food bags on the passenger side of the truck. The scent of stale french fry oil still lingered, though. She fit nicely in the middle between the two friends. Off they went, all starving and ready for some Italian food.

After lunch, the guys willingly meandered through several antique shops with her, but none of the tables struck her fancy. The trio packed itself back into the truck's cab and meandered home with Alissa in the middle, listening to the endless banter of these two men who seemed just as comfortable around her as she was around them.

And that's the same spot in Brad's truck cab that Alissa found herself a week later on Friday night of Labor Day weekend. Only this time, Chloe was on her lap, and Brad was throwing a tarp over their luggage in the back. He hopped into the driver's seat and noticed the cat.

"You better put her back inside now," Brad said. "It's seven o'clock, and we're ready to go, just like we planned."

"She's going with us," Alissa said.

Brad looked at Jake and then back at Alissa. "I don't think so," he said evenly.

"I can't leave her," Alissa said. "Genevieve and Steven are gone for a week with the girls, you guys aren't going to be around. No one is around to feed her for the next few days. She has to come with us."

Brad looked as if he were trying to be polite, but it was a real stretch for him. Alissa realized it would have been better if she had prepared him ahead of time. Or even if she had asked Cheri or Rosie to take Chloe. But this trip to Oregon had been pulled together so fast she hadn't thought of Chloe until the last minute.

"She's been on plenty of cross-country trips with me," Alissa said, stroking her cat's soft fur. "You won't even know she's here."

"Let's make a deal," Brad said. "If she jumps on me and claws my face while I'm driving, I get to throw her out the window. Okay?"

"Only if she claws your face?" Alissa said, trying to lighten up the situation.

"If she claws any part of my person, she becomes instant road kill. Deal?"

Alissa wouldn't take his outstretched hand. She calmly stated, "She won't be any problem at all. Believe me." Brad looked at Jake again and then at Alissa. "If you say so." He turned the key in the ignition, and their adventure was underway.

The plan was complicated, and Alissa wasn't sure she completely understood it. Lauren apparently had packed her furniture in a moving van along with the belongings of a woman she worked with. That woman was moving to Lake Arrowhead in the San Bernardino mountains, which was about an hour and a half drive from Pasadena. The moving van had arrived at Lake Arrowhead from Nashville last night, and now they were driving up the mountain to retrieve Lauren's things. They would load her belongings in the bed of Brad's truck as well as in the rental trailer he had attached to the back.

Then Brad, Jake, and Alissa would take turns driving straight through to some place called Glenbrooke, Oregon, where Lauren had driven earlier that week. It was supposedly cheaper than any other arrangements Lauren had tried to make. Alissa thought it had to be partially Brad's doing since he seemed like the kind of brother who needed an excuse to be there for his sister and to check out this new boyfriend without being too obvious.

They hit the freeway and found it less congested with the weekend holiday traffic than they had expected. They made it up the mountain and found the home at Lake Arrowhead with no problem. Alissa pitched in and helped load the trailer and truck. She decided she liked Lauren's furniture, and therefore she would probably like Lauren. The most intriguing piece was a dresser with a blanket wrapped tightly around it. Alissa wanted to see that one once it was unveiled in Oregon; it had to be a honey.

"Is there any fast food around?" Brad asked.

"There's a McDonald's at Arrowhead Village. That's about a mile from here on your way down the mountain," Roberta, the woman who had moved from Nashville, said.

"I can wait until we get to San Bernardino," Jake said. "How about you guys?"

"I can wait," Alissa said, getting back in the truck. She picked up Chloe from the floor of the cab where the cat had been furiously licking the car mat. Alissa guessed it was all the salt and grease embedded in the carpet. Those ingredients could make an interesting hair ball. Putting those thoughts aside, she quietly put Chloe back on her lap and waved good-bye to Roberta.

Brad backed up cautiously on the narrow street. He maneuvered the truck and trailer forward and backward six times before he could clear the neighbor's front light post. Alissa noticed the perspiration beginning to bead on his forehead, but he calmly wedged them out of the tight spot, and with a friendly wave to Roberta, he steered carefully down the street.

"Beautiful place to live," he said. "As long as tight parking places aren't a phobia for you."

"You did great," Jake said. "Let me know when you want me to drive."

"I figure I'll be okay until about two or three this morning," Brad said. "So if you want to sleep, this would be the time."

It was dark outside, and even though Alissa didn't know what time it was, she liked the idea of taking a nap, too. As they rambled down the winding mountain road, she put her head back and tried to sleep.

Suddenly a disagreeable sensation covered her lap. Chloe,

who had timidly remained in the cab of the truck the whole time they were loading up, had decided to relieve herself. The warm cat pee soaked Alissa's jeans and trickled down her leg.

"Stop the truck!" she screamed.

Brad jerked the wheel a little too fast on the narrow, winding road, then quickly corrected himself. "What?" he shouted.

Just then a pull-out came into view, and Jake, startled from his nap, yelled, "Over there!"

Brad pulled over, and Alissa cried, "Chloe peed on me! Let me out of here."

Jake opened his door and hopped out. Alissa slid across the seat, Chloe in hand, and took her aggravating animal over to the bushes. "Go, Chloe!" she said. "Get the rest out, if you have any left in there. Oh, look at me! I'm soaked." Fortunately, her T-shirt was unsoiled, but her jeans reeked.

Brad was beside her now and said, "I'm such a nice guy, I'm not going to tell you I told you so. Do you want to tape that creature to the middle of the road, or should I?"

"That's not funny!" Alissa yelled. "This cat has been with me through thick and thin for the past seven years. That's more than I can say for any human being I know! Don't even joke like that." Then, in a desperate wail, Alissa added, "She's the closest thing I have to a relative, so back off!"

Brad lifted his hands in surrender. Jake was standing next to them, watching Chloe. "Is she okay?" he asked. "Look at her."

Chloe was scrunched on her haunches, her furry frame rising and falling with a jerking motion.

"It's just a hair ball," Alissa said. "Thanks to your car mats."

"A hair ball?" Jake said, looking a little nauseated at the thought.

"My car mats!" Brad spouted. "It's your cat!"

"She licked all the salt and grease off your car mats." Alissa stood with her legs apart, her arms straight at her side, and her fists clenched. The smell and the feel of her wet jeans turning cold in the night breeze was becoming too much for her.

"Could you stop being a jerk for just one minute and get my suitcase? I have to change." With a sniff to try to control her emotions, she added, "Please, Brad?"

Chapter Nineteen

Without another word, Brad undid the tarp and went to work locating the luggage. He finally pulled out her bag and brought it to her. Jake had gone to the truck's cab and returned with a flashlight from behind the front seat.

"We'll be over here behind the truck," Jake said, offering her the flashlight. "Take your time."

Alissa sniffed, and carrying her bag, she high-stepped her way through the brush alongside the road, as she tried to find a secluded spot to change her clothes. She kept going until she found a place where the foliage seemed to hide her from the main road. She could see the guys leaning on the tailgate, their backs to her.

Alissa balanced the flashlight on top of some thick, green leaves and fished around in her luggage for the only other thing she had to wear, a pair of shorts. She had packed light: one pair of jeans, one pair of shorts, one skirt, and seven different tops.

With her jeans out of commission, there went one-third of her wardrobe.

She easily pulled off her wet, stinking jeans, but her legs were still wet. She had nothing to dry them with except some of the leaves surrounding her. Alissa plucked a handful and tried her best to at least dry the wettest spots. She convinced herself she could do a more thorough job when she had access to a restroom.

Brushing her hair away from her face with the back of her hand, Alissa crouched in the darkness and tried to finish her less-than-happy clothes change. When she made her way back through the forest growth, she held her wadded up jeans in one hand and her bag in the other. The flashlight was in her mouth. Alissa tucked her bag back in the open spot in the truck and found another cubbyhole in which to stuff her jeans. Hopefully Brad's sister had a washing machine wherever she lived.

"You ready?" Jake asked.

"Yeah. Hey, you guys, I'm sorry. Really. I apologize to both of you. I'm sorry I got so upset."

"Believe me," Jake said, "we don't blame you one bit."

"Don't worry about it," Brad added. "Let's get going."

They climbed into the truck and shut the doors. Then Brad asked, "Do you have the cat?"

"Oh!" Alissa spouted. "Where is she?"

Jake opened his door. "Here, kitty, kitty, kitty."

"Chloe!" Alissa called. "Come on, Chloe." The cat was still sitting where they had left her on the gravel, with a gross hair ball at her paws.

"I'd pick her up for you," Jake offered, "but you know…"

"I'll get her." Alissa scooped up the now exhausted old cat and gave her a good scolding before getting back in the truck.

Brad had left the motor running, and they were off in no

time. There was only one problem. Because the cat urine scent
lingered in the cab, the guys had rolled down both windows.
But it was so chilly, Brad had turned on the heater full speed,
which only drew out the smell of grease from the car mats. The
odor mixture would have made Alissa miserable enough in
and of itself. But what pushed her to the edge was that she was
freezing in shorts, and with Chloe spread out on Alissa's bare
legs, her skin itched terribly.

"By any chance, do you have a towel or a blanket or something?" Alissa asked Brad.

"You afraid she's going to go again?"

"No, I'm just a little cold, and she's making me itch."

They had arrived at the end of the mountain road. A
double-lane highway stretched out in front of them, leading to
the freeway a few miles away.

"We might as well stop for something to eat," Brad said.

"Over there on the right," Jake said. "Del Taco. What do
you think?"

"I think if they have a bathroom, I love them," Alissa said.

Brad pulled into the drive-through lane.

"I need to use the restroom," Alissa said, irritated that he
hadn't parked the truck.

"Go ahead. We'll meet you around on the other side."

Alissa gave Jake a look that said, "Sorry, but I have to
bother you again."

Jake read her face. He got out. She got out. Chloe settled
onto the floor. Then Alissa changed her mind before Jake
climbed back in, and she grabbed Chloe to take her along. It
wasn't that she didn't trust Jake or Brad, it was just safer this way.

The bathroom only had a hand blower and no paper towels. Alissa did the best she could washing and drying the affect-
ed area. By the time she was finished, her legs were red.

She met the guys at the front of the building. They already had the bags of food and looked just a little impatient with her. With Chloe in tow, Alissa climbed in. Brad handed her an old, smelly army blanket. "I keep this behind the seat for emergencies. I don't know if this is what you had in mind."

"That's fine. Thanks."

They hit the road, Brad driving like a man on a mission. All the little holdups didn't seem to be to his liking. Alissa determined it was time to lighten up. The worst was over.

"So what did you get me?"

Brad and Jake looked at each other and at the bag where Jake was pulling out the food. Neither of them said anything.

"What?" Alissa asked. She noticed then that Brad had a drink and Jake had a drink, but there didn't seem to be a third beverage. "Did they forget to give you my drink?"

"Go back," Jake said to Brad.

"I'm not going back."

"Here," Jake said, "you can have my drink."

"That's okay," Alissa said. "I'm not really thirsty. Just kind of hungry. What did you get me?"

Again, silence.

Alissa gave a little laugh. "What? You didn't think to buy me anything?"

The guys flashed guilty looks at each other.

Brad was pulling onto the freeway, carefully studying the side mirrors, trying to gauge his distance with the trailer on the back. Suddenly they felt a jerk inside the truck followed by a bump-bump-bump.

"Oh, man!" Brad said, slamming the steering wheel with his open palm. "The trailer has a flat." He pulled to the side of the freeway with an uneven motion and let the truck roll to a stop.

"Do we have a spare?" Alissa asked.

"I don't know." Brad looked bummed. "Did you bring your cell phone, Jake?"

"Yes."

"The 800-number for the trailer rental company is in the glove box. Could you call them and tell them to get somebody over here immediately to fix this thing? I'm going to check it out and put down some flares."

"Be careful," Alissa said as Brad edged his way out of the driver's door against the oncoming traffic. She took the bag of food from Jake as he rummaged through the glove compartment and then dialed the number.

It took more than an hour for a repair person to show up. The constant swooshing sound of the cars racing by became nerve wracking, not just because of the safety factor since the trailer stuck out a bit, but also because each car seemed to remind Brad that those people were all going somewhere, and he wasn't.

The three of them divided the fast food. It had become evident to Alissa that they had forgotten to order anything for her. True, it had been a hectic past few hours, and it was the middle of the night, but she had to work hard not to feel hurt.

The woolen army blanket had been too hot while they were sitting still, so Alissa had dropped it to the floor and let Chloe roll up in a ball on top of it. She was such an old cat. It had been a terrible idea to bring her along, and Alissa admitted it. But there was nothing to do but make the best of it.

By the time the trailer was ready to go again, Alissa was more than ready for some sleep. She was uncomfortable, even with the blanket all the way over her. The guys liked the windows open, and she felt prickly all over from the night chill and the scratchy blanket.

As they rolled into Los Angeles, all still wide awake but not talking much, Brad noted, "Well, this is about where we were…" He checked his watch. "A mere nine and a half hours ago. Does anyone else feel as if we've been on the road for days?"

When they hit the Grapevine, a steep pass over the hills into California's central valley, the sun was up, filling the sky with a sweltering summer blaze. "After we make it over this pass," Brad said, watching his side mirror for the semi-truck that was passing him as he chugged along in the slow lane, "one of you can drive, because I'm ready to crash."

The problem was, none of them had slept, so neither Alissa nor Jake felt ready for the task. This free-spirited adventure was not turning out the way any of them had thought it would. Even Chloe seemed disgruntled with the scratchy blanket in Alissa's lap and had opted for the floor mat between Alissa's and Jake's feet.

Alissa kept licking her lips and wishing she had something to drink. An hour earlier she had sipped on the melted ice in Brad's Coke cup. She was about to try for the last slurp, but Brad must have read her mind because he reached for the cup on the floor and took one last long draw on the straw. Then, tossing the cup on the floor, he kept the straw in his mouth, chewing on it as if it could help keep him awake.

She hated to ask but had to. "When we stop, can we pick up something to drink? That burrito must have had some kind of hot chili in it, because my lips still feel like they're burning."

"Sure," Brad said. "We need to get gas anyway."

The truck stop, complete with gas station, convenience store, and clean restrooms, was a welcome sight. Alissa hopped out, with Chloe in her arms, and took the rattled cat over to the dirt where she was commanded to do her duty. Then Alissa made good use of the restroom, washing her face, brushing her hair, and even brushing her teeth with the travel toothbrush in her purse.

When she looked in the mirror, she was startled to see her face had turned blotchy red. *Must have been the rough paper towels,* she thought. Then she stuck out her tongue and noticed that the burning sensation she had felt on her lips had gone to her tongue, too. "Those must have been some chilis!" She exited and found the guys in the truck, gassed up, and ready to go, with Jake in the driver's seat.

"I need to get something to drink," Alissa called out and hurried with Chloe in her arm into the convenience store. She grabbed a couple of bottles of water from the refrigerated section and tried to pay as quickly as possible.

"Next time," the woman at the counter said, "pets stay outside."

Alissa nodded her willingness to comply and dashed out in the warmth of the early morning. "Sure is hot for so early in the day," she said as she and Chloe slid past Brad and took their position in the middle.

"Ready?" Jake asked. She couldn't tell if he was irritated with her or not. Brad closed his eyes and leaned his head against the door jam.

"Sure, let's go." Alissa decided that at the next stop she wouldn't take so long since these guys seemed to be in some kind of race to Oregon. Before sticking her purse and the extra bottles of water under the seat, Alissa pulled out a pill box and pinched an antihistamine with her fingers. It was an old airplane travel trick she had learned long ago. Any kind of antihistamine tablet made her drowsy enough to sleep. She decided she should take one to get some sleep. That way she would be fresh and ready when it was her turn to drive.

Alissa swallowed the pill and settled back, glad now that she had on shorts instead of jeans. Her legs still itched, and she couldn't wait to take a shower.

Jake wasn't as much of an open-window guy as Brad. He

promptly closed both windows and turned on the air conditioning. Alissa adjusted the vents so they wouldn't blast right on her. She took one last look at the straight, flat stretch of the I-5 Freeway laid out before them and was thankful she wasn't driving. The monotony would lull her to sleep for sure.

The cold pill seemed to kick right in, and Alissa felt herself beginning to float into dreamland. She was almost asleep when, in the distance, she heard a shrill burring sound. In her hazy mind, she heard Jake talking. He nudged her, and she tried to open her eyes.

"My phone," he said. "Can you get it? It's in the door's side pocket."

Alissa leaned across Brad, who didn't stir a pinch as she fumbled to retrieve the ringing phone. She handed it to Jake and went back to sleep. Jake's voice seemed to fill her head, even though she wasn't tracking any of the words. He spoke more loudly.

"Brad. Hey, Brad. Wake up. I have to go back. They decided to move the shoot up because of the long weekend, and they need me there this afternoon. Sorry, man. I have to turn around."

Alissa didn't remember much after that. She was so, so tired. The truck kept rolling down the road, and Brad and Jake kept talking. When the truck suddenly stopped, she opened her eyes. They were at an airport.

"Is everything okay?" she asked, rubbing her eyes. For some reason they seemed to burn.

"Jake's flying back to LA," Brad explained. "We're in Bakersfield. Are you okay?"

"Yeah, just tired."

"You look kind of…" He stopped and turned his attention to Jake. "You need some extra money or anything?"

"Nope, I'm set. I'm glad you thought of this. It'll be quicker to catch this commuter flight than it would have been to drive back. You guys have a great trip, and I'll see you when you get back."

"Bye," Alissa said, her eyes still burning. All she wanted to do was go back to sleep. With the extra space in the cab, she stretched out and felt Chloe doing the same at her feet.

Brad hit the road and drove with the window down for hours while Alissa slept. He stopped for gas once, but she only woke up enough to make note that they were getting gas. They hit the road again with Alissa sound asleep. She didn't come around until the September sun hung low in the sky. Brad stopped again for gas and gently roused her.

"Hey, sleepy head, time to wake up. I need you to drive."

"Where are we?" She could barely open her eyes. They were swollen and sore. Her lips and tongue felt swollen, too. Alissa reached for one of her bottles of water. This dry heat must have taken a severe toll on her.

"We're in Redding. I just got gas so the tank is full. There's a Wendy's over there. If we get something to eat, do you think you could drive?"

"Sure," Alissa said, pulling herself upright and trying to focus on Brad. The first thing she noticed was that his lips looked swollen. "The heat seems to be getting to us," she remarked. "How hot do you think it is?"

"At least ninety, maybe hotter."

"I thought it would get cooler the farther north we went." Alissa rubbed the side of her face. It itched terribly. "We are going north, aren't we?"

Brad looked at her more closely. "Do you suppose it's heat rash?"

"What?"

"Look in the mirror," he suggested.

Alissa stretched to have a look and almost screamed at the

sight. Her eyelids were swollen twice their size, as were her lips. Her face was covered with red splotches. On closer inspection, so were her legs and arms. "I guess," she said trying to sound calm but realizing how ridiculous she must look. "Why don't we go over to Wendy's, and I'll wash my face there."

She tried washing and washing, but the redness and swelling didn't go away. Then she realized she couldn't put in her contacts because her eyes were so irritated. She hadn't thought to bring her glasses since she had been wearing her contacts constantly for the past few weeks. Without her contacts, she couldn't drive safely.

Meeting Brad in the chilly, air-conditioned restaurant, Alissa broke the bad news to him. He held a bag with extra food to make up for the oversight last time and offered her an extra large drink.

"If you can't see, you can't see," Brad said matter-of-factly as they walked back to the truck.

"I'm sorry."

"Don't beat yourself up over it. You can't help it. Must be the heat or something. I only got it on my mouth. I'll drive then, but if you can stay awake and keep me talking that would help."

"Sure," Alissa said. She felt relieved that Brad was being so understanding. This was turning into a nightmare of a trip, but he was hanging in there. Her esteem for Brad soared, and she started to think it might be kind of nice to be together, just the two of them. She climbed into the truck and kicked the hot blanket aside.

Brad got in his side. Suddenly Alissa froze. Her head stayed in one place, but her eyes scanned the cab first, then the parking lot in front of them.

"Brad," she scratched out in a thin voice, "where's Chloe?"

Chapter Twenty

Alissa drew in another deep breath and tried to stop crying. For nearly an hour tears had flowed down her red dotted cheeks. Now the truck was approaching the California-Oregon border, and each mile they traversed took them farther away from Chloe, wherever she was.

"Do you believe me that I didn't leave her anywhere on purpose?" Brad said, an edge to his voice. "I know I made jokes at first, but I'm telling you, she must have slipped out while I was getting gas between Bakersfield and Redding. When we go back down on Tuesday, we'll check every place I stopped. We can leave notices."

The more he talked, the more she wanted to cry. The area between Bakersfield and Redding was enormous. How could they ever find Chloe? She had believed him the first time he had told her he didn't do anything harmful to the cat. And she still believed him. It was just that in all the confusion and her deep sleep, her long-time companion had vanished. Alissa knew she would never see Chloe again.

All the tension had kept them both awake. Brad wolfed down Alissa's hamburger when she declared she couldn't eat anything. The good news was that the sun had set, giving them relief from the heat, and they were making good time.

"Brad," Alissa tried to explain, her tongue feeling numb and her legs itching like crazy, "I told you I believe you. I know you understand what Chloe meant to me. I should never have brought her along in the first place. I don't blame you, okay?"

"I still feel bad," he said.

"I do, too. Nothing we can do about that."

"You sure you don't want anything to eat?" Brad asked. "We can stop when we reach Ashland. I'll probably need gas again by Medford."

"I'm not hungry," she said and took another sip of the heat-warmed bottle of water from under the seat. "Thanks anyway. I'm just sorry I can't help you drive."

"Don't worry about it. I'll be okay."

Alissa's thoughts became consumed with a hot shower, cool sheets, and some good sleep. They drove on into the night, listening to the radio and watching the most enormous, butterball moon chase them onward. It might actually have been enjoyable if Alissa hadn't felt so hot and itchy.

When they arrived in Glenbrooke, Brad drove slowly down the main street, checking out the quaint shops on either side of the road. After two short blocks, he hit the residential area. Old houses lined the streets. In the light of the full moon, they could see that some had shutters, some weathervanes. There were white picket fences and tire swings hanging from gigantic trees. Gardens were full of tall corn, and bobbing flowers served as spacers between the homes. Alissa noticed that nearly every house had left on a porch light, exemplifying the "welcome" feeling of the hamlet.

"My sister gave up Nashville for this?" Brad said. He pulled a crumpled up piece of paper from his pocket and said, "We're supposed to go to the Victorian house on the top of Madison Hill."

"Must be that one at the top of the rise," Alissa said. The house's lights were all on, giving the huge dwelling on the hill the look of a lighthouse. "Is that where your sister lives? If so, I can tell you why she left Nashville!"

"Her friends live there. I guess they run a bed and break-fast of some sort. That's where we'll stay. She rented 'a little cot-tage,' she said. Could be any one of the houses we've driven by," Brad commented as they headed up the hill to the glow-ing mansion.

The circular driveway made it easy for Brad to pull in the truck and trailer. Two golden retrievers bounded from the back of the house, barking a cheerful welcome to the midnight trav-elers. Before they were out of the car, a young woman with short blond hair hopped up from the porch swing and came skipping down the steps.

"Is that your sister?" Alissa asked.

"That's my Wren."

"I thought she had long hair."

"She got it cut a year ago. Don't bring it up. It's still a touchy subject with her. I wonder if that's her Prince Charming," Brad said, eyeing the tall, dark-haired man who opened the screen door and called off the dogs.

"Only one way to know," Alissa said. "Let's go." They climbed out, stiff from the long drive.

"Hi!" Lauren called, coming down the stairs to meet them. "You guys must be exhausted."

"You don't know the half of it," Brad said. "This is Alissa

Benson. Jake ended up bailing out on us. You know the life of an actor in demand." Brad wrapped his arms around his sister, and she gave him a big kiss on the cheek.

"I appreciate your doing this so much, Rad. Thanks. Thank you, too, Alissa." She smiled at Alissa, and then in the porch light seemed to be taken aback at the sight of Alissa's face and swollen eyes.

"I'm Kyle, Kenton's brother," the man by the door said. "Welcome to Glenbrooke." He extended his hand to Brad and Alissa, but then he withdrew it before Alissa could touch him.

"If you don't mind my asking," Kyle said, "where did you get such a severe case of poison oak?"

"Poison oak!" Alissa and Brad repeated in tandem. Brad looked at her more closely.

"It's on her legs, too," he said. "And her arms."

"I have no idea," Alissa said, startled. Her mind whirled to put the pieces together. "Chloe!" she suddenly said. "When I changed my clothes in the bushes."

"That was it," Brad said, the light dawning on him, too. "How did it get in your eyes and mouth?" The minute he said it, his tongue peeked out, and he ran it over his own lips.

"The flashlight," Alissa remembered. "I put it in my mouth."

"Looks like you've got it in your mouth, too," Lauren said, examining her brother more closely. She looked at Alissa and back at Brad, an expression of pleasant surprise on her face.

"Don't go there, Wren," Brad said, reading his sister's thoughts. "There's some logical explanation. Trust me."

"I bet it was your straw," Alissa said. She studied her rash-infested legs, which took on a ghastly purple tinge in the porch light. They looked much worse than they had in the daylight. "So what do we do for this stuff? It's driving me crazy."

"I can imagine," Kyle said. "You came to the right place. Why don't we go in the house?"

"He's a paramedic," Lauren explained as they entered the beautifully decorated home.

Kyle led them up a wide staircase that wound its way to the second floor and the guest rooms. "We thought we'd put you in here, Brad," Kyle said. "And Alissa, you get the honeymoon suite." He smiled and then added, "I'm just kidding. Here you go. The bathroom is off to the right. I suggest you take a long soak in the tub. I'll bring up some lotion for you to put on and set it outside the door here. We can see about picking up a prescription for the itching tomorrow. Are you allergic to anything?"

"Poison oak, I guess."

"I mean medications," Kyle said with a smile.

"No."

"Good. May I bring in your luggage for you?"

"It's buried under all the furniture," Brad said.

"I'm sure I have an extra sleep shirt, if you want to borrow it," Lauren said to Alissa.

"That would be great. All I want to do is climb into that tub."

"I'll be right back." Lauren bounded down the stairs with a spring in her step. Alissa recognized it as the gait of a woman in love. If Brad didn't approve of Kenton, her guess was Brad would have a hard time convincing his sister to dump the guy. But then, if he was anything like his brother, Kyle, Alissa felt certain it would be a unanimous vote in Kenton's favor.

Lauren returned with a folded stack of fresh clothes and the bottle of lotion Kyle had sent back up with her. "Can I get you anything else?"

"No, this is great. Thanks."

Lauren lingered by the doorway. "I hope we have a chance to visit some while you're here. I know you're really tired tonight, but maybe tomorrow."

"Sure."

"I'll see you in the morning," Lauren said, smiling at Alissa. She tried to smile back, but her sore lips made it a challenge.

After following the instructions of the resident medic, Alissa slipped into Lauren's extra large T-shirt and tucked herself between the crisp sheets. She barely noticed the decor of the room. All she wanted to do was sleep.

Sometime in the late morning, when the bright sun had flooded her room, Alissa rolled herself out of bed. A look in the bathroom mirror showed that the rash still raged. She repeated the bath procedure and reapplied the lotion. No way did she want to go downstairs and face her host again. She put on the nightshirt and crawled back into bed.

Outside, she could hear a truck starting up and lots of voices. She went over to the window and pulled the sheer curtain to the side for a better look. Brad was pulling out with the trailer, and two other trucks were following. Perhaps he had enough help with Kyle and Kenton, and they didn't need her.

Alissa sneaked back into bed and was trying to decide if this would be a good time to invite herself to a pity party. She felt as if she were falling apart. A prayer came to her swollen lips before she could plan the words. It was a prayer of surrender and a plea for mercy. As she was finishing her communication with God, there came a gentle tap at her door.

She didn't know who was left to call on her. A maid perhaps? Alissa padded to the door and opened it slowly. A petite woman with short, blond hair stood in the hallway. She smiled at Alissa, and a noticeable scar curved up on her top lip. "Hi. How are you doing? I hope I didn't wake you."

"No, I was awake."

"I'm Jessica. Kyle wanted me to bring you this medication. Can I get you something to eat?"

"No, that's okay. Maybe later."

"It's no problem. We have french toast and soft-boiled eggs left over from breakfast."

"That would be fine," Alissa said, assuming Jessica was the maid. "And could you bring me some salt for the egg?"

"Sure."

Alissa closed the door and thought of how Chet had warned her to carry a packet of salt in case she had to eat her words about Brad. The way this nightmare was playing itself out, Alissa was certain she wouldn't have to worry about that. She would be doing well if Brad even spoke to her after this trip.

A few minutes later, the maid tapped on the door. Alissa answered and gratefully took the breakfast tray from her. It contained a vase with a big lavender hydrangea blossom in it, a cup of steaming water with several packets of tea and instant coffee beside it, orange juice, french toast, an egg in a china egg cup, and individual-sized salt and pepper shakers.

"This is great, thanks," Alissa said to Jessica. "I'm sorry I don't have my purse with me, but I'll make sure you get a tip before we leave. What was your name again?"

Jessica gave her a quizzical look before saying, "It's Jessica." Then she laughed a soft, charming laugh as if Alissa had just made a joke.

She was still standing there when Alissa closed the door. It almost seemed to Alissa that this gentle maid wanted to come in and watch Alissa eat. From all her traveling, she was used to staying in fine hotels and tipping well for room service. Perhaps this small-town bed and breakfast wasn't used to its guests being strong tippers.

The food was excellent, and it recharged Alissa. As she ate, she looked around the elegant room. Everything was in creams with subtle, pink rosebuds as the accent in little details like the teapot on the end table by the overstuffed chair. The room had a rich, classic look. By the overstuffed chair, which was covered in an ivory damask fabric, was a built-in bookshelf. It was angled in the corner and added to the room's charm.

The adjacent bathroom was also decorated in creams and soft pink rosebuds. Alissa decided this would be a wonderful place to recommend to her clients. That is, if any of them had plans to go through the middle of nowhere, which is where Alissa felt she was.

She left her tray in the hallway and noticed how quiet the place was. There must not be any other guests, or else they were all out enjoying the gorgeous weather.

Lauren had included a pair of slip-on shorts and a top with the clothes she had offered Alissa when they arrived. She put them on, pleased that they fit, even though the label indicated they were a size smaller than she usually wore.

Alissa decided to go for a walk in the extensive backyard. She loved the huge trees and rolling green lawn that made this place so typical of Oregon. A swing hung from the large apple tree to the right, and on the left was a white hammock, inviting Alissa to surrender to its embrace. She slipped into it and instantly felt relaxed.

About ten minutes later, she heard a car pull up in front of the house. She watched to see if anyone would come around to the back and discover her there. A few minutes later she heard the screen door open, and Lauren came toward her, two glasses of iced water in her hands.

"How are you feeling?" Lauren asked.

"Fine," Alissa said, taking the glass of water from her. "Thanks. I love this hammock."

"I do, too. I have one at my new house. My old college roommate, Teri, used to rent the same house, and she put it up. I think Kenton is going to get one right away for his place, too."

"They can be addicting," Alissa said. "Are you all moved in? Sorry I didn't help out this morning."

"Oh, no problem. We had plenty of help. The guys are still over there. I told them I'd pick up some food. You want to go back over with me?"

Alissa wasn't ready to face the world yet. The swelling had gone down considerably, and the lotion and medicine had taken care of the itch, but she was still red all over. Then it occurred to her that she couldn't stay in hiding the whole weekend, so she reluctantly agreed. The two women hopped in Lauren's Taurus and drove down the tree-lined streets.

"I appreciate your loaning me the clothes," Alissa said.

"Sure. No problem. I'm thankful you were willing to come all the way up here with Brad. He thinks very highly of you."

It could have been Alissa's imagination, but Lauren's delicate face seemed to take on a curious expression as she shot Alissa a sideways glance. Lauren's hair was pulled back, exposing her fine features. Alissa decided Lauren didn't look at all like Brad. She was fair, blond, and pretty. Alissa didn't think she looked like Lauren either, but she remembered Brad saying Alissa reminded him of his sister.

"He's a good friend," Alissa said. "If you're wondering if any kind of a romance is going on, it isn't."

A little smile played across Lauren's mouth as she turned the corner onto a street dotted with cute, one-story bungalows. "I know my brother," Lauren said. "And in his book, you take up a whole chapter. No other woman has done that before."

Alissa assumed she should be flattered. But she couldn't imagine what she should say in response.

Lauren pulled up in front of an old house painted mint green with ivory trim. "The painters are coming next week," Lauren said before Alissa could comment. "I can't stand the color."

"I've seen worse," Alissa said. "It's a cute place."

"Beats all the apartments I've ever lived in," Lauren said.

The guys stepped out of the house when they heard Lauren's car. Kenton jogged over to her open window before she could get out. He was tall with dark hair like Kyle's. The brothers resembled each other around the jawline, and they both had broad foreheads. Both were handsome men.

"We're done here. We decided to go to Kyle's where it's cooler. I'll come back with you tonight and help you unpack."

"Okay," Lauren said, reaching into the bag on the backseat. "You thirsty?" She handed him a can of 7-Up.

"Thanks, Wren." He kissed her softly on the cheek and then looked over at Alissa. "Glad to see you're feeling better. I heard about the poison oak and losing your cat."

She smiled her acknowledgment of his sympathy. She couldn't help but feel ridiculous, being covered with spots. At least Brad's sister and all her friends were being nice to her regardless of her unappealing condition.

Brad came around to her side of the car and said, "How are you doing? You're looking better." She knew she didn't really look better, but it was sweet of him to say that, especially in front of his sister and her boyfriend. "Do you want to ride back over with me in the truck?"

Alissa didn't particularly want to, but she guessed it would leave the front seat of Lauren's car available to Kenton, and he would probably appreciate that. She changed cars, and as they drove back, Alissa said, "Well?"

"Well, what?"

"Do you like him?"

"Kenton?"

"Of course, Kenton!" Alissa said.

Brad flipped his hair back from his face. "He's perfect for her, and I can't believe I'm admitting that to anyone."

"So you think maybe she made a good choice?"

Brad nodded.

"Are you guys starving?" Alissa asked.

"Not too bad. How about you? Did you get any breakfast?"

"Yes, the maid brought it up."

"The maid?" Brad repeated.

"I think her name was Jennifer. I told her we would tip her before we left."

Brad looked at her incredulously. "You told Jessica we would tip her?"

"That was her name, Jessica. Could you do me a favor and give her five bucks for me? She was very kind."

Brad looked at Alissa and then back at the road. Slowly and deliberately, he stated, "Jessica is Kyle's wife. They live in that house. We are their humble guests. No, I will not slip her a five-spot."

"Oh my!" Alissa felt her face turn redder than it had been, and she slumped against the door. "What an idiot I was."

"You won't hear any argument from me."

"Can we just leave, and maybe they'll forget I was ever here?"

Jessica was sitting in the porch swing when they arrived at the house. Alissa went up to her and quietly said, "I'm so sorry about the way I treated you this morning. I was mixed up and—"

"Don't worry about it," Jessica said. "You didn't know."

Alissa was relieved that Jessica graciously didn't explain to the others what the apology was about.

"You're looking a lot better," Kyle said, taking a seat next to his wife.

"Did you meet Kenton yet?"

"Yes, sort of," Alissa said.

"And this is junior." Kyle patted his wife's tummy.

"You're going to have a baby? That's wonderful. Congratulations! When are you due?"

"March. Hopefully sometime after the nursery add-on is finished."

"It'll be done by Christmas," Kyle said.

Jessica gave her husband a tender, teasing look that seemed to say she sure hoped so.

The rest of the afternoon the six of them sat on the wide, cool porch, visiting and rocking as if none of them had a care in the world. Alissa enjoyed the company of these two couples. But she found it hard not to see herself as part of a third couple, made up of Brad and Alissa. Lauren certainly seemed to view them as such.

After dinner they all pitched in and unpacked boxes at Lauren's two-bedroom home. Everything seemed to just fit, and Alissa got to admire the antique oak dresser with the beveled mirror.

"I bought it at a garage sale," Lauren told Alissa. "I love to restore old things."

"Is that why you fell for my brother?" Kyle teased her just as Kenton walked into the room.

"Did I miss something?" Kenton asked.

"We were just talking about Lauren's dresser, here," Kyle said with a wink at Lauren.

"I heard about this one," Kenton said. "She did a great job fixing it up, don't you think?"

"Definitely," Kyle said. "Lauren is a restoration specialist in my book."

Lauren and Alissa picked up on Kyle's double meaning. Alissa didn't know much about Lauren and Kenton's relationship other than it was almost all by mail. It was clear, though, that his brother was pleased with the arrangement.

Alissa liked these people. She liked the way they were

involved in each others' lives and showed in tangible ways how much they cared. She realized the appeal of Glenbrooke and these friends had become as real to her as it must have been to Lauren. Alissa wanted a slice of this small-town life. She wanted to live in a house like this with restored antique furniture and to eat wild blackberries every morning. She wanted to be a permanent part of this small circle of genuine friends.

Chapter Twenty-One

Later that evening, after the majority of Lauren's boxes were unpacked, Kyle and Jessica announced it was time for the six of them to take a dessert break. Kyle gave his wife a wink, and she smiled back.

Then Kyle led them to his truck and suggested that Jessica and Alissa sit in the cab with him. Lauren, Kenton, and Brad were offered the truck bed, which they shared with a large ice chest and a stack of woven Mexican blankets.

"I can drive my car," Kenton offered.

"Not where we're going," Kyle said. "What's wrong? You getting too old for a little adventure?"

"Never!" Kenton said, slipping his arm around Lauren's shoulders. She wrapped her arm around Kenton's middle, and Alissa noticed how nicely the two seemed to fit together.

Kyle turned to Alissa and said, "If you're not up for this, I would understand. Your rash looks better, but I know it must still be bothering you."

"I'm okay," Alissa said. "Where are we going?"

"A secret little dining spot we found," Jessica said as she climbed up into the truck. "I think you'll like it."

Alissa sat next to the window on a beach towel Kyle had brought along. He said it was so the seat's upholstery wouldn't irritate her, but Alissa thought it might be in case she was still contagious. She made sure she sat as far away from Jessica as she could and let Kyle open and close the door for her. They were all being kind and gracious about her poison oak, yet Alissa couldn't help but feel like a leper.

Kyle drove to the edge of town and then turned, with a sudden bump, onto a dirt road. A wail of protest rose from the trio in the bed of the truck along with some friendly fist pounding on the back window.

"We found a waterfall back here," Jessica confided to Alissa as the road grew bumpier. "It's not more than a trickle this time of year, but you should see it in May when the wildflowers are blooming!"

The truck came to an abrupt halt, and the protesting threesome jumped out of the back. Alissa waited for Kyle to open her door, but it was Brad who opened it. She made note of his kind act and thought it was nice the way his sister's friends were rubbing off on him.

"Hey, Kenton," Kyle called out, "give me a hand with this ice chest."

"This is no ice chest," Kenton said. "This is a refrigerator with handles. Doesn't it come with wheels? And where's the espresso cart?"

"You'll see," Jessica said. She handed Brad and Alissa flashlights and slipped a thin sweater around her shoulders. Kyle grabbed a couple more flashlights and stacked the blankets on top of the ice chest.

"This is so fun!" Lauren said. She held her light up for Kenton as he and Kyle blazed their way along the worn trail into the forest.

"I hear water," Brad said after they had walked about twenty yards.

"That's Heather Creek," Kyle said. "Over this way. There's a place I cleared."

"Yes indeedie, boys and girls," Kenton teased. "There's no need to fear when fire fighter Kyle is here. "

Alissa followed them into a clearing surrounded by huge ferns. Straight ahead was a ten-foot waterfall trickling into a small, dark pool edged with rocks. She flashed her light around the rocks and could see where the pool let out into Heather Creek, which was a hushed brook.

"This is incredible," Lauren said. "How did you guys ever find this place? I want to build a house right here."

Kyle put down the huge ice chest as Jessica began to spread out the blankets for them to sit on. He took a deep breath and said, "We bought it."

"How do you buy a waterfall?" Brad said.

"The property. We bought forty-three acres along this creek. We'd like to develop it into a camp someday. We were eager to show it to you guys, but when it's hot like this, the bugs are pretty bad during the day. Jess and I like coming here for midnight picnics." Kyle lowered his voice and tilted up his head. "Look up there."

Alissa followed his glance, up past the towering pines into the deep night sky. A thousand glittering stars returned her gaze. To the right, the moon, as round and bright as a beach ball, seemed to be balanced on the pointed nose of the tallest pine tree.

"It's beautiful," Lauren said. She moved next to Kenton and

wrapped her arms around him. Kyle sat on top of the ice chest and patted his knee, inviting Jessica to sit and watch the night sky with him.

Alissa and Brad stood about six feet apart. They awkwardly turned and looked at each other at the same moment. Alissa wished he would move closer. He didn't have to hold her hand or take her in his arms. After all, she was still covered with an unappealing rash. All he had to do was move one step closer.

But he didn't. Instead he stood his ground and turned his gaze up into the sky, checking out his sister and her boyfriend out of the corner of his eye.

See? Alissa told herself. *There's nothing between us. The attraction I feel for him is not mutual. I have no reason to feel so drawn toward him.*

She convinced herself that the moments she felt attracted to Brad were temporary feelings. He didn't have those feelings for her. He treated her like a chum, one of the guys. Not at all like someone who was close to his heart.

"Anyone interested in a little dessert?" Kyle asked as he and Jessica got up to open the ice chest. On one side a freezer-like compartment was packed with ice. The other side was dry with two large thermoses, six stoneware coffee mugs and a plastic bag full of spoons, sugar packets, coffee flavorings, and creamer. Alissa also noticed several tea bags marked "Irish Breakfast."

"What a great idea!" Brad said. "Hot and cold to go. You know, Wren, I'm beginning to like your friends more and more."

Lauren gave Kenton a squeeze, and looking up into his admiring eyes she said, "I knew you would, Brad."

"We have tea and coffee," Jessica offered. "Also marionberry pie and, of course, DoveBars."

"This is becoming a serious addiction for you, isn't it?"

Kenton teased. "Aren't you afraid your child will come out refusing to eat anything but chocolate-coated ice cream bars?"

Jessica blushed slightly in the glow of the flashlights and pulled out candles of varying sizes. She placed them on a flat rock behind them and began to light the wax sticks of soft light.

The forest was transformed into a secret place of celebration. Alissa settled herself on the edge of the blanket, allowing the warmth of the moment to envelop her.

Brad offered to help Jessica by cutting the pie. Lauren set about making two cups of tea, then served one to Kenton with a kiss on his cheek. Alissa felt wistful. Even if she hadn't found love, at least it was nurturing for her to be around people who had.

As Kyle handed her a mug of hot coffee, Alissa thought of Chloe and fought back the urge to sink into depression.

"So," Brad said, settling on the blanket with his slab of pie and pointing his fork at Kenton, "exactly what are your intentions toward my sister?"

"Radley!" Lauren snapped. "Stop with the Father-Knows-Best imitation."

"The way I see it, this guy convinced you to move all the way out here. So I have every right to ask his intentions."

"I didn't convince her of anything," Kenton said, his words smooth and even. "She was offered a teaching position at the high school. It just so happened that I had bought the town newspaper before I even had met her."

"Wait a minute," Brad said. "I hooked you two up on the Internet more than a year ago."

"Right," Kenton said. "To clarify, I bought the paper before we met face to face."

"So what you're telling me is that you two didn't really plan to end up together in Glenbrooke?"

Kyle spoke up. "To use our friend Teri's expression, it was a God thing."

Alissa had to agree. It sure sounded to her as if Kenton and Lauren's relationship fell into that category. The answer seemed to satisfy Brad's brotherly concern, too.

Slipping her first bite of marionberry pie into her mouth, Alissa thought of how someday she wanted that in a relationship with a man. She wanted to know in her heart that their coming together was a God thing. Until then, she decided, she ought to concentrate on enjoying the wonderful friendships God seemed to be bringing into her life.

Chapter Twenty-Two

About halfway through their long drive home Alissa went fishing for an opinion from Brad. "Would you ever want to live in a place like Glenbrooke?"

He paused before answering, "I don't know. Maybe."

Alissa had heard Brad telling his sister he thought she had made a wise choice. She had asked if he meant regarding Kenton or Glenbooke, and Brad had said, "Both."

"Why? Did that place capture you the way it did my sister?"

"Maybe a little. Do you think Lauren and Kenton will marry soon?"

"I hope not," Brad said. "They barely know each other. The only way to have a good marriage is to start with a long friendship. I think they should wait at least two years."

"Two years! That's ridiculous. What would they be waiting for? They're established in their careers; they're old enough to know what they want. I think they should get married at

Christmas. Why put that extra pressure on their relationship when they obviously are right for each other and deeply in love?"

"It's not the being in love part that matters. It's the being 'in commitment,'" Brad said, driving past an off-ramp on the freeway. "Remind me to pull off at the next one. That's where I stopped to get gas. We'll put up a sign for Chloe."

"What are you saying?" Alissa asked, noting his concern for her cat but wanting to get back to exploring his philosophy of relationships. "Is the commitment more important than being in love?"

"Of course. You can be committed to someone and be faithful without ever being in love. Look at all the arranged marriages in the world."

"You know, you just take the romance right out of it. How will you know when God brings the right woman into your life?"

"Oh, I'll know."

"And then what will you do?"

"Here's the off-ramp," Brad said, turning right and avoiding her question. He pulled into a small gas station with an even smaller garage and office. "Do you have some paper? Write down your phone number at least."

Alissa scrounged in her purse for something suitable while Brad filled the tank and washed off the windshield. They went into the garage together, looking for the manager so they could give him the lost cat information.

He took it willingly, but Alissa didn't feel hopeful that the man would actually post the information or do anything with it. They drove on to the next place where Brad remembered stopping for gas. This one was a large station with a convoy of trucks lined up waiting for diesel. Alissa felt sick to her stomach as she thought about Chloe meeting one of those eighteen wheelers head-on.

"Just forget it," Alissa said when they pulled back on the freeway. "I've accepted that Chloe is gone forever. Don't even bother to stop at the next place."

"I'll probably have to anyway to get gas," Brad said. "Besides, I'm not ready to give up. Have a little more hope, Alissa. She's probably made friends with some gentle soul who has fed her so well you'll never be able to unspoil her."

Alissa appreciated his optimism, even though she knew it was pointless. It made her realize that even though Brad wasn't afraid to pick a fight, he was also a fighter in the good sense of the word: he never gave up.

The final exit Brad took was called Kettleman. Several gas stations and a variety of fast food places greeted them. He drove past them all and headed down a two-lane road toward Fresno.

"Where are you going?"

"I got gas off the beaten path here. Sometimes the prices are lower if you drive a mile or two off the freeway and into the town."

The "town" they entered wasn't much to speak of. Graffiti etched the wall of the corner liquor store. Black wrought iron bars were on the windows of the small houses along the road, and the gas station that supposedly had the great prices was tiny and had no business.

Alissa and Brad got out of the truck and felt the rush of the afternoon heat rise from the pitted blacktop.

"Hello?" Alissa called out when she stepped into the garage. "Is anyone here?"

A faint "meow" echoed from the shade beside a stack of tires.

"Chloe?" Alissa raced to the tires. A big black blob of a cat lay with her belly against the cool cement. She had a white patch on her nose. "Chloe!" Alissa cried out in disbelief, scooping up her cat. "I can't believe we found you."

"Me either," Brad muttered.

A guy in coveralls stepped in from a back room and said, "That your cat? She's been hanging around here for a couple of days now. I tried to feed her, but she didn't eat much."

"Thank you for looking out for her," Alissa said, holding her thin cat close. She smelled like transmission oil and rubber tires. "Come on, you wayward little girl, you. Let's go home."

Chloe slept most of the ride home. It was seven long, hot hours. Alissa convinced Brad to run the air conditioner at least part of the time. They talked about their favorite movies and songs and sang along with some of the numbers on the radio. Their conversation didn't turn back to relationships or anything heavy. Instead they skimmed the surface of who they were in a companionable way. It was nice just being buddies together on the road, with Chloe making little snoring noises every now and then.

By Friday of that week Alissa's poison oak had toned down, and she had caught up on her sleep. But Chloe didn't seem to be able to stop sleeping, and she ate little. Alissa started to worry about her. When Chloe didn't snap out of it by the next Monday, Alissa called the vet and made an appointment to take Chloe over after work. The vet suggested Chloe stay overnight so they could observe her and run some tests.

On Alissa's way home, she stopped for Chinese food, this time trying Brad's Imperial Palace. She bought extra just in case he hadn't eaten yet and wanted to join her. Not that he would want to. The truth was, she wanted him to.

"Am I getting out of balance here, Father?" Alissa prayed as her car wound its way to their quiet street. "What am I supposed to do with these feelings that keep resurfacing? I convince myself he's just a guy. A grungy, outspoken guy who has absolutely no interest in me. And then…I don't know. He's back in my mind somehow."

That weekend she had seen Brad coming and going but hadn't stopped him to see if he wanted to talk. She had been on the go, too, shopping for some clothes in the next size smaller since everything in her closet was starting to feel baggy. The scale reported a loss of eleven pounds. Consistent exercise and a change in her diet seemed to be having a slow but lasting effect.

She pulled up in front of the duplex at the same time Brad pulled up. He got out of his truck wearing a cotton shirt and shorts—his work clothes—and holding a large white bag.

"Hi," he called out. "Have you eaten yet? I was in the mood for Chinese so I succumbed to your Red Dragon."

Alissa reached inside her car and pulled out her matching white bag. "And I thought I'd give your Imperial Palace a try. Looks like we have enough food to feed the neighborhood. Is Jake home?"

"No. He's testing for a walk-on part in a sitcom. I don't expect to see much of him this week. You want to eat at your place or mine?"

"How about the backyard? Nice compromise, don't you think?" Alissa asked.

"Fine with me, as long as we can talk. I think we need to work through something."

Alissa couldn't imagine what he was being so serious about. She met him out on the back patio a few minutes later and opened her bag of goodies. "Sweet and sour pork," she said. "And I don't remember what else. It all sounded good."

"Do you have chopsticks?" Brad asked. "I picked up extras." He handed her a pair and loaded up his plate with the bounty of food arranged on the table. After giving thanks, Brad said, "I've been thinking through some things, and I thought I should talk with you about them."

Alissa nodded, taking a drink of water. "What's up?"

"I want you to know we're not having a relationship."

Once again Brad had managed to shock her. "We are so having a relationship!" she shot back.

"I don't want you to think of it that way," Brad said.

"And how do you want me to think of it? We travel thousands of miles together, share deep secrets from the past, and both come home with Chinese food after thinking of the other person before buying it. What do you call that?"

"Dinner. We're just friends having dinner."

"Friends qualify as a relationship," Alissa stated. "Or are you saying you don't want to even consider me as one of your friends?" She began to wonder if he had been plagued by some of the same strong feelings that she had felt for him. This could be his way of trying not to let them get a hold of him.

"Let me qualify that," Brad said. "I'm not looking for a relationship. I don't see myself getting serious about anyone for at least another ten years. I just don't want you to get any wrong impressions."

"Wrong impressions from you?" Alissa wanted to laugh. "You are so verbal and honest about everything, how could I get any wrong impressions?"

"The trip to Oregon," Brad said, with a chunk of lemon chicken pinched between his chopsticks. "Everyone in Glenbrooke thought we were together."

"How did they get that impression?" Alissa challenged. She didn't want to let him off the hook so easily. He needed to make some defining statements here.

Brad popped the chicken in his mouth and chewed it thoughtfully. "Can I be honest?"

"I don't think you know how to be anything else."

"I had a long talk with my sister. I told her if, and that is a hypothetical if, I were looking for a relationship, you would be the kind of woman I'd be interested in. You are genuine and steady. You trust God in a big way, and you're beautiful. But then, you know all that. What I find intriguing is that you face me head-on. I don't know another woman who can do that. You take what I give you, and you dish it right back. That makes me think. It allows me to be myself, which is rare in my relationships with women."

"So what I hear you saying," Alissa repeated, "is that you like me. You like what our relationship—that we're supposedly not having—is doing in your life. But you don't want to have this relationship."

"Something like that."

"Am I supposed to understand this?" Alissa asked.

"I think you already do." He looked relieved now that his big speech was over.

"Then let me add something," Alissa said. "I didn't come looking for a relationship with you. It just started, and there it is. I think you should know that you have a powerful effect on me, too. I'm sure you already know that. Just don't get any ideas that I've been trying to trap you or something."

"I didn't say that," Brad said. "I hear what you're saying. I think considering the factors involved here, you and I should keep an amiable distance and not let our feelings take off on us."

Alissa couldn't believe how matter-of-fact he sounded. Was this the computer-geek side of him kicking into logic mode? What about emotions and seizing the moment? She thought of Chet and Rosie. What if they had been this phlegmatic when they first realized they had strong feelings for each other?

"Brad, do you think maybe instead of being practical all the time, it might be good and healthy once in a while to let down your guard? I mean, what if a person you cared for was only going to be around for a short time? Would you put all your emotions on hold?" She was thinking of Chet and Rosie and how it must have been for them right before Chet went off to war. They had spoken their hearts to each other, and the result was a relationship that endured for half a century.

"I don't see any reason to give in to emotions," Brad said.

Alissa knew he wasn't trying to do an impersonation, but he sure resembled Spock at that moment. She thought of what to say and realized there was nothing she could say. If he had spoken to her differently, stating that he wanted to follow his heart and see what God had in mind for their relationship, she would have responded in kind, saying she felt something deep and wonderful for him.

But she didn't even want to respond to this logic-oriented presentation. She didn't feel like eating anything else. Quietly excusing herself, Alissa said, "I'll see you around."

"Thanks for understanding," Brad said. "I knew you would."

"I never said I understood," Alissa said, turning sharply. "I'm just not into playing evaluation games. I believe things should be what they are, and that's it."

She went inside and slammed her back door. Turning on the TV and pulling down the shades so he couldn't see inside, Alissa tried to block everything out from the past hour. She missed Chloe. And she felt insecure and sorry she had ever opened herself up to a friendship with Brad.

When she stopped by the vet's on her way home from work the next day, he gave Alissa some news she didn't expect. "Chloe has cancer. It's quite extensive. It's not uncommon for cats her age. It's too risky to operate. We can put her to sleep, or you can take her home. She has perhaps a month to live. Maybe two."

Blinking back the tears, Alissa said, "Are you sure?"

The vet nodded.

"I'd like to take her home," she said. "Is that cruel?"

"No. I can give you some medication for her so she won't be in any pain. I'm sorry."

Alissa drove home with her dear, sick Chloe on the floor. After all they had been through together, including Chloe's most recent escapade, who would have guessed this would be the end?

They went inside, and Alissa fixed Chloe a special dinner of white tuna. Chloe licked it and walked away.

There was a knock on her door, and Alissa opened it up to little Anna, who had a plate of cookies in her hand. "My mom and I made these, and I brought you some." She looked up and added, "Are you crying?"

Alissa wiped away a tear and invited her little friend inside. Without meaning to, Alissa poured out her heart. "I just found out Chloe has cancer. They can't operate on it, so she's going to die, and I'm really sad."

Anna glanced at Chloe, who was curled up by the foot of the couch. "When is she going to die?"

"The doctor said she has a month or maybe two to live. That's all."

"That's so sad," Anna said. "First Shelly leaves and now Chloe."

"I especially appreciate your cookies, Anna. They'll cheer me up. Thank you."

"You're welcome. I have to go now. Bye." She slipped out the front door. Alissa wondered if she had scared away Anna with the confession about Chloe. Maybe it would have been better to say nothing.

Three days later, she was getting ready to run to the vet's to pick up a different medication for Chloe since her cat wasn't taking the first kind he had sent home with her. That's when Alissa discovered that Anna had taken the news of Chloe's illness to heart.

Anna was in the backyard playing with her little sister. Through Alissa's open window she heard Anna say, "She's going to die. She told me. I don't think she has told anyone else. She has a thing called cancer, and the doctor said they can't operate on it. So I think we should be really nice to her, because she only has two months to live."

Mallory had taken in every word wide-eyed and solemnly. "Okay," she agreed. "We'll be real nice to her."

Alissa heard the back door close on the other side of the duplex. She couldn't see if it was Brad or Jake. She had kept her distance and brushed from her mind any lingering thoughts of Brad. Grabbing her shoulder bag, she headed out for the vet's. As she opened the door, Brad stood on her doorstep, hand poised, ready to knock.

"Hi," he said slowly. There was a long pause. He didn't seem to have anything else to say.

"Excuse me," Alissa said, pulling the door shut and walking past him. She still felt angry with him and was in no mood for more spewing of his hurtful logic. "I'm in a hurry."

"Where you going?"

She answered, "Out," because she knew if she said "vet," she would have to give a long explanation about Chloe, and she would be late to the clinic. Perhaps Brad had overheard Anna and Mallory, and in his own, unemotional way, he was trying to offer his condolences. It didn't matter. He was the last person she wanted to talk to right now.

After the vet's she stopped by the dry cleaners and then went to the pharmacy for some more lotion for her nearly cleared up poison oak.

When she arrived home, the sun was setting. The sky was

aglow with soft pinks and gentle, fading blue behind the bend-
ing trees. Summer was tiptoeing out gracefully and doing so
with a radiance that filled Alissa with awe for the beauty of
God's creation. For the few weeks of late summer that
remained, there was a promise of many more elegant sunsets.

Alissa loved them. Sunsets meant a gentle quiet between
the bright glare of day and the deep silence of night. If she had
her choice, she would live her whole life in the sunset hour.

With her arms full, she turned the key in her front door
and stepped inside. The sight that met her eyes shocked her.
The plastic wrapped dry cleaning slid from her arm into a
puddle on the floor.

In her living room, on the coffee table, the couch, the
chair—everywhere—were thick bouquets of flowers. Bachelor
buttons, roses, daisies, and sunflowers. It looked like a florist
truck had lost its way and backed up into her living room.

Brad stepped out from behind the kitchen counter.
"Genevieve helped me," he said. "I wanted to get your attention."
He was dressed up, face shaven, clean shirt. Alissa couldn't figure out what was going on. He came over to her and took the
packages from her arms, glancing at the pharmacy bag before
setting it on the counter. "Come in here," he urged her.

He moved a bunch of flowers from the love seat to the
floor and sat beside her, taking her hands in his for the first
time ever. "Alissa, I was wrong."

She sat still, in shock.

"Alissa," he said, his voice more tender than she had ever
heard, "I can't ignore the truth of my feelings any longer.
There's no point in being so logical when it's our lives we're
talking about here. You were right. It's not good to put our
emotions on hold."

Brad looked into her eyes. A tinge of blue rimmed the cool
summer green eyes she had found so irresistible more than

once. He drew her hands to his smooth chin, and holding them against his jaw, he said in a deep voice, "I love you, Alissa. Say you'll marry me."

Chapter Twenty-Three

$\mathcal{A}$lissa couldn't help herself. She laughed. Then she pulled her hands away from Brad, looked around the room, and said, "You can come out with your camera, now. Very funny."

But Jake didn't appear. Brad remained steady, serious, and maybe a little wounded.

"You think this is a joke?"

"Well," she tried to swallow her laughter and smoothed her hair back in an attempt to regain some dignity. "I find it hard to believe you're serious."

"I'm completely serious. Ever since we talked on Monday night I've been tortured, knowing I wasn't being true to myself, nor was I being true to you. I'm fooling myself to think it's a good idea to wait ten years. We never know what tomorrow will bring. We have to take each day and embrace it."

Alissa tried hard to digest all of this.

"I don't care if we only have a short time together. The

important thing is that we're together. Everything just suddenly fell into place for me. I realized I love you. I knew we had to get married."

Her skepticism began to dissolve. She felt as if her squelched feelings were being set free. "Are you sure you mean this?"

"Completely sure, with all my heart," Brad said.

When she still hesitated, he readjusted his position and spoke to her softly. "Alissa, the first time I saw you that day at Starbucks I felt something for you I've never felt for anyone. When I saw you again at the travel agency, I felt I had to do something to keep in contact with you. So I left the number for the duplex when I heard you making phone calls for an apartment."

Alissa absorbed his words.

"It was my way of testing to see if the Lord would bring us together again. I know that may sound crazy, but it made sense to me at the time. Then you took the duplex, and that first day when you caught me rewiring the outlet, I thought you were going to bite off my head. I figured my feelings weren't to be trusted; so I put them away and approached you on a purely platonic level."

Brad's hand went up to her face where he touched her cheek. Then he slid his fingers through her hair. "You are so incredible to me. I love everything about you, Alissa. This is the real me speaking from my unhidden heart. Will you marry me?"

Alissa felt her lower lip quiver as she released in a whisper the answer that came directly from her heart. "Yes."

Brad slowly moved toward her, his eyes fixed on hers. She sat still, ready and waiting. Her eyelids lowered in unison with his, and their lips met in a tender kiss.

If she questioned his words or his wacky, impulsive actions, his kiss removed any doubt. This man loved her heart and soul. He was the first man who ever had. He was the first one to kiss her like that.

Wrapping his arms around her and drawing her close, Brad said, "I know it's going to take a lot to pull it all together, but do you think we can get married next weekend?"

"Yeah, right," Alissa laughed softly.

"I'm serious," Brad said, kissing her on the temple. "It won't be a big wedding, but it can be beautiful. We could hold it here, in the backyard. Then we'll go to Venice for our honeymoon."

Alissa pulled away and studied his face. "You are serious, aren't you?"

Brad nodded. She couldn't get over the sudden transformation in this man. What had happened? Did an angel come down and command him to marry her immediately? That's the way he was acting.

Just then the doorbell rang, and Alissa rose to answer it. "Don't go away," she said, looking over her shoulder at Brad. "If I'm dreaming, I don't want to wake up."

Chet and Rosie were at the door. They greeted Alissa with a big bouquet, hugs, and kisses. "Brad called and told us to come right over and bring flowers. What's the big news?"

Alissa welcomed them in and looked at Brad.

"I just asked Alissa if she would have me as her husband, and she said yes."

"I knew it!" Chet said, pulling a plastic bag from his pocket and handing it to Alissa. "I told Rosie I might need to give you this." It was a salt shaker. "You ready to eat your words, missy?"

Alissa laughed. "I guess so. It's all happening so fast. Come in."

Rosie added her bouquet to the already full coffee table, and the two of them sat close on the couch. "It looks like it was an awfully romantic proposal," Rosie said, glancing at Brad and the abundance of floral arrangements.

"You know, I never heard how Chet proposed to you," Alissa said, sitting back down next to Brad. His arm went around her shoulder, and he drew her close.

"He didn't," Rosie said.

"And she'll never let me forget it, either," Chet said. "I asked her if June was soon enough to pull everything together or if we needed more time. She said the middle of June, and that was that. We put our plans together, and here we are, hitched."

Alissa was glad Brad had gone all out in making his proposal so romantic. She would never forget this day. If only she could convince herself it was really happening.

The four of them chatted another twenty minutes or so, and then Chet and Rosie graciously got up to leave. "Whatever date you two settle on," Rosie said, "we'll be there."

"And I already know what we'll buy you for a gift," Chet added. "Salt and pepper shakers!"

Alissa laughed and promised Brad she would fill him in on the joke later. They showed their friends to the door, and Brad kept his arm around her as they waved good-bye. She turned to wrap her arms around his middle, resting her head on his shoulder. It felt so good to be in his arms, to see the future opening up before them.

"We have so much to decide," Alissa said. "Do you want to start planning tonight, or should we wait until tomorrow so the shock can wear off a little bit?"

"It wouldn't hurt to start with some of the basics tonight," Brad said. "Do you have some paper handy?"

Alissa reached for a pad by the phone.

"I think we're going to need more paper than that," Brad said when he saw the little square of note paper. Alissa found a yellow pad in a drawer of her desk and wrote at the top, "Brad and Alissa." She felt like a schoolgirl, doodling the name of her boyfriend on the front of her folder.

"Put down the minister, a cake, Lauren. We have to see if she can fly down on such short notice."

"And end up here instead of Alaska," Alissa added. A twinge of sadness came over her as she realized she didn't have a single relative to contact. At least she had Rosie and her enthusiastic support.

"Put down tux rental and dress for you. You don't like those big hoop skirts, do you?"

Alissa shook her head.

"Good. Get something lacy around the neck."

"Any other specifications, oh master? It is traditionally the bride's choice, you know."

"Get whatever you want then. Just no big skirt. Oh, and music. Let's have someone sing one of those old hymns you like so much." Brad headed to the refrigerator looking for sustenance. "I like harps. Do you like harps? Shelly used to play harp music, and I decided I liked it. Maybe we could have someone play a harp. I'm eating the rest of this chicken. Do you want any?"

The room began to spin around Alissa. Too much was coming at her too quickly. "No. Go ahead." Brad was already acting as if they were married, but she was beginning to doubt herself and her answer to him. How in the world could she have said yes to him just like that? She barely knew this man.

Brad walked up with a chicken leg in one hand and a paper towel in the other. "Hey, are you okay?"

Alissa tilted her head down and drew in a deep breath. "Does it seem hot in here to you?" she asked.

Brad immediately put down the chicken and came to her side. "Maybe you should go lie down. Come on, I'll help you to your room. Are you in pain?"

"No, of course not," Alissa said, rising as he led her by the elbow into her room. He moved the stack of magazines from the end of the bed and helped her to lie down. "I'm okay," she said. "It just all hit me so fast."

Brad sat on the side of the bed next to her. "Do you want some water? What about the medicine you brought home? Do you need to take any of that?"

"No. I'm fine. Really, it's nothing."

"Honey," Brad said, stroking her forehead, "it's okay. I know. You don't have to pretend to be strong. We're going to face this thing together. And we'll fight it. I'm praying that God will heal you outright. Even if he doesn't, I'll be with you every step of the way."

Alissa opened her eyes and scrutinized her babbling fiancé.

"It's okay. I know everything," Brad said softly, answering the question in her eyes. "I overheard Anna out in the backyard. And I want you to know that I'm going to stick with you through this. We're going to find a new doctor. Get a second opinion. So many forms of cancer are treatable now, I can't believe that—"

"Cancer!" Alissa squawked, bolting upright. "You think I have cancer?"

"You don't?"

"No, I don't have cancer! Chloe has cancer." A shocking realization washed over Alissa, and she sprang to her feet. "Is that why you proposed to me? All the flowers and the sweet words? You thought I only had a few months to live, didn't you?"

Instead of defending himself, Brad snapped to his feet and shouted, "Chloe has cancer?! Why didn't you tell me?"

"Because only four days ago you were the one saying you wanted me to keep an amicable distance! You told me you didn't want a relationship. That's what you said. And now, here you are with flowers and kisses and accusations that I didn't tell you about my cat; so it's my fault that..." Alissa felt her face getting redder. "Get out of my house right now. I don't want to see you ever again!"

Without a word, Brad obliged. He took long strides down the hall and slammed the door on his way out. Alissa flopped on the bed and lowered her head into her hands.

She remembered all the reasons she had put up her defenses and shut down her emotions after the Phoenix church disaster. This was why. Whenever she allowed herself to be vulnerable, she got hurt.

If some man is going to walk into my life, rip my heart right out of my chest, and stomp on it, it's going to be a better man than Bradley Phillips, I'll tell you that! He has no right to...

Alissa didn't know how to finish that thought. No right to fall in love with her? But he had. She knew he had. His kiss told her so. So did his eyes. His heart definitely had come through when he proposed. Even his decision to marry her, thinking she only had a few months to live, was actually rather romantic.

So then, why did he storm out of here? If he meant his words, he would have stayed. He's a fighter. I ordered him out of my condo the day I moved in, and that didn't phase him a bit. Maybe this was all too much for him, too, and he needs some time to think it through. Wait a minute! What am I doing, making excuses for this guy?

Alissa, still feeling foggy, moved into the living room. "Here, Chloe. Come here, Chloe." The two of them needed to be together to ride this emotional tidal wave. "Chloe, come, girl."

Alissa found her curled up in her favorite spot by the side of the couch, sleeping. Reaching down, Alissa picked up her only true friend and held her in her arms, rocking for a long time. It felt as if the world, which only an hour ago had been spinning wildly, had come to an abrupt halt, and Alissa, Brad, and Chloe had all fallen off.

Chapter Twenty-Four

$\mathcal{S}$aturday morning Alissa met Genevieve out front for their usual walk. Alissa had already decided she wasn't going to tell Genevieve everything that had happened with Brad. She needed more time to process it herself.

"You seem awfully quiet," Genevieve said at the end of their walk. "If you want to pop by later today and talk some more about anything, I'll be home all day."

"I need to go to the beach. Newport has become my special thinking place; I'm going to spend the day there. Thanks anyway. I really appreciate you, Genevieve."

"And I you," Genevieve said.

Alissa took her time getting out of the house. The last time she had gone to Newport, only a few short weeks ago, she had been searching for someone, a person from her past who might give her some encouragement or whom she might encourage. Instead, she had found the presence of the Lord to be very real.

He was, after all, a person from her past—her past, her present, and her future.

Today she knew she could lie on the beach and talk to God. She could think things through and find him faithful to comfort and direct her. Maybe it was because of that realization that she didn't want to go. She wanted to cry a little more. Or go back in time and feel Brad's hand across her cheek and his fingers in her hair when he had proposed to her. Surely she could have done something to alter the events of last night.

But what? She couldn't have changed the situation. She knew she couldn't have controlled Brad or the feelings she still had toward him. But there had to be something she could have done differently.

When she arrived at the beach, instead of settling in the sand, Alissa decided to walk. On and on she walked, her footprints being washed away a moment after she placed their imprint in the sand. She thought and prayed until, exhausted, she finally gave in. "It's all in your hands, Father God. You are the almighty creator. It's within your power to give and to take. I'm yours, God. Do whatever you want in my life."

Then the peace came. Not peace like a river, but peace like an ocean—still moving but calmed and rhythmic and no longer raging. It was as if the Lord had finally heard her frantic shouting, and with two words, "Be still," he had calmed her heart.

Alissa began the long walk back through the sand. As she rummaged through the contents of her straw bag to find her sunscreen, her hand grasped a piece of paper. She pulled it out and read as she walked. The paper contained the words to one of the hymns she had found. She had written it out, planning to memorize it several weeks ago, and then she had forgotten about stuffing it in her beach bag:

Be still, my soul; the Lord is on thy side
Bear patiently the cross of grief or pain
Leave to thy God to order and provide
In every change He faithful will remain.
Be still, my soul; the best, thy heavenly Friend
Through thorny ways leads to a joyful end.

Be still, my soul; thy God doth undertake
To guide the future as He hath the past
Thy hope, thy confidence, let nothing shake
All now mysterious shall be bright at last.
Be still, my soul; the wave and winds still know
His voice who ruled them while He dwelt below.

Be still, my soul; though dearest friends depart
And all is darkened in the vale of tears;
Then shalt thou better know His love, His heart,
Who comes to soothe thy sorrows and thy fears.
Be still, my soul; thy Jesus can repay
From His own fullness all He takes away.

Alissa stopped at those final words. God was right there.
She knew it. She reread the line, "Then shalt thou better know
His love, His heart."

"I want to know Your heart, God. Keep teaching me,
please. It doesn't seem to get any easier, does it? What am I
supposed to do about Brad? I love him. I know he loves me.
But I know we're not ready to get married."

She walked on, reading the last stanza again and silently
praying, "God, I need you to soothe my sorrows and my fears.
I don't know how to do this very well, but I want to learn to
trust you."

When Alissa looked up she realized she wasn't far from where she had parked the car. She went to put more quarters in the meter. Then she sauntered onto the sand and found a nice open spot to stretch out in the sun. It took no time at all for her to drift off into a peaceful sleep.

Sometime later, she stirred on her beach towel, half awake, half asleep. A deep, resonating voice spoke to her softly. "So this is your thinking place," Brad said. "Well, I've been thinking, too. There has to be something in the middle. Not an overnight wedding in Vegas and not a decade of relationship testing. Something sane and wise. A balance of friendship and love, if there is such a thing."

Alissa didn't open her eyes. She let Brad's soothing voice wash over her. A slight smile on her lips let him know she was listening. She wondered how long he had been at her side, thinking, waiting, watching her sleep. Maybe sleeping women were as irresistible as sleeping men.

"All I can say is, I'm sorry," he went on. "I rushed in without thinking, and I hurt both of us. I guess what I'm saying is, I want to be there for you."

He paused and then added, "When it comes to dating relationships, my growth has been stunted. I admit it. I'm a klutz. I've never been in love. Until now."

She could tell he was waiting for her to respond, but Alissa waited to see if he had anything else to add. "I love you, Alissa. I want to commit myself to a relationship with you. Only it needs to be a step at a time, not all at once. I think I'm finally beginning to understand that."

The silence was filled by the sound of the waves rushing in and receding, right on schedule.

"Aren't you going to say anything?" Brad asked.

Alissa opened her eyes a slit and looked up into the face she knew she wanted to greet every morning for the rest of her life.

"Well?" Brad asked.

With a playful grin, she closed her eyes again and calmly said, "So, what took you so long?"

To silence those lips, Brad leaned over and kissed her.

"I mean it, Alissa," Brad murmured. "I love you."

"And I love you," she said, looking up into his eyes. They were so green, she almost felt she could dive right into them. "You need to know, Brad, that you are the first man God has ever granted access to my true heart. The only one."

A confident look crossed Brad's face. "I know that," he said.

She stood up and took his hand. Overhead, the evening sky surrendered to the Master's paintbrush. "Come on," she challenged. "Let's go down to the water."

Slowly, silently, and with contentment, they walked together to where the sunset, alive with vivid reds, oranges, and pinks, met the edge of the Pacific.

There, hand in hand, Alissa and Brad moved toward the sunset, the way a bride goes forth to meet her beloved.

Dear Reader,

When I started writing *Sunsets,* I knew Alissa would meet Brad, but I didn't know she'd meet Chet and Rosie. This charming couple didn't appear anywhere in the outline or original summary of the book. They just "showed up" at Alissa's desk one day, and I knew I wanted to get to know them.

About halfway through the writing of *Sunsets,* my husband and I went for an evening walk. He asked how the book was coming along. I told him about Chet and Rosie and all the hard times Rosie had been through. That day I had written the scene in which Rosie and Chet were finally married.

As we watched the sun take a colorful bow into the west, I told my husband there was something simple yet grand about this old couple marrying. Then all of a sudden I got choked up and started to cry.

The bigger picture had become clear to both of us. Rosie and Chet were a depiction of Christ and his Church as it is talked about in Ephesians 5. All the terrible stuff we endure in this life won't matter in the end. We have a wonderfully patient Savior who is waiting—longing—for the day when we will be united with him.

I guess that's what Alissa needed to learn. A relationship with God is so much more than coming to him and asking forgiveness for past sins. God desires a living, breathing relationship with his bride, a relationship that includes promises made and promises kept. When we surrender to God's love, he receives us and forgives us. Then he adorns us in pure white. And that's how he sees us coming down the aisle toward him. We're no longer wearing the thin rags of our inadequacies, but we're clothed in Christ's righteousness.

It's such a beautiful mystery. The ultimate love story. Us and God—united at last.

I pray for you, my dear readers, that you will come to know his forgiveness and his love. When you do, he will give you his Holy Spirit, which is his "engagement ring" or promise. (Ephesians 1:13-14) Wear it well. One day we will get to the end of this long aisle and see his face.

Always,

Robin Jones Gunn

P.S. You are invited to come visit me online at www.robingunn.com.

Sunsets Recipe

Alissa's Bongo Fest Potato Salad
(sans pickles)

Every summer, around the Fourth of July, I miss my mother-in-law something fierce. Kay used to make the best potato salad for all our summer family gatherings. My husband let me know our first summer together that the nicest gift I could ever give him would be if every summer, for the rest of his life, I made potato salad the way his mom made it.

I followed Kay around the kitchen on the afternoon of July 3rd for several years in a row, taking notes in an attempt to learn her secrets.

"No secret to my potato salad," she told me. "Unless it's the onions. Nice big onions. Sweet ones, if you can find them. Make sure they're chopped up real fine. And no pickles. Of course you want to be generous with your salt and pepper. And make sure your celery is fresh. Snapping fresh. That's all. No secrets. Oh. Maybe one secret. I only use real mayonnaise."

In chapter eleven of *Sunsets,* when Alissa decided to contribute something to the picnic before the Bongo Fest, I knew right away she'd bring the potato salad. And I knew exactly how that potato salad would taste. Now you can, too!

The ingredients are listed with approximate amounts since this potato salad is like Brad and Jake's Bongo Fest: it works best if you create as you go along. Feel free to improvise!

Boil six to eight large potatoes in their skins in a covered pot until they are tender. Chill the potatoes for several hours. Peel and cut them in small cubes.

Chop and add:
6 hard-boiled eggs
1 large onion ("sweet, if you can find them")
1 medium stalk of fresh celery ("snapping fresh")

Season well with salt and pepper, cover and place in the refrigerator for one hour or more

Add about 2 cups of mayonnaise mixed with about 3 tablespoons of mustard. Mix well. Sprinkle paprika on the top and keep covered in the refrigerator.

By the way, this potato salad almost always tastes better the second day. So plan to make it a day before your next summer outing.

The Glenbrooke Series

Come to Glenbrooke...
A quite place where souls are refreshed

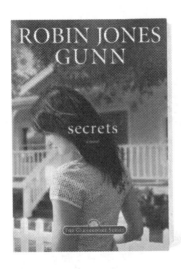

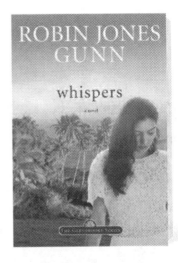

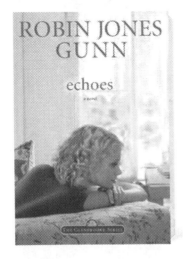

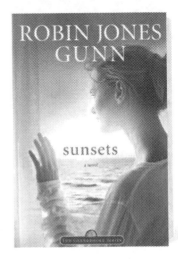

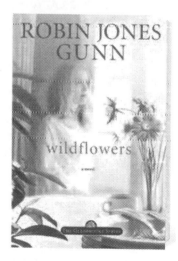

Join Jessica, Terri, Lauren, Alissa, Shelly, Meri, Leah, and Genevieve as they encounter love, life, and a growing faith in the small town of Glenbrooke.

Read excerpts from these books and more at WaterBrookMultnomah.com!

SISTERCHICK®

Adventures by

Robin
Jones Gunn

"A friend loves at all times…"
—PROVERBS 17:17A (NASB)

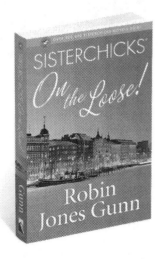 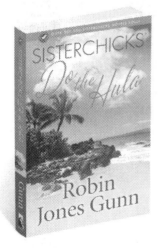

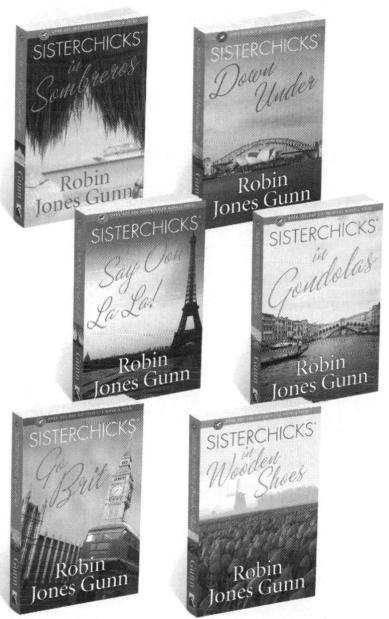

Read excerpts from these books and more at WaterBrookMultnomah.com!

Grace...IT BIDS ME FLY
AND GIVES ME Wings

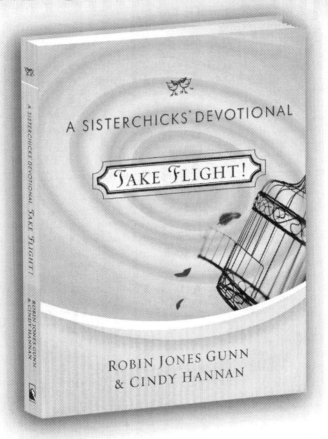

A SISTERCHICKS' DEVOTIONAL

Take Flight!

A SISTERCHICKS DEVOTIONAL TAKE FLIGHT!

ROBIN JONES GUNN
& CINDY HANNAN

ROBIN JONES GUNN
& CINDY HANNAN

For every Sisterchick seeking a fresh time with God, this devotional/ponder/prayer/excuse-to-gather-together book will send you soaring. Inside, you'll find a collection of insightful devotions, key Scripture verses, and wit 'n' whimsy wisdom for the journey, along with Sisterchickin' suggestions for further reading, space to pen a peep or two, and more!

Connect With Robin

Facebook – robingunn.com/facebook

Twitter – robingunn.com/twitter

Robin's Nest Newsletter Sign up at

robingunn.com

Robin's Online Shop

Forever ID Bracelets

T-Shirts

Key Chains

Posters

Books

Visit Robin's Online Shop at

shop.robingunn.com

CAN'T GET ENOUGH OF ROBIN JONES GUNN?

Christy Miller Collection, Volume 1 (Books 1-3)
Christy Miller Collection, Volume 2 (Books 4-6)
Christy Miller Collection, Volume 3 (Books 7-9)
Christy Miller Collection, Volume 4 (Books 10-12)

Sierra Jensen Collection, Volume 1 (Books 1-3)
Sierra Jensen Collection, Volume 2 (Books 4-6)
Sierra Jensen Collection, Volume 3 (Books 7-9)
Sierra Jensen Collection, Volume 4 (Books 10-12)

Printed in the United States
by Baker & Taylor Publisher Services